The Sun

And The Shadow

For anyone who has ever believed
in magic.

Published by Independent Publishing Network

First edition 2021

Copyright Ilya Ellis 2021

Cover content created by Shutter Stock

Author's Note

Due to some sensitive subject matter in The Sun And The Shadow, I have felt it suitable to include this content warning for any readers who may need it. If any of these subjects are triggering or upsetting to you please read with caution.

Brief discussions and implications of consent

Descriptions of blood and mild gore

Descriptions of panic and anxiety attacks

Discussions of death and mortality

Descriptions of drowning

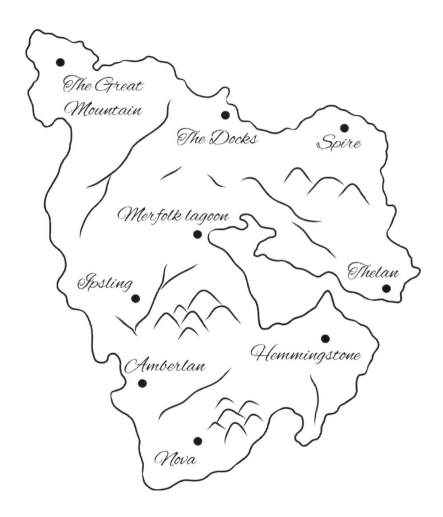

The Great Mountain

The Docks

Spire

Merfolk lagoon

Ipsling

Thelan

Amberlan

Hemmingstone

Nova

Part One

One

A slight frost had kissed the ground, covering it in a sprinkle of white that glittered as the sun rose and greeted it with a cool light. It was a little unusual for a frost to still be present in early June, though not entirely unheard of. Nathaniel stepped out onto the wooden balcony that looked down over the city of Spire and placed a steady hand onto the wooden railing in front of him.

He felt the warmth seeping from his skin and watched as it crept along the wood. The tiny specks of ice melted then dripped down onto the balcony beneath his feet. He smiled to himself as he glanced up at the sky; despite the slightly bitter but crisp feeling in the air he knew it was going to be a good day.

He flourished in the sun; he could feel his body reacting to the rays before he had even stepped outside. There was a glow thrumming through his pores, desperate to seep out and explode up into the sky to collide with the brightness and consume its warmth. He closed his eyes and took in a deep breath. Spire always had a wooden scent engulfing it, which came as no surprise as the entire city was nestled in trees, built entirely out of wood so it looked like part of the landscape. Nathaniel had to marvel at it, how perfect the city appeared to an outside eye. It seemed that they had embraced the nature surrounding them with full force. In reality, it was the opposite.

One thing about Spire was that it didn't stand a chance against the power of the forest. Back in the early days, before Spire even had a name, the inhabitants had cleared the area of all trees and wildlife. It was a vast empty expanse of land that seemed barren, but a perfect place to start building on. Yet for every tree that was cut down another would grow at an alarming rate out of the abused earth, they would grow with a strength and intensity that had never been seen before and defied all laws of logic and nature. It got to the point that there ended up being more trees in the area than what there had been originally. The people realised that they had no choice but to reluctantly embrace the trees and built their homes around and within them.

Now that Spire had been established it looked like living with the trees had always been the intention, and the Spirans took great pleasure in naming themselves the city chosen by magic.

Magic. Nathaniel laughed to himself. He had never believed in it as a child, not even when all the children his age did. He was never convinced by stories of Santa or the Tooth Fairy–and he absolutely did not believe that there were monsters living underneath his bed (no matter what his brother told him). Yet he was now in a place where he could not deny the existence of magic; it literally ran through his veins and consumed his every moment.

How long had it been since he discovered what he could create? How long had it been since he knew just how powerful he could be? He could remember snippets of his previous life, small segments that didn't fuse together no matter how hard he tried. He knew that fairies didn't exist back where he came from, he knew that no one could harness an element and use it to either protect or create harm. The island had called to him; he had heard its voice carrying on the wind and he followed, blindly, but he trusted the voice to get him to where he needed to be. He never looked back.

He couldn't remember his parents, their names, his own true name. Henry had insisted that it was Nathaniel, but Henry often lied. In fact, he *always* lied. Nathaniel even wondered if he really was his brother or if that was another fable he came up with on a whim. For all he knew Henry was still alive somewhere and his death was just him taking one of his pranks too far. He wished that was the case. God, he missed him.

Henry's death felt like such a far off memory he wasn't even sure if he properly grieved for him. He felt a sadness within himself when he thought about him, but, back then, when it all actually happened, he was sure that all he felt was numbness. He still remembered his face. Thin lips that stretched out into a wide smile that made him look a little goofy, especially when he laughed. His hair was short at the sides, longer on top, but always a mess no matter how he tried to style it. Even the fairies got frustrated with how messy he always looked. What Nathaniel remembered most about him though was his unique ability to create far-fetched and unbelievable stories out of thin air. He could recall the Princess with the glass slipper, the Prince who switched places with a pauper...a pea under a mattress. Such tales floated effortlessly out of his brothers mouth, he knew every detail, could answer every question that Nathaniel or the other boys had, no matter how obscure it was. Why didn't the glass shoe shatter when the Princess walked? She was as light as a feather, of course.

"I don't see the sun I was expecting." A voice came from behind Nathaniel, pulling him swiftly out of his memories, and he turned to see King Raesh behind him. The King was dressed like he usually was, in dark coloured clothes that clung to his skin—accentuating every sharp line of his body. Around his waist was a gold link belt adorned with different coloured gems that twinkled no matter the light that they were under. Over his left shoulder was a cloak the colour of damp moss that appeared to be made of crushed velvet and made Nathaniel recoil slightly whenever it brushed against his skin. He was pale, having not seen the sun in several months and not wanting to venture outside when the snow had settled on Spire—which made his jet black hair stand out even more than it usually did.

Raesh cleared his throat then raised an expectant eyebrow at Nathaniel. "Well? I was expecting bright sun, can't you do something about that?"

"I can't control the weather," Nathaniel said dryly and looked back out over the balcony. The King moved up beside him, Nathaniel's skin pricked as he felt the velvet material of this cloak press firmly against his arm. Raesh moved his hand up to the side of Nathaniel's face and took a strand of his shoulder length brown hair into his fingers and twirled it around slowly.

"If I ask for the sun I should get it." His voice was steady and sure, a weight behind it that Nathaniel knew all too well was not a good thing.

He turned and smiled at his leader. "You will, it is early, the sun hasn't had chance to rise fully yet, but you can feel the warmth already."

Raesh's lip twitched slightly. "If you say so...I have a meeting with the games masters today and we planned on walking around the arena. I don't want my guests getting cold." Nathaniel gave a nod. The games masters. How had he forgot that they were coming?

"When will they arrive?" he asked.

"A couple of hours. You should get yourself ready." Raesh looked him up and down. "I can't have you by my side looking like...well...this–" He waved his hand at Nathaniel lazily. "You look like death." Looking like death seemed like a bit of an exaggeration on the King's part; he had washed and ran a hand through his hair that morning, which had to count for something.

"I will get myself ready immediately, Your Highness." He dipped his head to his King then felt the other man hook a finger under his chin, causing him to look up at him again.

"You will report to my private chambers tonight Nathaniel, do you understand?" He felt Raesh's eyes boring into his. "I need your company."

"Yes, Your Highness." Raesh smiled and dropped his hand away from Nathaniel's face while making a satisfied noise in the back of his throat.

"Good. Now, meet me down in the throne room in an hour, there's a good little pet." He turned while Nathaniel fought the urge to conjure a fireball that he could aim at his head. Killing the King the day the games masters were due to arrive was not a good idea. He shook his hands, cancelling out the small flickers of flames that were daring to rise from his palms and stuffed them into his pockets. No. Not today.

Two

Rica managed to let out a gasp as the air was pounded out of her lungs. She lolled her head to the side and eyed the moss beneath her body accusingly. It was meant to protect her from falls, cushion the blow, not make her chest feel like it was going to explode. She drew her attention to the light that was dancing through the gaps in the leaves on the trees and squinted her eyes so that they blurred together. She could feel her lungs finding their breath again but each inhale of air was painful as she lay on the forest ground. A shadow loomed over her and the blurred light above her was obstructed by the form.

Pan looked down at her. "Get up," he muttered, jaw clenched. Rica grinned at him, not daring to show just how winded she was. His brown eyes narrowed at her. "Seriously, get up," he repeated so she reluctantly got herself into an upright position.

"The trees here are different," she said and gestured to the tree in front of her that she had fallen from moments before. "The bark, it isn't right."

"...The bark...isn't...right..." Pan cocked his head as he continued to look down at her. "They are exactly the same as the trees that we have on the other side of the island." He stepped towards the large trunk and placed his hand on the rough bark. He seemed to be considering something for a moment but then looked over his shoulder at her and tutted. "They are no different, Rica."

Rica shook her head and finally stood up again. "Nope, they are all wrong." She kicked the base of the tree with her bare foot which made her wince in pain and immediately regret the decision to do it. "I don't feel...the glow, you know?"

"You mean the fairies?" Pan leaned back against the wood, arms folded across his chest.

"Exactly. The fairies. I haven't seen one since we got here, they are everywhere back home, you can't move without seeing a bloody fairy."

"They do live here, but the people of Spire don't live in harmony with them like we do. Fairies are seen as more of a nuisance than anything;" he explained then glanced down at her knees. "You've got a hole in your trousers."

"Shit–" Rica bent down to inspect the damage then let out a long groan. "My dad is going to kill me. Did you know that–"

"The trousers were made from woven spider silk found in the mountains?" Pan grinned. "Yes, Rica, I am very aware of how your trousers were made." Rica straightened herself and lifted her chin with a sniff.

"Then you will know that you need to fix them." She pointed to her knee while looking at the man expectantly.

Pan laughed airily. "Sorry, do you think I carry a needle and spider silk with me?"

"No! Use your hands," she tutted.

"Your Highness, with all due respect, I am not here to fix your garments, but I am sure we can find a fairy around here who has the talents to mend them for you. But first, I need you to get to the top of the tree without falling down."

Rica narrowed her eyes at him then huffed. "I think you want to see me fall."

"Yes, because seeing you tumble out of a tree really is the highlight of my day." Rica couldn't tell if he was being serious or not, she never really knew with Pan. She gently pushed him away from the trunk then stepped back a few steps to get a run up. Within seconds she was leaping through the air, her hands jolting out to grasp the lowest branch and then she was scaling the tree like she was one with the bark. Pan watched from below, his eyes trained on her the entire time. He knew her limits, how far she could realistically fall before getting hurt. She was the future, he was never going to let any harm come to her.

Nathaniel stood behind Raesh on his right hand side like he always did. He followed two paces behind as the King walked and talked with the game masters and did his best to look like he wasn't listening to every word of the conversation. He had changed his clothes, like Raesh had requested, and was now wearing a tunic the green colour of the Spiran flag, pulled in at the waist with a gold belt much like the King's. Only his was not adorned with jewels. His black trousers were tucked into black shiny boots, he had washed them before putting them on.

It had been ten years since the last games and he knew full well that Raesh was nervous. The King had won the past four games with his chosen competitor with relative ease, but this time there were rumours about some serious contenders.

It wasn't just glory up for grabs, the crown itself was the big prize. Raesh had never lost. The six main cities in the land competed every ten years for the chance to rule, with a few other settlements joining in, though none of those stood a chance. The crown went to whatever city was victorious. Spire had certainly benefited from being the Capital for the past forty years; its strength and wealth outweighed the other cities in extreme measures, making the whole prospect of the games a rather daunting idea to other cities.

Raesh had mentioned from time to time that he felt a shift in the air, that he could feel a rising brewing and the thought was unsettling. Nathaniel even felt uneasy with the idea of people turning against Raesh; he had been hand chosen by the King to be his confidant–his right hand man. No matter how much he disagreed with the way Raesh governed Spire and dealt with world affairs, the people would just see him as an accomplice.

"Nathaniel–" Raesh snapped, jolting the brunette out of his thoughts for the second time that day.

Nathaniel blinked at him. "Sorry, Your Highness, I was distracted."

"Obviously." Raesh pursed his lips together. "I was saying that you could meet the Princess from Nova this afternoon. She is due to arrive with her convoy over near the lagoon. We don't want the *savages* getting to her now do we?" Nathaniel flinched at the term. The merfolk were anything but savages, but they were ruled by no one, a force that Raesh would never be able to control.

"Of course, I can do that," he said quickly. "And what of the other rulers?" he asked. "When are we expecting them to arrive?"

"You should know that already," one of the game masters tutted. "What is the use of having magic if you don't use it? Surely you can see when they will arrive?" Nathaniel had to bite his tongue; he didn't know how many times a day he was reprimanded for not using magic that he simply did not have. He could do a lot of things, but seeing into the future was not one of them.

"I think you need to watch your tongue," Raesh warned and the man's eyes widened. "Nathaniel is very special to me, you should show him some respect." Nathaniel looked to his King in surprise. Raesh very rarely spoke up when someone was being rude to him, though he guessed that this time he was just using it as an opportunity to assert his dominance over the man.

"I, um, well, I apologise," the man stuttered as he bowed his head. "I did not mean any offence."

"Nathaniel is a very skilled magician. I do not appreciate anyone suggesting that he is not using his power to its full potential." Nathaniel could practically see the hidden meaning behind the King's words, feel them hitting him from all angles. For it was Raesh who was the one who pushed for magic, who constantly questioned the boundaries of Nathaniel's abilities, who accused him of not being enough. "Anyway!" Raesh clapped his hands together. "We really must discuss the order of the rounds, hmm?" He looked at Nathaniel. "Head to the lagoon and make sure our guests get to us safely."

Nathaniel would venture out to the lagoon every now and then to speak with the merfolk, usually when Raesh was out in other settlements, to find out what whispers were floating throughout the island. It took him a good three hours to get from Spire to the white marbled rocks and bright exotic flowers that surrounded the magical area. The lagoon was always bathed in beautiful golden rays from the sun which encouraged the flowers there to always be in bloom no matter the seasons elsewhere. It truly was an enchanting place–but deadly for those who did not venture there with caution.

"Nathaniel!" He heard his name before he set sight on any movement in the water, a usual occurrence, so sat himself down on a rock that was bathed in sunlight and let out a content sigh. "Hi, Nathaniel." A smiling face emerged from the water in front of him and he sat forward slightly to give his full attention to who had greeted him.

"Priya." He smirked as the mermaid pulled herself out of the water to sit on the rock to his left side. He glanced at the scales that covered her arms and climbed up her neck to decorate her cheeks. They shone iridescently in the light, creating an ethereal glow around her.

"Did you miss me?" she asked and placed a cold kiss to his cheek. She wrapped a wet, webbed hand to the back of his neck, he could see from her stiff expression that she was fighting the urge to pull him violently into the water.

"Of course," he answered then noticed her arm twitching before moving her hand back to rest on her glistening white tail. "Have you been lonely without me?"

"Not at all," she laughed. "Why, I have many visitors during the day. The fairies come to see me all the time." Nathaniel shifted slightly and pulled his legs up to sit crossed legged beside her. Dangling his legs near the water was not a good idea. He knew from experience.

"And what stories do they tell you?"

"What will you give me if I tell you?" She smiled at him and flicked her long silver hair over her shoulder.

"This–" Nathaniel said and reached into his overcoat pocket to pull out a small pink enamel music box. He twisted a brass screw on the back four times then opened the lid to show a small ballerina inside who turned around to the sound of twinkling music.

"Nathaniel!" Priya exclaimed and snatched the box away from him. She held it close to her face as she watched the small figurine turn in circles until the music slowed and it came to a stop. "Poppy-leaf told me that they have been watching a new group who have been sailing to the island," she said once she had finished inspecting the box.

"A group?"

"Yes." She nodded. "Men, on a boat, she didn't say much else. There have been a lot of whispers of strangers in the area. I've also heard that Pan has been seen again."

"Pan?" Nathaniel frowned. Even the mention of the man's name made the hairs on the back of his neck stand on end.

"Yes. I have not seen him myself, but Poppy-leaf wouldn't lie to me, she is a good fairy." Nathaniel wasn't so sure of that; he hadn't encountered Poppy-leaf many times, but the times he had he could tell from the high pitched bell chimes of her voice that her tales were told with added flourish. It was hard to decipher what was true and what was a fabrication.

"Pan has not been seen in forty years," Nathaniel told her. "And if he had, everyone would know about it. Do you think he would creep around in the shadows? No. He would come back to take the crown."

"If you say so." Priya shrugged then let out a yawn, her small fangs creeping over the edges of her lips as she did so.

"When did Poppy-leaf tell you that she saw Pan?"

"This morning," Priya yawned. "Oh, Nathaniel, darling, let's not speak of Pan, I've told you that I can drown him if he comes down here, if you want me to. Why won't you let me?"

"I don't want you to kill him if you see him." Nathaniel chewed on his bottom lip as he thought of the possibility that Pan might actually be back. It was far too absurd to think about. "Besides, Pan is not the reason I am here. There is a convoy passing through from Nova. I need to make sure that you don't stop them from getting to Spire."

"Now what makes you think that I would do that?" Priya asked innocently before flashing a smile at him. "I haven't seen a convoy, what are they doing coming all the way from Nova?"

"They are here for the games."

"The Crowning Games?" Priya asked and sounded slightly surprised. "It has been ten years already?"

Nathaniel nodded. "It has."

"That could be why Pan has been spotted then." She placed the music box down beside her tail then stretched her arms out into the air, sending small droplets of water cascading down to her elbows to drip off onto the rock below her. "I will be sure to let the others know not to attack any convoy passing through. But any stragglers are fair game. We have to eat." She looked at him, her dark eyes like water themselves, rippling black pools that seemed to go on forever. Nathaniel could feel himself falling into them, could feel the icy cold grip of her wet fingers circling his wrists and the powerless feeling started to make his arms go numb.

"Let go." His voice was stern but weak as he looked at her, blinking rapidly to break whatever trance she was trying to put him in, he couldn't ignore the small feeling of fear that was building in his chest. It would only take her a few seconds to pull him into the water and hold him there until his lungs were filled and his breathing stopped. She looked back at him, her eyes showing no emotion, but eventually let go of his hands and slipped back into the lagoon silently, not leaving a single ripple as evidence that she was ever there.

He focused on the music box she had left behind as he willed the warmth and feeling back into his arms. He hated how quickly she did that, how he hadn't even noticed her hands gripping his, he didn't even notice the magic slipping away from him, rendering him easy prey for the mermaid.

He let out a puff of air and rubbed his wrists, he could feel fire crackling beneath his skin and swallowed thickly. The magic that had momentarily abandoned him was back with a vengeance, looking for whoever had silenced it.

"Stop," Nathaniel commanded as small sparks danced on his fingertips. "Not now, please." The magic seemed to be considering what he was asking as it flared more then burned down to nothing a second later. "Thank you." He released the tension in his shoulders and and took a deep breath, his gaze aiming for the blue sky above him. Clouds moved lazily across the hazy canvas and the sun looked down at him nonchalantly. He wanted to fly. He wanted to just rise up into the sky and touch the sun, maybe then the constant pull he felt towards it would subside and he would be free.

Three

Rica chewed on the end of a small twig as they walked. She could feel Pan's eyes on her each time she held the wood between her teeth then yanked it out as hard as she could. She knew full well what he was thinking, *"Don't do that, it will break your teeth."* Well, maybe she wanted to break her teeth. Maybe she wanted to have small shards of white in her mouth opposed to the perfect set she had now. She heard the man clear his throat so she narrowed her eyes to look at him.

"Pan? Do you have something to say?" she asked and gave the twig another hard pull, which actually hurt that time, but she didn't let that pain register on her features.

"We are near the lagoon." The response from Pan was not what she was expecting, not what the rest of her entourage was expecting either. A couple of guards pulled their guns from their holsters and got ready to aim, but Pan simply raised a hand and signaled for them to relax. "I know an easy way past it," he informed them. "Unless it is somewhere you would like to visit, Princess?"

Rica flicked the twig to the ground. "Are the stories true? About the mermaids?" Pan nodded. "Then, yes, let's go that way. I have never seen one before and if I am meant to be Queen then I think I should really know about all the creatures on this land." She noticed how Pan tensed when she spoke about being Queen. His broad shoulders holding all of his anxiety. Surely he believed that he would win these games for her and her family? Wasn't that what he had promised them?

"I don't think we should go that way," one of the guards said nervously. "I've 'erd that them merthing's they pull ya into the water. Drown ya."

Pan looked at him thoughtfully. "What you have heard is completely correct. Many people have lost their lives to the merfolk. Their song is enticing, as is their appearance. They can make themselves appear as your deepest desire. Best not look them directly in the eyes. And that is assuming we will actually see them."

Rica pouted. "You mean there is a chance that we might not even see them? They might not be there?"

"They will be there," Pan confirmed. "They will be watching. They just might not deem us important enough to show themselves to." With that Pan pulled the hood of his black cloak up over his head, casting his face into shadows. "If they are there. Do not look at them in the eyes. Remain friendly and polite. Don't give them reason to kill you." He moved past the guards and took position at the front of the convoy.

"Did you encounter the merfolk a lot?" Rica asked as she pushed through her guards to walk beside Pan a short while later. "When you lived here?"

"There were a few that I considered friends, actually," he admitted. Rica had to jog lightly to keep up with Pan's long strides. "I guess it is foolish to think of any of them as friends though."

"They never tried to kill you?"

Pan laughed. "Of course they did! I was pulled under the water more times than I care to admit. There was always someone there to save me though."

"There was?" Rica asked, intrigued. "Do you mean to tell me you had a real life human friend who liked to save you from drowning?" she scoffed. "Nope, can't picture that Pan," she chuckled, her black curls bouncing as her shoulders shook. "No one could stand to voluntarily spend time with you."

"You do."

"Well, I am one of a kind," she said proudly. "Everyone else is scared of you. Why is that Pan?" she asked with a hum and an arched eyebrow.

Pan blew air between his lips in exasperation. "I am the enemy. Or I was. I hardly expect people to just accept that I am no longer working against them. You weren't even born to know what it used to be like."

"You mean when you were in charge?"

"Exactly." Pan looked over his shoulder to make sure that the guards were keeping up. He stopped a moment later and pointed to a sloping bank to the left of them. "The lagoon is just down there. I will go first, come down with the Princess once I give you the signal."

"What's the signal?" the same guard that spoke earlier asked.

Pan blinked slowly at him then raised his hand up to his shoulder. "When you see me raise my hand, you can come down." He didn't wait for a reply, just turned and cautiously made his way down the bank until he reached the white stones at the bottom.

The lagoon was peaceful, not a single ripple on the water. It had been a long time since Pan had been out there but he had never seen it so quiet. Part of him considered the idea that the merfolk had moved on, that this was no longer their lagoon, but deep down he knew that wasn't the case. His eyes scanned the water, waiting for something, anything to move and greet him, but nothing came. He was about to raise his hand when he saw the figure sitting to the side of the water and his breath caught in his throat.

Nathaniel.

Nat. *His* Nat. He looked the same, maybe his hair was a bit wilder, his skin paler than before, but everything else looked like he had been frozen in time. Pan could even make out the familiar pattern of freckles that crossed over the other man's nose and cheeks from where he was standing, small dots on his skin that he had once pressed his lips to many years ago. He fought back the urge to cry.

Nathaniel stood up and started to make his way over to Pan, a strange arrogance in his walk that he couldn't remember having seen before. He stood a few feet away, which was good, there was no way he could make out any of Pan's features under his heavy cloak, he didn't need Nathaniel knowing he was back. Not yet.

"Are you part of the convoy from Nova?" Nathaniel asked, he sounded tired, strained, the carefree lightness of his voice had long gone. "My name is Nathaniel, I have been sent to escort you to the King." Pan didn't speak, he couldn't, he knew that Nat would recognise his tone straight away.

Instead he raised his hand to signal the others, which made Nathaniel step back and raise his own hand in warning. Pan could see an orange glow in the other man's palm, he was ready to attack. The fire had not dimmed.

Rica and her guards came down the bank and stopped behind Pan. The Princess looked between the two of them then stepped forward, her bravery showing no bounds. She stood tall, her shoulders drawn back to show her stance as strong, just as Pan had taught her.

"My name is Rica Therault, Princess of Nova. We are passing through to get to the city of Spire for the Crowning Games. You will let us pass." Nathaniel lowered his hand immediately, the flame that had been threatening to grow extinguished. He bowed deeply, hand across his waist, then raised back to his full height. He had grown, Pan thought, not much, but he wasn't as small as he used to be.

"Princess, my name is Nathaniel. I have been sent from the royal court of Spire to greet you and ensure your safe passage from here into Spire." He smiled at her and Pan saw that glint of sunshine that he so used to admire in the man. "I am honoured to meet you."

"This is my personal guard, Kaz," Rica said and gestured to Pan. He was relieved she had remembered not to use his actual name. "My other guards will follow behind but Kaz is to stay by my side."

"Of course, Your Highness," Nathaniel nodded. "Please, follow me, King Raesh is looking forward to meeting you." Rica slumped her shoulders a bit, obviously not feeling the need to keep up her dominant posture and walked forward towards Nathaniel with a warm smile.

"And I am looking forward to meeting him!" She reached out her arm and linked it with Nathaniel's, something that the man seemed surprised at. He tensed at the contact but Rica didn't let go. Pan couldn't tell if she was trying to be friendly or if she was trying to be assertive, but he stepped back behind her as they started to walk.

Nathaniel had never come across someone like Rica before. She was bright, in that she exuded a happiness that he hadn't witnessed in years. Spire was a relatively peaceful and happy place but no one had the same persona as Rica—he could tell even from being with her for a short amount of time. She had deep dimples in her cheeks every time she smiled, dark brown eyes that sparkled with every new thing that she saw. Her skin looked clear, soft, the colour of the trees but kissed with a droplet of gold. Her black hair was curly—not fly away curls like Nathaniel's, but tight curls that seemed to have a purpose, decorated with dainty golden beads. She was beautiful. In a way he wanted to warn her away from Spire, away from Raesh, he knew that the King would view her as someone to conquer, a prize rather than a person.

"Since being here I have not seen any fairies," Rica pointed out, her smile dropping a bit from her lips. "Why is that? There are so many back in Nova."

"Well. Like everywhere else Spire does have fairies, but, it is hard to maintain relationships with fairies so not many people put the effort in." Nathaniel explained.

Rica made an agreeable sound in her throat. "Well, I know how difficult they can be. My fairy, Fern, well, she still isn't talking to me at the moment. I told her to stay at home while I went to the games. She...isn't the brightest of fairies, she gets lost very easily. I didn't want to risk her getting lost in a place she didn't know," she laughed lightly. "But, I couldn't imagine her not being around. Do you have a fairy or did you...not put in the effort?"

"I have a fairy," he confirmed. "His name is Tippy-toe and he has a horrible attitude most of the time. He is pretty lazy too, very rarely leaves our home. I don't know what I would do without him though." Nathaniel had a relatively good relationship with the fairies. He owed a lot to them, he wasn't even sure if he would still be alive if it wasn't for them.

The day that he tumbled through the branches of the trees and landed harshly on the forest floor Nathaniel thought that his life was over, and not just from the injuries he had sustained from being dropped out of the sky. His ankle hurt, he was positive that it was broken and he could see blood running down his face from the corner of his eye. Wounds would heal, but whatever was going on inside of him would not.

He felt like he was being ripped apart from claws within his stomach, burning hot pain that shot through his entire body. He hated the world around him, hated how everything seemed to be aging and dying and now he was part of that too. Pan was gone. He had betrayed him and this feeling was the punishment for what he had done. He wanted to laugh again, to feel happiness, bask in the sun that used to beat down on his skin. He wanted Pan back.

Pan. Bloody Pan. This had all stemmed from him, this was all *his* fault, Nathaniel couldn't take the blame for it all. Every time Pan tasted power he became hungry for more. More power, more land, more magic. He never changed. Nathaniel only did what he thought he should do to protect his friend, his partner.

He had never felt regret before, not like this. It was almost like he couldn't comprehend the feeling, it was overwhelming and all consuming. It hurt. He raised his hand to his face, his fingers blurring as he tried to muster up some kind of magic. If he could he would turn back time, he would go back to when it was just him, Pan, and the other boys. He wanted to see the smile on Pan's face, his black hair shimmering under the sun. If he could he would memorise every golden freckle on Pan's brown coloured skin, join them together with his fingers like a dot-to-dot puzzle. He missed his voice, and the wonderful feeling of never being lonely.

It was Tippy-toe who was there to help him. Him and about a dozen other fairies. They had mended his wounds, fixed his broken bones and cleaned up the blood from his face. Tippy-toe had laid on his chest and told him stories of the adventures that they had shared when Nathaniel was younger, most of which he had forgotten as he had got older. One fairy brought him a flower filled with a sickly sweet nectar that he was told to drink to stop any infections spreading through his body. Its petals were a vibrant purple, he had never seen a flower like it before or since that day.

"Natty, get up," Tippy-toe whispered to him once the other fairies left. "We need to go home."

"Where is home, Tips?" Nathaniel let out a pained sob as the realisation that his home had gone ripped through his body.

"The Lost Boys have called it Spire. That is home now," Tippy-toe told him, his dainty voice of tiny bells rang out with certainty. "We must go there and report to the King and hope that he does not kill us on sight."

Nathaniel stirred and finally sat himself up causing Tippy-toe to slide down off of his chest and into his lap. "Do you think that Raesh will have us killed?" he asked and wiped his eyes with his sleeve.

"Yes, probably."

"Then why did you and the others heal me? Why bother if the King will simply have me killed?"

"Well, there is also the possibility that he won't." Tippy-toe adjusted the tiny little acorn hat that he had perched on top of his head. "Besides, we can't just lay here forever can we? I'm cold." Nathaniel held out his hand for Tippy-toe to climb onto, once he did he lifted him up and placed him into his pocket–the one place Tippy-toe liked to be so he could sleep.

"Let's take a chance on Raesh..."

Four

Pan stood back as Rica was introduced to Raesh, hood still up, hiding all of his features. The King was thinner than Pan remembered, in fact he looked a little like a corpse. His skin was paper white, hair blacker than the darkest night, his thin frame was hugged with tight black clothes that accentuated each jutting bone in his body. Pan was sure that he could blow and knock the King over. The only thing that held any weight on him was the heavy green cloak over his shoulders and large golden crown on top of his head.

Nat stood to the King's right hand side which made Pan bristle with anger. How could he? It was one thing to go running to Raesh after Pan was defeated, it was another betrayal entirely to be standing at his right hand.

"The other royals from across the land will also be arriving today," Raesh said to Rica from his throne made of twisted wooden branches. "To celebrate I will be throwing a feast in all of your honour this evening. It has been a long time since we have all been joined together and I intend to make it a joyous occasion." The King smiled, a crooked thing which showed off less than desirable teeth. "You may also stay in my palace if you have not arranged any other accommodation for your stay." Pan had to hold back a laugh. *Palace*. The place was a prison, just because the walls were made of wood and appeared to have accessible exits did not make it any less of one.

"If you are extending an invitation for us to stay with you in this beautiful palace then I will gladly accept," Rica said, showing off her charm yet again. Pan could see the King looking down at the hole in her trousers, it was clearly bothering him, which was good, he didn't want him to be comfortable with her.

"Would you like a personal tour of the palace and the gardens?" Raesh asked as he stood from his throne, he had grown since Pan had last laid eyes on him. The last time Pan stood a good couple of heads taller than him, now he appeared to be just as tall as Pan, if not taller. Nat looked tiny next to him, but height had never been an issue for the magician before, he had more power in his little finger than Raesh could even dream of. He was safe, Pan knew that much.

"I would love to," Rica beamed.

"But first–" Raesh smirked. "I need to know which one of your guards will be fighting on your behalf in the games." He gestured to the people standing back with Pan. "I'm sure that you are well aware that we need to know, for fairness, who your competitor is before you meet the other royals. All names are given to my right hand man, Nathaniel, and kept secret until the official announcement. I will not know your choice either."

"Has your choice already been submitted?" Rica asked, which caused a brief expression of disgust to cross over Raesh's face at being questioned so openly.

"But of course," he said and placed a jeweled hand over his heart. "I play by the rules, Princess."

Rica smiled. "Then of course, may we speak in private, Nathaniel? I do like all the secrecy and intrigue," she laughed. Nathaniel looked to Raesh who gave him a nod so he gestured for Rica to follow him into another room. Pan was close to insisting on going with her, but he knew the rules of the Crowning Games, he just had to trust that Nathaniel would let no harm come to her.

He didn't have to worry for long as only a couple of minutes later Nathaniel came back into the throne room with Rica close behind him.

"That was fun!" she exclaimed and Pan groaned under his breath. She was too excitable, treating the games like a holiday rather than a serious political event. He didn't feel like bringing her down though; she was much better company than her parents. "Now, we can have the tour?" Raesh nodded and moved away from his throne and offered his arm for her to take. Rica did so without any hesitation and Pan fell in behind them as they started off around the palace.

Kaz Bresis. Nathaniel had never heard of him and it irked him. Of course he didn't know every single person who was under the rule of Spire in the land, but he knew of the important people. That included those most likely to be chosen by their cities to compete. The name Kaz Bresis had never been whispered to him by a fairy and he wondered where this mysterious man had come from. It didn't help that he hadn't lowered his hood at all, not even when meeting the King which was, well, quite frankly rude, and he was surprised that Raesh hadn't reprimanded him for it. Still, there was something oddly familiar about him, his figure was known to Nathaniel, it was the way he carried himself, so light, like he was walking on wind. There was only one person who had ever had that air of grace about them and there was no way that Kaz was him, it was impossible.

He took a deep breath and ran his finger over the ink displaying the man's name on the parchment in front of him. Raesh hadn't named a competitor yet, but there was a space above Kaz's name for Raesh to put it there once he had decided. It was the same every time. Raesh would wait until Nathaniel had gathered all of the names and then study the list before deciding who he was going to enter into the games. It was cheating, pure and simple, but the only person who knew about it was Nathaniel and it wasn't like he was going to expose the King.

He didn't have any clue who Raesh might be wanting to enter this year either. Usually he had some idea who it might be, but Raesh had been very quiet about it, to the point where Nathaniel wondered if he even had a worthy competitor to enter.

Tippy-toe yawned from his small bed beside the window, which was a large brown leaf filled with tufts of grey wool. Nathaniel looked over to him and saw his silver wings flutter as he slowly woke up. He blinked a few times as he lifted his head, his dark brown hair poking out at all angles as he looked at Nathaniel blearily.

"Good evening Tips, nice of you to actually wake up today." Nathaniel went over to him and held out a corner of bread he had saved from lunch. "Hungry?" Tippy-toe looked at the bread then took it, but lay back down and cradled it in his arms.

"I don't want to be awake," the fairy groaned then took a bite of the bread and chewed slowly. "I want to die."

"Oh come on Tips," Nathaniel said with a frown. "She will be back."

"Oh it is easy for you to say!" Tippy-toe wailed and threw the bread out of his bed in a huff. "It took her eight years last time. *Eight years.* How can I survive another eight years without her?" Nathaniel picked up the bread and placed it closer to the bed, knowing that the fairy would want it again.

He had been in a slump since Mildew had left. Mildew had once been Pan's companion, and, since he left forty years ago, she would often go out on expeditions to try and find him. Tippy-toe was right, sometimes these trips lasted years, and she never found Pan no matter how hard she tried. It always left Tippy-toe completely and utterly heartbroken, and fairies were not known for being able to handle more than one emotion at a time, so that heartbreak was all consuming.

"She always comes back, Tips, she loves you, she wouldn't ever leave forever."

"You know nothing of love," Tippy-toe spat back and pulled a piece of wool over his head. Maybe the fairy was right; maybe he didn't know anything about love and the pain that could come with it. He thought that he was in love once, but that was a very long time ago.

Five

"P an!" Nathaniel called after the boy ahead of him and watched as he jumped with ease from rock to rock, lingering in the air for a few seconds each time. "Pan, I can't run that fast!"

"Then fly!" Pan shouted back at him which made Nathaniel huff in frustration.

"I can't! I don't know how." He stopped running and panted as he watched Pan get even further away from him. He felt tears pooling at the corners of his eyes and let out an involuntary sob that caused him to start openly crying in the middle of the forest. Within seconds he felt arms wrap around him and a warm breath on his cheek.

"Don't cry," Pan whispered. "I'm sorry, I forgot you can't fly. Let's walk instead." It was an out of character suggestion, one that made the hair's on the back of Nathaniel's neck stand up. Pan was many things, but he was rarely kind and he *very* rarely showed any signs of affection. "I promised your brother that I wouldn't let you cry," Pan said, as if reading his mind.

"You did?" Nathaniel sniffed and pressed the palms of his hands to his eyes to stem the flow of his tears.

"Of course I did. Boys don't cry, they are not allowed."

"That's not true." Nathaniel frowned. "Boys can cry too, anyone can cry...I just don't like crying. Henry said it was okay to cry if you felt sad."

"I've never seen a boy cry before." Pan scoffed then laughed.

"But, I've seen *you* cry before, Pan."

"Okay, okay, okay." Pan raised his hands in defeat. "I only cried that *one* time, never before that and not since then either." Nathaniel knew that was a lie. "Now, let's get walking and find the pirates." Pan took Nathaniel's hand into his and they walked together at a much slower pace than they had been moving before.

"The pirates aren't really real, are they, Pan?" Nathaniel asked after a while which made Pan stop in his tracks and look back at the boy with a solemn expression.

"Of course they are real," he said seriously. "They would take over the whole island if it wasn't for me. That is why we need to keep checking, to make sure that they have not come back."

"But, I have never seen a pirate. What do they even look like?"

"Oh, well, they look like...they look like..." Pan frowned deeply as he spoke and cocked his head to the side as he thought. "Well, now come to think of it, I am not really sure."

"You have seen them though?"

"Well of course I have!"

"Then, why don't you remember what they look like?" Nathaniel asked, an innocent and inquisitive expression plastered across his face.

"I don't know what they look like because they hide in the shadows," Pan explained. "They never let you see their faces, but I have heard that they are so ugly that if you did look at them they would frighten you to death!" Pan pulled a gruesome face and stuck out his tongue which made Nathaniel gasp softly.

"So, we need to follow the shadows and we will chase them away from the island?"

"Exactly," Pan pronounced proudly and turned to start walking again. Nathaniel felt frightened at the thought of these grotesque shadow pirates; they could appear out of anywhere and he kept looking around at any small movement that was made in the forest. It didn't occur to him then to question Pan and his version of what a pirate really was; Nathaniel had never seen one so what Pan said was the only truth he knew.

They never found any shadow pirates on their excursions into the forest, but even when Nathaniel got older he would still be wary about travelling too deep into the trees on his own in case a sudden darkness consumed him and he found himself surrounded.

It wasn't until Pan had gone and Nathaniel had spoken to other people about pirates that he found out that Pan had been lying about what the pirates really were. They were not mysterious shadows. Sure, some of them were not particularly attractive, but they weren't monsters like Pan had portrayed. They were men. Plain and simple.

The Lost Boys created a very different picture of the pirates. They insisted that Pan was the one who ignited the feud with them, that actually the pirates wanted to live on the island peacefully but Pan had tormented them to the point that the captain, a Mr James Hook, couldn't take it anymore.

Hook.

The name always felt familiar to Nathaniel but he couldn't place why, Pan had certainly never mentioned him that's for sure.

In fact, there was a lot of things that Nathaniel found out about Pan that the man had never talked about, important things that Nathaniel was sure were key moments and memories for Pan.

It was difficult to know fact from fiction when it came from the whispers of The Lost Boys, no one really knew the truth and the stories passed down over the years became elaborated and sensational–Nathaniel was even guilty of flourishing a few facts to make them more interesting himself. Not that he wanted to make Pan into something that he wasn't, no, he wanted to add to his legacy and make him the magical and wonderful creature he used to be, not the villain he had become.

One of the stories that Nathaniel created was the story about how and why Pan had started to grow up. For Nathaniel, Pan growing up was not a bad thing; it was a sign of Pan and the island that they lived on becoming something new, a completely exciting and shiny new era that Pan should have embraced if he hadn't of been so scared. No one aged normally; Nathaniel knew he was much older than the twenty years he appeared to be, yet the aging process was reduced to such a rate that he could have actually been in his hundreds. Which meant that Pan was even older. A boy that never grew up was magical, to children. But, a man who aged and kept his youthful looks and bright spirit–that was magic for an adult. If only Pan did keep his spirit, that ray of sunshine that shone so brightly from day to day was ripped away from him. He turned into a bitter and angry man who showed no signs of his once youthful and happy ways. He became a darkness, he became the shadow that people feared, he forced out everyone, including Nathaniel.

Six

Nathaniel looked around the throne room and noticed that Kaz Bresis was suspiciously missing. Rica had referred to him as her personal guard, so, it made no sense for him not to be around her at an affair like this. Raesh had his own guards stationed around the palace, but that didn't mean that the place was safe. Since that afternoon Nathaniel had greeted a further six royals from various parts of the land and added another six names to the competitor list.

He watched those competitors now as they mingled with the royalty, eating food from the grand feast Raesh had arranged for them. Richly colourful fruits, salted meats, freshly baked breads and cream cakes adorned a giant table in the middle of the room. There was a lot of showboating on evenings that led up to the games, which is why it was strange for Kaz not to be there. Rica should have been showing him off, amplifying his strength and ability to intimidate the others. Then, that could have been her intention by not having him there. He was now a mystery, a cloaked man who no one had heard talk and no one had seen. The more Nathaniel thought about it the more clever it became. Rica knew what she was doing. She had a very carefree and excitable personality, but she was focused and she clearly had eyes for the crown.

"Beautiful isn't she?" Raesh was by his side and he wished he could sense the King before he appeared the way he did. He was looking at Rica with intent. "Do you think she would offer herself to me?"

"Offer herself?" Nathaniel couldn't help but scowl. "In what way?"

"Preferably as a wife," Raesh said and took a sip of his dark red wine. "Though, I am sure I could take her as a mistress and that should be enough for her. No one really believes that the crown is going to be taken from me. She would be lucky to be accepted and taken by me. Two great cities joined. Even if someone was able to take my crown, I would still have Spire, and Nova would be joined to it," he explained. "I should make her my wife before the games start." Nathaniel looked over to Rica. She clearly had no idea about what Raesh was planning for her; if she did she wouldn't have been there.

Raesh had taken twenty-two wives in the forty years he had ruled as King. None of them lived very long. "I just need to wait for the right moment to speak with her."

"What if she refuses?" Nathaniel asked.

Raesh laughed bitterly. "She won't. And if she does, well, I won't take no for an answer. I will chain her down and force her to join with me if she refuses. And, Nathaniel, this doesn't change the order I gave you this morning. I expect to see you in my chamber tonight. Do not make me wait."

Nathaniel walked through the dark halls quietly. He knew his way to the King's room with his eyes shut—and he hated it. Yet, he felt like he had no other option. The King had spared his life all those years ago, even put him in a position of wealth and power, and this was the price. The only person who knew about the anguish it caused him was Tippy-toe, who had, more than once, threatened to put poison in one of Raesh's drinks. Nathaniel knew he would do it if he asked him to as well, but he didn't want Tippy-toe to kill anyone, especially not for him.

The first night he had been called to the King's room he had been naive enough to think that it was for an innocent talk. He had cried himself to sleep that night and washed his skin with such intensity it had been left red-raw.

Raesh always had a lover lined up for each night, Nathaniel was just a fill in, a strange desire for the man that he had to indulge in every now and then. Luckily, that desire seemed to take over the King less and less but it still made Nathaniel feel nauseous whenever he was summoned to his bed chambers.

He kept his eyes down as he walked until he noticed a presence that was not normally there at night. It wasn't out of the realms of possibility that someone else could have been roaming the halls given that they had so many guests staying, but when he looked up and saw the cloaked figure his breath caught in his throat. Kaz Bresis.

Nathaniel didn't know what to say, but he felt he had to say *something*. "Are you okay?" The man opposite him shifted from foot to foot and gave a nod. In the dark of the night it was even harder to try and see his facial features, especially with that damn hood still over his head. "You know, we are inside, there is no risk of rain in here, you can lower your hood." Kaz let out a laugh, a husky sounding thing that was not what Nathaniel had imagined for him.

"I could make it rain if I wanted to," Kaz said. Nathaniel was expecting to find his voice familiar, but it wasn't, it rang no bells in his memory, which squashed any hope that it could have been Pan. It was a ridiculous fleeting thought anyway. Priya should never have mentioned him.

"So, you can do magic?" Nathaniel asked. "No wonder your Princess chose you to fight for her. Magic is a very, *very,* good advantage to have."

"So they say," Kaz said as he lowered his hood from his face. Instead of the brown curls that Pan had, this man had bright red hair, though his skin was a similar tone to the warm brown that Pan possessed. He was handsome, a scattering of facial hair accentuated his defined jaw line and he had the deepest blue eyes that Nathaniel had ever seen. "I hear you are quite the magician yourself? Will the King enter you into the games?"

Nathaniel couldn't help the laugh that escaped his lips. "No, he wouldn't enter me into the games. He has far better fighters than me."

"But, you said yourself, magic is a good advantage. You do not need strength if you wield magic."

"Maybe not, but you cannot win on magic alone. It takes more than that."

"You would know," Kaz commented somewhat bitterly.

Nathaniel narrowed his eyes at him. "What do you mean by that?"

"Well, you watch the games with your King each time they are held. I simply meant you would know how they play out, what approach is best. Maybe I should have a private chat with you sometime, find out all of your secrets." Kaz grinned at him, his thin lips pulling across his face to show a devilish smile.

"I highly doubt my King would allow that," Nathaniel smiled back. "And it would be an awful conflict of interest."

"It would?"

"Of course. I am assuming you are wanting to win for Nova to become the capital and gain the crown? I am loyal to my King, and to Spire, any secrets stay with me."

"Pity," Kaz sighed and stepped closer to him, so close that Nathaniel could feel his breath on his cheeks. "I would have liked to have got a foot up on the competition. Though, really, I don't think that I will need it." He stepped around Nathaniel and pulled his cloak back up over his head then continued to walk down the corridor away from the now bewildered Nathaniel.

Pan watched as Rica stuffed an absurdly large strawberry into her mouth. As she bit down the juices squelched and spilled out of her mouth at the sides then ran down to her chin before dripping off onto her bed covers. She hadn't even finished chewing before she was placing another one of the berries into her mouth but when she reached for a third Pan battered her hand away.

"Hey!" she protested as juice flew out of her mouth and sprayed on Pan's face. He scowled and wiped his skin quickly then moved the bowl of fruit away from her.

"You eat like a pig," he scolded. "It is disgusting. You are not a child."

"The fruit here is better than any I have tasted," she reasoned. "Seriously, it is amazing. How could I not cram it in my face?"

"You can enjoy food without eating it like an animal."

"The King couldn't keep his eyes off of me earlier, even when I was eating like a pig, as you say."

"I noticed," Pan said solemnly. "Don't let your guard down around him. The way he was looking at you, it was not in admiration, Rica, he was looking at you like you were a prize."

"Oh come on," Rica rolled her eyes at him. "Are you worried that the King is going to get all touchy feely with me? If he dares to do anything I don't like I will break his jaw."

"I don't doubt that," Pan conceded. "I am just warning you, to be careful. Especially with what we are trying to pull off."

"You mean the "grand plan", the most magnificent thing we have ever come up with?" She smiled. "We will pull if off Pan, I know it. I have Kaz out there patrolling the halls as we speak to ensure that he is seen."

"With his hood down?"

"I told him to be mysterious but to also allow someone to see his face. I quite like the intrigue surrounding him, or you, already. No one will see it coming and we will win the games." She stood up on the bed and started to jump happily before Pan yanked her leg and caused her to fall back down on the mattress with a thump.

"Will you just stop?" he said harshly. "Just stop. We don't have any guarantee of anything. There are more complications here than I expected."

Rica rolled to sit up and bit her lip as she looked at him. "Do you mean a certain right hand man who you can't stop staring at?"

"What? No! I wasn't staring at him," Pan said with a blush creeping up his cheeks. "But, yes, he is an issue. I knew he was here, but I didn't know he was Raesh's right hand man."

"Why is he such a problem?" Rica asked as she reached for another strawberry and managed to get it before Pan could stop her.

"He is an...old acquaintance. If you can call him that. He knows me, definitely knows my face, my voice, if he figures out who I am then the whole plan is ruined."

"That is why we have the real Kaz walking around until the games begin, then you take his place. You just have to hide out in here until the games begin," she said simply.

"The games are not for another week. You will be expected to mingle and meet with diplomats and royals. I need to be by your side, so I will have to keep up the disguise during the day too."

"Pan how am I going to explain why my right hand man always has a hood hiding his face? And what if they ask you anything? You can't remain silent, someone will get suspicious eventually. Besides, Kaz can do magic, he will keep me safe in your absence. I trust him."

Pan shifted uncomfortably. "I don't feel particularly happy about that."

"Aww Pan!" Rica squealed and moved over to him to wrap her arms around his shoulders. "See? You do like me!"

Pan shrugged her off of him. "Like is a very strong word."

"Sure, sure it is." She grinned and kissed his cheek lightly. "You're the best, Pan."

Seven

Back before Spire was established, before the Crowning Games existed and way back before Pan was missing, the former leader of The Lost Boys would adventure across the island with Nat by his side, looking for adventure, trying to avoid trouble, or sometimes causing it.

Nothing can be a strange thing. Depending on the situation nothing can mean everything or simply nothing. For Pan and Nathaniel, nothing was a blessing. They had been living on the old boat down by the docks in the east for the whole summer without any incident. No one from The Lost Boys came to bother them and they were not disturbed by any other strangers from the island.

It felt very much like it did when they were children, exploring the land without a care in the world. Nathaniel let his mind be taken up by all things Pan. He loved seeing the joy on the man's face and that made him happier than he could ever remember being. They stayed out late on the deck of the ship every night and counted the stars. Pan told him what each one was called, though he often got confused and couldn't remember which star was which, not that it mattered at all. They fell into such ease with each other that it was like they had been together forever.

There were times when they were apart, of course. Pan liked to go out to parts of the island on his own, Nathaniel guessed it was to clear his mind of whatever haunted him. The older man had nightmares. Nathaniel found this out after the first night of being on the ship with him. Some were worse than others but they came every night and took over his dreams and left him a trembling mess. Many times Nathaniel had got down on the floor with him and held him in his arms until he settled down. Other nights he would find that Pan had made his way into his bed and cuddled up to him like a child seeking protection. He looked vulnerable in those hours and Nathaniel wanted to protect him with everything that he had.

They never mentioned the nightmares to each other; Nathaniel put it down to Pan being embarrassed or simply not realising that Nathaniel knew about them. Pan had always been headstrong, he had no weaknesses–that's what he wanted people to think anyway. The adult Pan was not really any different to the child Pan that Nathaniel once knew. He was still full of his own self importance, smug and authoritative and there were times where Nathaniel just wanted him to just *shut up*. Half of the stuff Pan spoke about was clearly lies, and Nathaniel wasn't too anxious to call him up on those lies like he was when he was a child.

"What?" Pan had frowned one day. "You don't believe that I fought off twelve tigers all on my own?!" The whole suggestion of it was absurd–simply down to the fact that there were no tigers on the island in the first place.

"Where did you find these tigers to fight?" Nathaniel asked in amusement. "Or did they find you?"

"Well, they were in the forest, of course," Pan said as he sat back on the deck of the ship then played his wooden flute happily.

"Right. And...did you kill them or just scare them away?"

"Killed them," Pan said when he removed his mouth from his flute. "They would probably track me down if I left them alive."

"You know, that's a real shame, Pan," Nathaniel smirked. "You might have killed the only tigers in the land, now no one will ever know they were here." Pan narrowed his eyes at him and raised an eyebrow.

"You still don't believe me?" he asked in disbelief which only made Nathaniel laugh.

Other days Pan gave complete re-enactments of his adventures. These would last hours and would involve Pan dressing up with old clothes that had been stashed away on the ship. He would even rope the fairies in to join in with his performances. Nathaniel loved these the most; it was wonderful to see joy in Pan's eyes again, to hear him laugh and parade around the ship with happiness.

One evening Pan lit candles and placed them on the deck, creating a beautiful glow that even the fairies seemed jealous of. Nathaniel was taken aback by how much effort he had gone to for whatever adventure he was going to play out next and was even more surprised when Pan told him that he wasn't going to be telling any stories that night.

"It's your turn," he smiled and gently took Nathaniel by the hand and led him to the bow of the ship. He had made a cosy area on the floor using blankets from the bed and had even set out a plate of fruits and nuts.

"My turn for what?" Nathaniel asked as he let Pan pull him to the deck and they made themselves comfortable.

"To tell me a story, of one of your adventures. I know you must have had some...from when I was gone?" Pan picked up an apple and bit into it, crunching down on it loudly.

"I don't know if you would really call them adventures," Nathaniel said and tucked a strand of his hair behind his ear. "Nothing like the ones we used to have as kids anyway."

"Oh, come on, there must be something that you can tell me."

"Hmm...okay," Nathaniel smiled after a moment and popped a blackberry into his mouth. "There was this time that Raesh was convinced that a flock of birds was trying to get into the village down near the ridge." He watched as a smile spread over Pan's lips. "He said that there were thousands of them, giant birds that he had seen flying over head one day. He told us that they were hiding out in the north-west, so he sent a group of us out there to find them."

"To fight birds?" Pan laughed and took another bite of his apple. "What did he think they were going to do? Make too many nests?"

"*Giant* birds, Pan," Nathaniel corrected him but he had a smile on his face as well.

"Did you find them?"

"No, though there was a huge nest right at the foot of the Great Mountain, it was massive. And there were broken pieces of egg shell too–one shard was even bigger than me. So, like, if that is how big the egg was imagine how big the birds were."

"Hang on." Pan placed down his apple. "Are you saying that there *were* giant birds?"

"There was a giant *something,* most likely a bird. But, it had gone by the time we got there and no one has seen them since Raesh did." He shrugged and ate another blackberry.

"I haven't been to the Great Mountain in years, maybe we should go there, see if that nest still exists?"

"Why?" Nathaniel laughed. "It's just an old nest."

"Would be awesome to see though, plus it would be quite nice to spend a day exploring with you. I could even show you the crocodile, everyone thought it was dead but it wasn't, it just went into hibernation in the cave behind the lagoon." Pan picked up his apple again and took a few big bites around the edge of it–crunching just as loudly. A light wind brushed past them both, tickling the flames of the candles, threatening to put them out. Nathaniel took a deep breath and closed his eyes. When he opened them again Pan was looking at him intently.

"What?" Nathaniel asked with a frown.

"Has anyone ever told you how pretty you are?" Pan asked which caused Nathaniel to let out a nervous laugh.

"No," he said and looked down at his hands. Pan reached over and tipped his chin up gently with a smile.

"Don't be embarrassed, it is a compliment, not many pretty people around here."

"Not even the women in the town?"

"Especially not the women in the town." Nathaniel swallowed thickly as he felt Pan's gaze start to intensify. He parted his lips as if to speak but Pan sat back again and started to shove berries into his mouth.

"Don't you want to meet any of the women in the village, Pan?" Nathaniel had no idea where that question came from, it had been building in the pit of his stomach and before he knew it the words had tumbled out of his mouth.

"No," Pan mumbled. "I'm not interested in them."

"Who are you interested in?" Nathaniel asked and, yet again, he didn't know how these words were forming from his lips.

"I'm not interested in anyone," Pan said after a painstaking few seconds of silence. "What about you Nat?"

"Am I interested in the women?"

"Sure." Pan nodded.

"I don't know. Maybe." He shifted uncomfortably. "I guess the only thing I want is to not be alone."

Pan frowned. "You've never been alone, Nat."

"I was when you left."

"You were with the other boys, that is hardly alone, is it?" Pan scoffed.

Nathaniel chewed at his bottom lip as he looked at Pan. "You still don't understand what it was like, do you? When you left? You were gone for years."

"I am aware of how long I was gone for."

"I had lost Henry, you were my closest friend. The others...well...they were not you," Nathaniel explained. "You got scared and you ran away and left me. Did you not think I was scared too?"

Pan slammed his hand down on the deck angrily. "It isn't all about you Nathaniel!" he shouted, which caused Nat to flinch back. "I looked in that mirror and saw a man staring back at me. That was never meant to be my story. Never."

"Everyone grows up, Pan," he said softly to try and calm the other man down. "Everyone."

"I wasn't supposed to." Pan stood up and kicked the plate of fruit, sending it tumbling across the deck. "You might have been able to accept it, but I couldn't. I still can't." Nathaniel opened his mouth to say something, but Pan had already turned from him and stormed back into the cabin. He took a deep breath and looked up at the night sky. The conversation had played out many times before and always ended the same way. Nathaniel could never get over the hurt of Pan leaving, he didn't think he ever would. And Pan, he would never get over the fact that he grew up.

Eight

Nathaniel blinked his eyes open. He felt like he hadn't slept a wink. It felt real, like he was on the deck of the ship with Pan again. The memory was so fresh yet so far away and he could feel the pounding of a headache right in the front of his skull. He turned on his side to look at Raesh who was asleep next to him. The previous night hadn't been that bad in comparison to other nights. The King seemed content on getting his physical need over and done with and swiftly fell asleep. Nathaniel had stayed awake for longer, but he had eventually drifted off into a restless sleep and now felt more tired than when he originally closed his eyes.

Pan. It was a complete fantasy that he would return, and what would he even say to him if he did come back? He hardly expected the man to be friendly with him, if anything Pan would likely try and kill him after what happened. Then again, he might try and kill Pan too. Parts of what happened felt like a blur, like someone had erased it from his memory–but badly, they had left parts of words and phrases there that didn't make sense on their own. How was he meant to piece it all together?

A burning sensation started to creep up his arms and he closed his eyes to will the magic away. He could feel his chest getting tighter, like his skin was being pulled tight over his lungs and ribs, compressing down until he couldn't breathe. The prickling heat started to become more intense as he tried to take deep breaths. Not now. This couldn't be happening to him now.

He got out of bed, scooping up his clothes from the floor and pulled them on as quickly as possible, not bothering to see if they were the right way around or if he looked presentable. He looked back at Raesh momentarily who was still sleeping soundly. He wouldn't be pleased that Nathaniel had left his room without permission, but the alternative was him burning down the place—which wouldn't make Raesh happy either.

The cool air out in the hallway was a blessing, but not enough to stop the burning that was now thrumming through his entire body. He avoided the looks of the guards who were stationed outside the King's room and hurried down past the guest rooms until he got to the bottom floor. It was then he started to run. His lungs were flames, burning up to his throat and he could feel sparks piercing through his skin. The quickest way out was through the kitchen, so he pushed through the staff who mumbled under their breath as he raced past them out the back door and into the vast gardens of the palace.

When he got far enough away he fell to his knees and let out a scream, his hands slamming down onto the earth in front of him. Fire plunged into the dirt causing it to crack along the earth, leaving black scorch marks in its wake. Nathaniel could feel the magic pouring out of him, the fire seeping deep into the soil and reaching out so far that anything green around him turned yellow and then to dust.

It hurt. His hands were tingling from the heat and lack of oxygen flowing through his body. Breathe. Breathe. Pan used to rub his back and tell him it was okay, it was okay to feel that way. He groaned and felt another rush of flames escape him–a flower bed to his left catching alight almost instantly. He looked over his shoulder at it and sighed before finally taking a deep breath. It felt like breathing for the first time after being submerged in water. It was painful, but so needed. He took another breath, then another as he heard footsteps behind him. There was a voice, distant at first, but then he realised that whoever was speaking was crouching down on the floor beside him and resting a hand on his shoulder.

"Are you okay?" He turned his head to the voice, his eyes blurred with tears, but he could make out the mass of beautiful black hair and he realised it was Rica beside him. He jerked away from her which caused her to pull her hand away suddenly but she didn't move from the position beside him.

"You need to get away from me," he whispered and wiped a burning hot hand over his equally hot face. "I could hurt you."

"Like you did those flowers?" she asked and nodded over to the flower bed that now had servants throwing buckets of water over it. "I think you are done now, don't you?"

Nathaniel flinched. No one had been this close to him during one of his attacks, no one apart from Pan. "You aren't scared?" He could feel the heat subsiding, slowly, but it was subsiding, but his breath was still getting caught in his throat, tripping on air and plummeting back into his lungs painfully.

"Of what?" She frowned and placed her hand back on his shoulder softly.

"Me," he gulped, his throat a desert. "I lost control."

"Nah," she shrugged. "If you were going to set fire to anything else I figured you would have done it by now. Want to go for a walk and cool off?" He couldn't understand how she was so flippant about what had happened, she might not have seen the extent of what he could do, but no one had ever got that close to him after a loss of control. Still, her talking to him and her steady hand on his back had grounded him in a way he wasn't expecting.

"A walk?" He pursed his lips together as she raised her eyebrows at him.

"Are you going to deny a Princess her request?"

"Well...no...I guess not." He swore he felt a rush of cold spread over him, emanating from her palm pressed against him.

He found himself getting to his feet, even though they felt like they didn't belong to him, and he was sure he was going to walk like he had been drinking rum all morning. Rica stood as well, dropping her hand, and waited for him to find his balance then she kicked at the dry earth beneath them with her black pointed boots.

"The way Raesh was gloating about his beautiful gardens yesterday I am going to assume that he is going to be pissed about this," she laughed, her bright voice reminding him of the way fairies communicated to each other, in high, happy tones. Twinkling bells.

Nathaniel looked down at the ground. The cracks and scorch marks were vivid against the green beauty of the rest of the garden. "No, I imagine he will be quite furious..."

"Best we leave the scene of the crime then?" Rica gestured for them to walk. He looked back at the staff who had now managed to put the fire out then gave her a curt nod. "Wonderful idea."

Rica moved with nature much like Nathaniel had seen some fairies do. She seemed to move slightly with the wind, she breathed and the wildlife around her took a breath too. She ran her hand along the rough bark of the trees as they passed them, fingertips gently caressing the brown surface with grace. He was so enamored by the way she moved that he didn't notice when they came to the large wooden fence that surrounded the edge of the palace gardens and she looked up at the large structure with a deep frown.

"Why cut off the gardens from the people?" she asked with a quiet tut. "These gardens are so beautiful, they should be for everyone to see."

"Have you been into the city yet? Spire is like this, full of trees, flowers, having a fence here really isn't hiding anything from anyone."

"Then why have it at all?"

"For protection."

"From who? The people?" Rica let out a disbelieving laugh. "It seems to me that the King is keeping the person he needs protection from in the palace with him."

Nathaniel regarded her with a slight sneer. "Are you referring to me?"

"Yes," she said bluntly. "I have seen magic before but I have not seen someone destroy earth like that. You were...powerful. Does it happen often?"

"You said you weren't scared of me," Nathaniel said bitterly.

"I'm not." She shrugged. "I just want to know why that happened. I thought that those who had magic were able to control it. That is kind of the point isn't it?"

"I don't think that anyone knows the point of magic. It isn't something that is taught to you, control is something that comes with time."

"And you still don't have it?"

"Why is it any of your concern?" he snapped. "King Raesh trusts me, that is enough."

Rica put her hands on her hips and laughed airily. "It isn't about trust, Nathaniel, I was worried, okay? I guess I just wanted to understand why it happened. Magic is still something that is a mystery really...I am just trying to understand."

"I don't lose control very often," Nathaniel said after biting his bottom lip for a moment. "I have panic attacks."

Rica blinked then gave an understanding nod. "That must be awful." She reached out and placed a hand on his shoulder. He felt the chill again. "I'm sorry that it causes you to lose control of your magic too. It can't be nice."

"It isn't," he agreed. "But, look, Raesh doesn't know the extent of what happens when I get like that. I don't want him to know. Please, don't say anything to him."

"The less I talk to your King the better," she whispered with a playful grin. "Bit of an arse isn't he?"

"I...can neither deny or confirm that," Nathaniel hesitated. "Actually I should have just said no shouldn't I?"

"Don't worry, I won't utter a word about what happened. But, will you keep a secret for me too?"

Nathaniel took a deep breath and eyed her skeptically. "What secret is it?"

"I am going to climb over the wall and go and explore the city. Obviously my guards will have a fit if they find out."

"We can arrange a tour of the city for you?"

"No, that's no fun is it? I want to be a runaway Princess, have an adventure, just like in the stories. So. I won't tell if you won't tell?" Nathaniel frowned, a deep feeling of conflict brewing inside of him. If anything happened to her he would be held responsible, and he didn't want her to come into any danger either, but who was he to stop her? She was old enough to make her own decisions and he was not going to get into the habit of telling royalty what they could and couldn't do.

"I didn't see you and you didn't see me," he agreed. "Just...be careful okay? Spire is pretty safe but you do get the odd person who is just out to cause trouble."

"I love trouble," she had a glint in her eye, the same spark that Pan used to have, in fact Nathaniel was sure Pan had said the exact same thing to him before.

He smiled. "Then, have fun Princess."

Nine

Pan had heard the commotion below his window and hung his head out as far as he dared to see what was happening. In the gardens below there was a flurry of what he assumed were palace staff, given that they were all dressed in the same grey uniform, and they were trying to put out a fire. No sooner had they doused one fire with water another popped up in the garden, which was a rather odd game for them to be playing. Pan smiled to himself. He remembered when Nat would light a flame in his palm from wherever he was hiding and Pan would follow the light to find him. The smile fell from his face when he realised that these flames were probably something to do with Nathaniel as well. His eyes swept over the garden but he couldn't see the messy haired man anywhere, only scorch marks on the ground and burning flower beds.

He had once woke to smoke flooding into his lungs. It tasted like he had been chewing on ash and when he opened his eyes they stung from the heat. He heard Nat crying, no, *screaming* from somewhere, but he couldn't see through the smoke to know where he was. He rolled off of the bed and found that he could breathe easier on the floor, the air slightly cleaner, not yet polluted.

Then Pan saw him, he saw Nathaniel in the corner of the bunker, fire pouring from his hands as he screamed. Pan had never seen anything like it, the fire, the fear, the utter devastation on Nathaniel's face. He crawled to him, coughing as more smoke cradled his lungs, but he made it to him, he placed his hands over the other boy's and gritted his teeth at the pain it caused him.

Nathaniel was boiling, and the fire that had been falling from his palms to the ground around him now crept up Pan's arms and bit at his skin–sharp and angry.

"Stop, Nat, stop," Pan whined, the fire reaching up to his neck and grasping his throat hungrily. "You will kill us."

"I don't know how," Nathaniel sobbed, but Pan felt the flame retract, felt it float back down until it rested on his arm. He couldn't believe his whole body wasn't alight, his clothes untouched. "I can't."

"You can, you're doing it now." He tried to sound calm, but he didn't know how successful he was being. He had to get them both out of the bunker, if the smoke didn't suffocate them then the flames that were licking at the tree branches certainly would. "See? You are doing so well," he said through a cough. "I'm holding your hands, they are getting cooler. It is going away. I just need you to breathe, breathe, you can do that, can't you?" Nathaniel nodded slowly at him. "Good, good. Now, we need to get out of here. Can you move?"

"I–" Nathaniel started, looking unsure. "I don't know." The smoke didn't seem to be effecting him the way it was Pan, there was no coughing or wheezing coming from him at all. "I mean...yeah, yes, I can." Pan felt a rush of relief wash over him, it only lasted a second before he could feel the heat that was surrounding them prickle at his skin again.

Moving in the bunker that they passed through everyday seemed baffling. The hours they had spent there with the other boys, telling tales, hatching plans, creating treasure maps, it all felt like a distant dream. Pan could almost grasp the familiarity of it, but with it plunged in smoke there was no finding it. The only thing that helped him figure out where to lead Nat was the little glimpse of fresh air that he could taste somewhere in the distance.

They climbed. The entrance to the bunker concealed down a tree. Perfect for hiding from enemies. Not so well thought out when you needed to escape.

Breathing in the air from outside was like plunging into a cold lagoon on a boiling hot day. They both collapsed on the lush green grass that carpeted the forest, chests heaving as they greedily took in large mouthfuls of air over and over again. Pan didn't know when his breathing calmed, or when Nathaniel rested his head onto his chest in exhaustion. He just slowly became aware of him, aware of the strong steady beat of his own heart beating underneath Nathaniel's cheek.

"What happened?" His words broke the peace that had settled over them and he felt Nathaniel flinch. "What happened Nat?"

"I couldn't find anyone," he replied quietly. "I was alone. It...it was so dark."

"Dark?" Pan shifted which made the younger boy move away from him. He sat up and looked at him laying down beside him, both of them tinged black from the fire. "What do you mean?"

"I woke up," Nat sighed and picked a blade of grass from beside him. He brought the piece to his face and inspected it closely. "The light wouldn't come in. I was in a room. A bedroom. Not one from here." He flicked the piece of grass out of his fingers and then picked another piece.

"A bedroom? Not from here?"

"Nothing that I have ever seen here before."

"What are you talking about?" Pan frowned.

"I don't know." He dropped the second piece of grass and looked up at Pan. "I don't know...I was confused. I called out for you, but you didn't answer. I panicked. I thought you had left me." Something pulled in Pan's chest, something he had never felt before and could never start to explain.

"I would never leave you Nat," he said surely. "Never."

Why had he lied all those years ago? The memory haunted him, even when he thought he had long forgotten it, it crept back just to remind him of the many promises he broke when it came to Nat. Now, looking down at the gardens that were charred and still smoldering, all he could think of was Nathaniel. It was obviously his doing, fire magic was not common and he was sure that Raesh wasn't hiding anyone else in the palace who could wield such power. Something must have happened to make him unleash his magic like that though, something that scared him. He knew Nat. He knew how his fear could build up, how panic struck him in a flash and he knew exactly how that manifested in his magic. The thought of Nathaniel having an attack and not having someone there to comfort him left an unsettling feeling in the pit of Pan's stomach. It was guilt. Rica had told him that many times, that uneasy feeling was one-hundred percent guilt. Emotions had never been his strong point. He had lived so many years without knowing or simply caring about anything other than happiness that when other emotions came flooding in at all angles he didn't know what he was feeling half of the time. Now, though, guilt was something he understood. Guilt was his default setting, something he was never going to lose.

Ten

The roster for the Crowning Games was missing one important name. Raesh had yet to decide who he was going to enter to fight for him and for Spire, despite the announcement of the competitors looming. Nathaniel knew that he wasn't going to get any names from Raesh that day, not after his precious palace gardens had been set alight. Surprisingly, he hadn't blamed it on Nathaniel. He was expecting the King to be furious and had been anticipating some kind of punishment. It never happened, which, in its own way, was rather unsettling.

"I am looking forward to the competitor announcement," a young Prince said as they all sat eating dinner at the large wooden table in the banquet hall. Nathaniel did know his name, Roman, Ryan, something along those lines. Unimportant. He was never going to win. Spire didn't even trade with his part of the island either, Nathaniel only made a note to remember those who posed a threat.

However, there were about four guests who could potentially steal the crown from Raesh. Yulia, Regent of Thelan, a large woman who towered over everyone, her shoulders broad, body powerful. She could have probably entered the games herself. She seemed strong enough. Her competitor was another woman who had a very similar build, her name was Luger and Nathaniel was sure she could crush him with one hand. The second was a Princess from Ipsling, a small village to the south of Spire. She was quiet, but she seemed to be taking everything and everyone in. Her competitor was a man who could manipulate the earth, a strong element, difficult to beat. The third was a boisterous man named Char, he had the audacity to call himself a King, even in front of Raesh. Nathaniel was surprised that he hadn't been sentenced to death. Yet. He boasted about his competitor, who was only known as 'Grim'. Nathaniel hadn't seen him, but Char insisted that his water magic was a force to be reckoned with.

Rica was who Nathaniel had his money on though. She was quietly confident, her competitor also held the same reserved confidence that Nathaniel admired. He was intrigued by them, he hoped that she would be victorious. She seemed like she would be a good ruler. Plus, it would be nice to actually have someone other than Raesh in charge.

"I must say, I have a very good feeling about the games this year," Char said through a mouthful of honey roasted vegetables. He waved his fork in the air as he spoke which made Raesh narrow his eyes at him in silent judgment. "I don't mean to boast, but I do think you will be handing over that crown to me, Raesh." He grinned at the King and Raesh gave a tight smile back.

"Is that so?" he responded in amusement. He picked up his goblet of wine and swirled it in his hand. "And what would you do differently, if you were King?"

"Open trade with all, why cut anyone off? We are all here on this island, might as well be friendly with each other."

"Trade is really the least of my concerns. As a royal, there are far more important matters to attend to." Raesh sipped at his wine. "Like keeping the peace."

"With the pirates?" Rica asked and all eyes locked onto her. "Is that who you are trying to keep the peace with?"

Raesh laughed. "Pirates? Those are just tales we tell children."

"Oh, come on now, you know that is not true." Rica smirked. "We all know they existed. Once. That they posed a great threat to us. Well, not really us exactly, but to Peter Pan. And The Lost Boys" Nathaniel took a sharp intake of breath. "That was way back when our little island was known as Neverland though, wasn't it? Or do you think that is also a tale for children?" He felt Raesh's body language stiffen, he could feel the anger emanating off of the King in small waves that only got stronger as Rica spoke. It was one thing to mention Pan, it was another issue entirely to mention the island by its true name.

"Do you realise how offensive you are being?" Raesh spoke after an agonising minute of silence around the table. "To mention that tyrant and the name he bestowed on this island? He is a blot in our history. The name Neverland died with him." Raesh sounded calm, but Nathaniel could sense the sharpness to his tone. The unease around the table was horrendous, a few people moved in their seats uncomfortably, while Char was making noises like something was stuck in his throat.

"A tyrant?" Rica placed down the cutlery she had been holding in her hands. "You think Pan was a tyrant?"

"I don't think. I know. He killed children. Hundreds of children. Everyone knows that," Raesh said simply and gestured to one of the servants to fill up his goblet of wine.

"Now, *that* is a tale," Rica laughed. She actually laughed. "A story that has been twisted over time. To say he got rid of The Lost Boys would be more accurate. He didn't kill them. Just sent them home."

"You are an idiot," Raesh said and let his calm demeanor slip. "If you think that Pan was an innocent child then you really are stupid. Stupid. I knew Pan. I was under his rule." He slammed his now full goblet down on the table, sending wine sloshing over the edges. "I respect that you are a Princess, but I am a K*ing*, and I demand that you remove yourself from my table." Rica looked to Nathaniel but he couldn't look her in the eye.

She raised her chin and stood defiantly. "As you wish, your majesty." She stepped back and bowed to him, an over exaggerated gesture that was clearly meant to offend rather than show any respect. She turned on her heel and left, her footsteps echoing across the wooden floor behind her.

"I will not tolerate any mention of Pan or Neverland in my palace. It is forbidden," Raesh said seriously as he looked at his other guests. "Anyone who breaks that law will be punished. You might be my guests but I will not have anyone disrespecting me." He turned his head to look at Nathaniel. "Let us leave our guests to dine in peace, we have a lot of preparation for the games to be getting on with."

"Of course." Nathaniel nodded. He didn't glance at the others around the table, he didn't want to see if anyone was going to dare and defy Raesh. He knew what the outcome would be.

Raesh punched his hand into the wall with such force Nathaniel was surprised that he didn't break any bones. He growled angrily and hit the wall again, this time breaking the skin on his knuckles.

"That *bitch*," he spat. "How dare she sit there and talk to me like that? How could she mention him? Pan? Pan!" he shouted. Nathaniel stood dumbly in the middle of the room as he watched his King pace back and forth. "Do you think that is what they believe in Nova? That Pan was some misunderstood hero?" He looked at Nathaniel expectantly, but he wasn't sure how to answer.

"I have heard no word of any rumours like that from Nova," Nathaniel said when he realised that Raesh wasn't going to move on until he said something. "I can send a fairy if you want me to."

"Send a fairy?" Raesh scoffed. "Bloody little liars. The lot of them. You need to get rid of her."

"Get rid of her?"

"Don't act dumb with me, Nathaniel," Raesh raised his voice angrily. "Get rid of her, turn her to ash for all I care. I want her gone."

"Your Highness," Nathaniel said carefully. "With all due respect, don't you think that the other royals will find it odd that she is missing after your altercation?"

Raesh seemed to consider what he said for a moment. "No. I don't care. I am still King. I will still be King, even after the games. I can have her executed."

"Then execute her," Nathaniel said simply. "After the games, make an example of her in front of everyone. To do so now might make people think you were threatened by her and her competitor in the games," he warned. "Now is not the time to let anyone see us as weak." He could feel his heart racing, he didn't want Rica to be another fatality in Raesh's history. No one deserved to be dwindled down to that kind of statistic.

"What if she wins?" Raesh asked and rubbed at his bleeding knuckles. "What then?"

"She won't"

"What makes you so sure?"

"Because I will compete for you in the games."

Part Two

40 years ago

One

Dark black sails flew violently in the wind, smacking hard against the mast that they were attached to and tangling in the ropes that hoisted them up. They had once been decorated with a skull and crossbones, but over the years the weather had torn them to such extremes that you would never have known that they once had an image sewn onto them.

The ship used to sit proudly in the dock, wood shining and windows glistening–a far cry from what it had been reduced to now. The glass in every window had been shattered, leaving sharp, angry shards of glass prickling at the frames. A few had been boarded up with wood, but most were left to let the weather make itself at home within the ship. The decks were covered in a dull green algae that caused anyone who stepped too suddenly on it to slip and fall, especially now they were covered in a thick frost.

Inside the ship it was surprisingly homey, made that way by those who inhabited it. The cabin had been filled with autumnal leaves, the floor was covered in the rich colours of red, orange and brown which created a warm and soft carpet for feet to enjoy. The bed, which had once belonged to the captain of the ship, was adorned with animal pelts, knitted blankets and the odd stuffed toy. During the night the room was filled with the warm glow of fairies, who returned to the ship every evening and holed themselves up in nooks and crannies of the cabin. In the center of the room was a large wooden table, it used to be polished so expertly you could see your reflection in it. It was dull now, carved with patterns and covered in various trinkets that had been collected from the island. The only thing that remained on the table that the new inhabitants had not moved was a large wooden box, lined inside with red velvet and locked with a gold clasp. It was rarely opened.

Nathaniel had only been to the ship a few times, most of those times being when he went there with Pan, when all they did was want to explore, many years ago.

Before Pan left.

He had avoided the dock since Pan went to live out on the ship alone, he was scared to see him, to be faced with the man they once told stories about. Part of him also didn't want to see him. Pan had abandoned him, abandoned them all without a second thought. Rumours had been circulating for months that Pan had returned. He had left in such a state of distress, none of The Lost Boys thought that he would ever come back. Nat had got near to the ship a few times, but had never ventured any closer than the trees surrounding the dock.

This time was different though; he needed to know if Pan knew anything about the new strangers on the island. They had appeared from seemingly nowhere, unsettling to say the least. Whispers had floated around the village of The Lost Boys that they were something to do with Pan. That he was going to build an army against them. He was going to kill them all.

Nathaniel wrapped his arms around himself, pulling his handmade overcoat to his body tightly to try and protect himself from the unforgiving wind. He spotted Tippy-toe hovering above the deck and raised his hand in a greeting to the small fairy who smiled in response. His feet slipped as he made his way up the ladder onto the boat; he had never been very good at climbing, and trying to make his way up a threadbare ladder was hardly a fun activity for him. It was one of the reasons why he had chosen a solid wooden ladder for his own tree house—it was far more secure, his home wasn't that far off of the ground either.

He surprisingly made his way to the top without incident and peered over the edge of the boat to see the waves crashing against the wood harshly. He had heard stories about how pirates would make their captives walk the plank—to be plunged into those murky depths and never take a breath of the cold air again. He shivered as he moved away from the edge and Tippy-toe beckoned to him, lighting the way to the cabin door which had been left ajar. His fingers trembled as he pushed it open with ease and was hit by a wall of warmth that flooded over his entire body in seconds. He let out a sigh of content, then quickly picked up his posture as he stepped inside of the cabin. Several fairies looked up from where they sat or lay to see who had dared to venture inside, but when they saw that it was Nathaniel they looked away with disinterest.

It only took a few seconds for him to notice the dark figure hunched over in the corner of the room, their back to him as they mumbled under their breath.

"Pan?" Nathaniel called out, his voice sounding distant and small as it was consumed by the cabin. Pan turned when he heard his name, his head lulling over his shoulder lazily as he looked over at Nathaniel with dark circles framing his eyes.

"Have you come to return my teeth?" he asked, his once light voice gravelly and worn. Nathaniel blinked slowly as he took in his appearance. His clothes were ripped, jagged and frayed at the edges, with dark stains that could have been anything from dirt to blood. Everything about him mirrored the angry weather outside, his usual golden aura had gone.

"Your teeth?" The question was not something that Nathaniel was expecting. He remembered having a strained conversation with Pan many years ago when they were kids about teeth, but he didn't think that related to what Pan was talking about now.

"I had them, in a white cloth, wrapped up." Pan stood from his crouched position and turned fully to face Nathaniel. "They were in a drawer in the desk. I was keeping them, for when I lost my adult teeth." Nathaniel was slightly taken aback at how tall the other man had grown, he now loomed over Nathaniel, a good foot taller than him. It felt surreal to see him again, after so long, after so much had changed. His beautiful skin that complimented the colour of the trees was thick with dirt, his usual sun kissed dark hair lank and greasy.

"I don't know what you are talking about."

"You must have taken them, you are the only one who knew about them." Pan waved his hand in the air to swat away Tippy-toe who had decided to flit around his head in excitement. "Stupid fairy," he muttered which earned him a nip on the ear from the young fairy who then flew to sit on the desk and watch the exchange.

"Pan, why would I take your teeth? I haven't seen you since you left, what would I even do with your teeth?" Nathaniel asked and felt Pan's eyes on him, taking in every inch of his body.

"You told me that I was losing my teeth because they were baby teeth. I figured that once I was no longer an adult I would be able to make use of them again."

"What? Once you lose your baby teeth, that is it, Pan. You have your adult teeth until you die." Nathaniel could see him moving his tongue along the teeth at the front of his gums and resisted the urge to ask him if he had been brushing them. "It was probably one of the fairies who took them."

"Maybe." Pan looked around at the glow from the fairies who had decided to live with him, he wouldn't put it past any of them to take them. "If you didn't come here to return my teeth then why are you here Nathaniel?" He ran his slender fingers through his curly hair and leaned back against a wooden chest of drawers in the corner of the room.

"I wanted to know if you had come up with a happy thought."

"Not yet."

"Good." Nathaniel said quickly which made Pan raise his eyebrows in surprise. It had been a rumour that Pan could no longer fly. A rumour that now appeared to be true. "So. You can't fly?"

"Do you not want me to leave Neverland?" Pan ignored the question, he stood straight again then stepped closer to the smaller man.

"It's not up to me if you leave or if you stay."

"That's not what I asked."

"I don't know." Nathaniel shrugged then stood his ground as Pan stepped even closer.

"How old are you now Nathaniel?" Pan asked and reached out his hand to touch Nathaniel's cheek softly.

"I don't know the answer to that either," he sighed. "How old are you Pan?"

"No one knows." Pan gave him a crooked smile and dropped his hand away from him. "Do you have any happy thoughts?"

"Not anymore."

"Not even about your brother?"

"I'm surprised that you even remember him." Nathaniel tensed at the mention of Henry.

"Of course I remember him." Pan frowned and took a step back. "I remember most things now, I don't know if it is a good thing, though."

"So, you remember leaving us?" It was Pan's turn to tense up this time and he cleared his throat awkwardly.

"Yes," he admitted. "You know that I didn't want to leave you behind though don't you?" Nathaniel took a deep, shaky breath at the question. He should have been able to talk about what happened freely after so many years. But being faced with Pan again was something he hadn't been able to prepare for.

"I don't want to talk about it."

"So, the only reason you came here was because, what? You wanted to know if I was leaving?"

"Yes." He didn't know why he wasn't asking about the other people on the island. He didn't know if he would get another chance and he was here wasting it.

"I don't see how me being here or not makes any difference to you though," Pan said coldly and sat down on the edge of his bed.

"It doesn't." Nathaniel spoke with the same cold tone that Pan had given him. He gestured to Tippy-toe, a slight nod of the head that said that it was time to leave. He saw Pan's eyes widen for a split second as he turned away and made his way out of the cabin and off of the ship.

Two

A roar of voices rumbled up through the tree trunks, erupting into the many wooden tree houses that were perched on strong, sturdy branches. Nathaniel woke up with a start, his hand on his chest as he felt his heart pounding hard against his ribs. He could smell fire before he realised that there was a slight glow creeping in through his windows. At least it wasn't him who had started it this time.

He was out of bed within seconds and leaned out of his window to get a glimpse of what was going on underneath him. There was a crowd forming around the pole in the center of the village and it was only then that he saw that a hastily made bonfire had been lit.

Raesh, the oldest of the boys, was standing in front of the flames, looking into them with such an intense expression that Nathaniel could see it from all the way up in the trees. Movement was happening from all of the abodes around him—boys throwing themselves down ropes and ladders haphazardly to get to the action that the fire called them to. A loud cry broke out over the excited voices that petered out into a low groan of pain and it was only then that Nathaniel grabbed some warm clothes to wear and made his way down to where the other boys were gathered.

He pushed his way through the crowd until he got to the front and stood beside Raesh, who was still looking into the fire like he was possessed.

"Raesh?" Nathaniel asked in alarm. "What's going on?"

"We caught a spy," Raesh said bluntly and tore his eyes away from the flames to point at a man who was gagged and bound to the side of the bonfire. Nathaniel didn't recognise him, and his mind immediately went to the newcomers on the island. He was old, his hair grey, thinning, dry like straw. Dark wrinkles surrounded his eyes and his cheeks plunged down from his bones so his face resembled that of a bulldog.

"What are you going to do with him?" Nathaniel kept his eyes on the man as he spoke, he could already see the sweat pooling on his skin from the heat of the fire.

"Burn him." Raesh grinned as he too looked at the man and the boys who had been listening let out a cheer.

"Why?" he asked bitterly as he looked at Raesh.

"If we don't kill him, then he will return and tell the others about us, about what he has found out."

"And what has he found out, exactly?"

"About us, of course." Raesh spoke seriously and narrowed his eyes at Nathaniel. His gaze was piercing, his eyes reflecting the dancing flames in front of them.

"If we hold him captive, then we can find out more about him, about what he is doing here on the island."

"We have already questioned him, we have enough." Raesh smiled. "Besides, we haven't had a good bonfire in a long time, we need a little fun every now and then." Nathaniel looked back at the man who was struggling in his restraints. He knew that it was the way that they had functioned ever since Raesh had taken over from Pan–that anyone who was against them was to be put to death. Burning was Raesh's favourite form of execution. It was slow and painful, he liked to watch as the flames consumed whoever was unlucky enough to get caught. He would often stay in front of the fire until it was reduced to a few smoldering embers. Nathaniel, on the other hand, could not stand the smell. Flesh bubbling away from bones was not something he could get used to, and the smell lingered for days.

"Did he say where he was from?" Nathaniel pressed, wanting to find some way to avoid the burning.

"Yes, we will talk about it more tomorrow. But now–" Raesh said and clapped his hand on Nathaniel's back. "Just enjoy the show." He motioned for a few of the boys to lift the man and cruelly throw him onto the fire like he was a pile of wood. Nathaniel couldn't stand it–the scream that came from the man was so unnatural, completely haunting and desperate, it gave him chills. He turned away from the sight just as the boys surged forward to get a good look at what was happening. He allowed the crowd to move in front of him, happy for them to watch what was happening as it meant he could get lost in the crowd and make his way back to his home.

It was incomprehensible. The boys had been so vocal about how cruel Pan used to be, and he was, but he never burned anyone like that. He never paraded someone's death around like some kind of morbid celebration. When he killed it was done quietly.

Raesh had taken the reins from Pan with style. He was the one who encouraged the boys to build their own homes in the trees for safety, to build a wall around their village to keep others out. There was no real threat to them in Neverland though. They would occasionally come across a hostile group, but really their defenses were uncalled for.

Raesh was paranoid, and Nathaniel had the suspicion it was actually Pan he was wanting to keep out. It was Pan who he wanted to burn. The problem was Raesh never brought any magic to the boys. Seeing Pan fly was a thing of wonder, he told them stories, introduced them to mermaids and fairies. Raesh would welcome any new lost boys with rules, a long list of things that they could and could not do. The number one being do not speak of Peter Pan. If Raesh ever found out that Nathaniel had been to the ship that day to visit him then he would be the next one on the fire.

The screams from the man seemed to go on for hours and it was difficult to imagine just what kind of pain he was in. Nathaniel wondered if it got to a point where he might just become numb, when the pain became so much that the nerves in his body would just shut down. More often that not whoever was on the fire would end up dying from smoke inhalation before they died from the flames, but that was when they were dangled above the flames rather than thrown directly into them. Nathaniel pulled his pillow over his head, muffling out the sounds until he fell into a restless sleep.

When he woke in the morning it was silent. The air in the room felt damp and clung to his skin which trickled down his spine in cool waves. He knew within moments of waking that he wasn't alone. He turned in his bed to find another person beside him. He should have been surprised to see that it was Pan sleeping soundly next to him, but part of him expected him to show up, just not in his bed.

Nathaniel sat up and looked down at him. Pan looked no older than twenty years old, but he knew that wasn't the case. He himself looked the same age, and despite not knowing just how old he was, he knew he was a lot older than twenty.

Pan looked peaceful as he slept, his mouth hanging open slightly as he breathed slow and steady breaths. His cheeks were no longer round like they had been as a child, they were sharp and showed off his cheek bones. He was a little gaunt, his whole body just slightly too slim. Nathaniel recalled that Pan used to practically live off of nothing when they all lived together. He would tell stories about how he would steal food from the birds that flew around Neverland, but he didn't fly anymore, so goodness knows what he was doing for food now.

It was a little presumptuous of the older man to think he could be there without Nathaniel waking and killing him. Maybe that was what he hoped to happen, or maybe he just knew that Nathaniel didn't see him as the enemy.

"Pan," he whispered and a small smile crept onto his lips as he slowly opened his eyes.

"Tippy-toe told me what house was yours," Pan said when he blinked his eyes open a few times then sleepily focused on Nathaniel. "Your bed looked so comfy I couldn't resist."

"If anyone finds you here then we will both be killed."

"No one will find me," Pan said surely as he yawned and sat up, his curly hair sticking out at all angles, it had definitely been cut by the fairies at some point. "You need to leave with me though."

"What?" Nathaniel laughed. "I am not going anywhere. Especially with you."

"It won't take long. Just, come with me."

"Pan, we have not spoken in years. Why do you think that I would go anywhere with you?"

"For the same reason that you are not angry to find me in your bed." Nathaniel opened his mouth to speak but his words caught in the back of his throat. "You know I would only come here if it was important."

"Is it about the new people on the island?"

"You already know about them?" Peter frowned.

"We all do." Nathaniel nodded. "Raesh caught one of them yesterday. He was killed on the bonfire last night."

"So that is what that smell is." Pan scrunched up his nose in disgust. "Did he get anything out of him before killing him?"

"Apparently. He said he would tell me about it today." Pan looked like he was deep in thought and he sucked in his lower lip to chew on it absentmindedly.

"Talk to Raesh," he said eventually. "Then when you have spoken to him come out to the ship and I will show you what I have found."

"It was hard enough getting to your ship yesterday, the weather has turned really bad Pan, I might not be able to get out of the village by this afternoon."

"If I can do it you can do it." Pan smiled and maneuvered himself out of the bed. His clothes appeared cleaner than they did the day before, in fact they were most likely a new set given that they weren't torn to shreds. Nathaniel doubted that the fairies would have been able to fix them that well in one night. He also seemed to have had a wash, his hair seemed a little shinier and his nails were no longer caked with dirt.

"The boys will be waking up now," Nathaniel told him. "How will you get out without anyone noticing you?"

"Now, that is a secret." Pan lifted his chin cockily and placed his hands on his hips. Nathaniel knew that he was supposed to hate him. It had been drilled into him practically every day since Pan decided to leave him.

Peter Pan was the villain.

He was not to be trusted.

Yet seeing him standing there in front of him with that smug look on his face was so familiar and comforting that Nathaniel felt everything but hate for the man.

Raesh lived in the largest tree house that sat at the back of the village. It had taken the boys several weeks to build as they had to follow Raesh's exact instructions which changed on a daily basis. He originally wanted the floor lined with moss but had quickly changed his mind after stepping inside and disliked the sponge like sensation beneath his feet. The moss was swapped out for hard wooden planks that the boys had acquired from an old paddle boat that had been deserted by the lagoon.

Every piece of treasure that was discovered on the island was first taken to Raesh who would inspect it and decide if he wanted to keep it or not. Despite his home being the largest it was by far the most cramped; every inch was covered in cumbersome furniture and trinkets that you could barely move without stepping on something. It was always cold too, something that Nathaniel had trouble understanding because Raesh always complained about having a chill, yet he slept with his windows wide open and allowed the freezing air to come in whenever it felt like it.

"There is a group of men that are planning to raid our village," Raesh said as he sat crossed legged on his bed and ran a comb through his black hair. He looked at his reflection in a silver hand held mirror and gave himself a satisfied smile. "We know of their plans now, of course, there is no way that they will succeed."

"Where did they come from?" Nathaniel pressed, wanting to get as much information as he could, and quickly, so he could try and get to Pan.

"He said that they have always been on Neverland, just like us."

"We haven't always been here though, Pan found us, most of us. The others found their own way here. I don't think anyone has been born on Neverland in decades."

Raesh scowled at the mention of Pan. "Maybe he forgot." He shrugged. "You don't remember where you came from originally, neither do I."

"No, but I know that I wasn't born here." Nathaniel felt a sense of irritation as he watched Raesh pull the comb through his hair over and over again.

"It doesn't really matter anyway." Raesh let out a yawn and placed the comb and mirror down on the bed. "What matters is that we have foiled their plan. News will quickly spread about what happened to the man we captured. The others will not dare to come here."

"If you say so."

"I do say so." Raesh stood up and went to stand uncomfortably close to Nathaniel. "Do you think that I don't notice your distaste for me, Nathaniel? How you question me in front of the others?"

"What?"

"You've changed in recent years. You are not the same boy that I once knew. I don't think that I trust you anymore. You need to fix that."

"How?" Nathaniel asked as Raesh stepped even closer which caused him to step back and hit softly against the wall behind him.

"You need to pledge yourself to me."

"I've already done that, Raesh."

"You need to do it again. I will arrange it. It needs to be done in front of everyone. I can't have even the slightest inkling of distrust in my boys, you understand that don't you?" Nathaniel nodded his response and felt a lump forming in his throat. "Now, run along little Nathaniel." Raesh smirked. "You will be on patrol tonight."

The snow storm felt like it came out of no where. It seemed like it only took mere minutes before inches of cold white crystals were building up on the ground and the boys were burrowing themselves away in their homes. Nathaniel looked out at the vast white expanse that sat outside of his window. There was no way he would make it out to Pan.

Now that the snow had settled in, it would be there for months until it melted away to reveal the cold dead land beneath it. He should have just gone with him without asking any questions, should have just followed him and then he would have been holed up with him on the boat to see out the snow.

The information that he had got out of Raesh was useless, the whole thing a ruse for him to just go there and get a talking down. Despite not particularly liking Raesh or supporting his many bad decisions, he didn't want to be on his bad side. Sometimes he thought what it would be like to be exiled from The Lost Boys. To no longer have the support system that he had come to rely on—the family he had made.

Was it really family though? There was no one who he could really depend on if he needed someone, he couldn't even think of one boy he would go to if he found himself in trouble. Tippy-toe was his only true companion, the only one who he actually enjoyed spending time with. He looked over at the fairy who was sitting in the small crevice he had decided to make into a home. He had acquired a piece of moss covered bark from one of his outings and was fashioning it into some strange looking pointy hat. Nathaniel knew better than to criticize Tippy-toe's sense of fashion. The last time he had made a comment about an unusual looking pair of shoes the fairy was wearing he woke up to find holes stabbed in most of his trousers.

"Tippy-toe?" Nathaniel called over to him and he saw the fairy place the hat down and look over at him with a smile. "You wouldn't be able to fly in this blizzard, I know that, but once it stops do you think that you could do me a favour?" Nathaniel studied the small face of his friend and he could see the range of emotions flickering over his features as he thought out his answer.

"Sure." He shrugged.

"Thank you." Nathaniel smiled at the response. "I need you to get a message to Pan for me." A small mischievous look spread over the fairy's face which caused Nathaniel to laugh. "What? What is it?" he asked as Tippy-toe flew over to him and whispered into his ear.

"I took his teeth."

"You stole Pan's teeth? Why? Where are they?" Tippy-toe pointed to his tiny bed and when Nathaniel looked closely he saw a white piece of cloth hiding behind it. "You can take those back to him, it's not funny Tips." Despite his words Nathaniel grinned as Tippy-toe burst into a small fit of laughter—his voice sounding like tiny bells vibrating off of the walls. "You are such a little sod."

Pan's teeth were not the only thing that Tippy-toe had stolen over the past year, but the teeth were the first to be noticed. He liked to stash away small tokens that belonged to Pan in Nathaniel's house in the hopes that the man might find them one day and be reminded of the adventures he used to have with him. Tippy-toe saw it as a game, with the reward for winning being that he might be able to fly with Pan again, maybe even with Nathaniel too. Yet, to his dismay, Nathaniel never noticed the odd thread of clothing, or shiny button placed neatly beside his bed. If he did notice them he never said anything, which of course made Tippy-toe mad. Being mad made Tippy-toe forget about everything else that was going on in his mind, which in turn made him forget about the things he had taken from Pan.

He did sometimes take things that belonged to Nathaniel and leave them on the ship for Pan to find too. Pan was much better at the game than Nathaniel and always found each item no matter how tiny it was. But, the items made the man cry, which was not Tippy-toe's intention and he would leave feeling full of guilt which would stay with him for days. Taking the teeth was a spur of the moment thing, and something he regretted almost immediately because they were heavier and more cumbersome than he thought that they would be. He had yet to hide them for Nathaniel to find when they had gone out to Pan's ship, so in a way that round of the game was ruined, but at least it had got the two men talking. For Tippy-toe that was a roaring success.

Three

When the blizzards finally stopped and the snow melted away three whole months had passed. The bright light of the sun threatened to break through the dull grey clouds and tried to kiss the land with such passion that the flowers bloomed almost immediately. The air smelt new and crisp, a welcome scent after months of stagnant air that still held the odour of a burning body. Nathaniel inhaled deeply as he stepped outside of his home, the air was still slightly cool, but there was a hidden warmth that caressed his skin and brought a smile to his lips. This was new. This was welcome.

His first thought was to go to see Henry's grave, it had been a long time and the stones that marked it would probably need re-painting, but that was not where he went. He wasn't the only boy to leave the village the first chance that they got, many of them ran out into the forest to start exploring again, eager to be set free after hibernating for so long. So, it wasn't strange for Nathaniel to leave and start making his way to the docks. It felt odd to be going to see Pan, he didn't think he would ever feel a need to see him again. But, the excitement he felt building inside of him as he neared closer and closer to the ship was immeasurable and Tippy-toe flew along with him as he walked with just as much joy.

Pan was out on the deck when Nathaniel finally arrived and smiled at him when he saw him using the ladder up the side of the ship.

"Mildew!" Pan called out. "We are being invaded!" A green haired fairy burst out of the cabin with a face like thunder, which only relaxed slightly when she saw Nathaniel and Tippy-toe boarding the boat. She flew over to Tippy-toe and it only took a matter of seconds before the two of them got into a heated argument.

"She's feisty," Nathaniel said as he brushed off his clothes from the climb.

"They always argue," Pan said dismissively. He had bulked out over the snowy months and had more colour to his cheeks since the last time Nathaniel had seen him. He looked good.

"I'm sorry I did not make it out here before the snow set in."

"It's okay, you would have just got stuck on the ship with me if you had come, and I know you wouldn't have liked that."

"Why wouldn't I?" Nathaniel smiled.

"You hate me," Pan stated simply. "I would have had to have slept with one eye open from fear of you killing me." Nathaniel let out a quiet huff after Pan had finished talking.

"Why do you think that?"

"I know that all of you hate me. It is hardly a secret is it? I also know that you have spoken to the merfolk about drowning me."

"Now, that isn't strictly true," Nathaniel said as he crossed his arms over his chest. "They suggested it, I told them that drowning you was not a solution to anything. So, yes, we have spoken about drowning you, but, no, it was not something that was ever going to happen."

"Why would they suggest it then?" Pan smirked. "You must have expressed a strong dislike for me for them to come up with such a thing."

"I told them that you killed my brother."

"But, I didn't kill Henry!" Pan shouted, his mood changing as quickly as Tippy-toe's.

"You keep saying that, but if you didn't kill him, then who did?"

"I swear that I would never hurt him."

"If you didn't kill him, Pan, then who did?" Nathaniel repeated his question with irritation laced in his voice.

"I don't know," Pan snapped, but there was something about his demeanor that told Nathaniel he was lying. "Anyway, you didn't come here to talk about Henry, did you? You came here to tell me what Raesh said about the prisoner."

"He didn't have much to say at all, it was pointless." Nathaniel turned away from him to look out to sea, it was nice to see that the waves were lapping gently against the boat this time.

"I have found out a lot of things." Pan moved to stand beside the smaller man and looked out at the sea as well.

"How?"

"By watching. I found a trail that wasn't effected too much by the snow and was able to get out there to their camp to watch them for most of the winter. I don't think that they are bad people, they seem pretty normal actually."

"Yeah? Why are they here then?" Nathaniel tipped his head to look at him.

"I don't know. Why is anyone here?" He shrugged. "But, they do have guns, and there are a lot of them too. Not just men either, women as well."

"Really?" Nathaniel couldn't help the surprise in his voice, he couldn't remember ever seeing a human woman before in Neverland, he had heard stories about settlements that used to include women, but as far as he was aware, they were long gone.

"Yeah, loads of them. Some are quite pretty too." Pan had his usual smug expression on his face as he spoke and for some reason it made Nathaniel's blood boil.

"And have you made friends with any of these women?"

"No." Pan grinned as he saw a faint red blush spread across Nathaniel's cheeks. "Are you jealous? I'm sure that we could easily introduce ourselves and you can become acquainted with some of them."

"Why would I want to be acquainted with them?" he asked bitterly.

"Do you not know what you can do with a woman?" Pan laughed which made Nathaniel's cheeks flush an ever deeper shade of red that crept up to the tips of his ears.

He knew what men did with women, The Lost Boys spoke about it all the time. Some even boasted about doing some of those things which was ridiculous as he was sure none of them had ever seen a woman in Neverland either. They had even come up with some pretty creative made-up scenarios that involved the mermaids, but Nathaniel knew full well that they were lies. Some of the men had eventually grown intimate with each other, removing the problem of no women being around completely, none of it was news to him.

"I know what can be done with a woman." Nathaniel kept his eyes out to sea as he spoke.

"Well, then, you know why it might be nice to be friendly with them. I was going to show you where the camp was before the snow came."

"Why? So I could see some women?"

"Well, no, not back then." Pan continued to smirk. "I was going to show you so that you were aware of them, I didn't want you getting hurt." Something wasn't sitting right with Nathaniel. Pan didn't look out for him, he hadn't looked out for him for years, it seemed ridiculous to think he would start doing so now.

"Why? If they were a threat then I would have reported it back to Raesh, I was under the impression that you wouldn't mind if Raesh got killed." Pan laughed at Nathaniel's words and ruffled his fingers through his messy hair.

"Nothing would bring me greater pleasure than seeing that lunatic get killed, but I wouldn't want to hear about you or any of the boys getting hurt. I know what they all think of me, but there was a time when we were inseparable."

"Back when we were younger, sure. They are men now, we all are, we don't need you looking out for us, you really only need to worry about yourself."

"Maybe." Pan shrugged yet again. "If you don't want to know where the camp is, then you can just leave." Nathaniel didn't move for a moment as he contemplated what to do next. It would be an advantage to know where these new people were, if Pan was wrong and they were dangerous he would at least know where they were attacking from. On the other hand, he would have to tell Raesh how he found them, he certainly couldn't mention Pan, but Raesh was good at sniffing out lies and he didn't want to feel his wrath. Or, he could just not tell Raesh anything. "I'm heading out there in a little while." Pan interrupted Nathaniel's chain of thought as he spoke again which made him sigh quietly.

"Okay, I will come out with you. But not to see the women, this is purely for strategic purposes."

"Sure, you keep telling yourself that Nathaniel."

"Is Nathaniel your real name?" Pan asked, pulling his attention away from the fighting fairies that were flying beside them.

"Hmm? I'm not sure. Maybe...maybe not." Nathaniel frowned slightly.

"What was your proper name then?"

"I wish I could tell you, I've just been Nathaniel for so long now that I can't remember what my parents used to call me."

"Do you remember anything about them?"

"Only a few things."

"Tell me?" Pan gave a reassuring smile to him. "I know I used to forbid people talking about their parents, but, I guess I want to know a little bit about what you remember from back home. What is that called? When you want to know something?"

"Intrigue? Curiosity?" Nathaniel hummed.

"Then tell me, to help my intrigue and curiosity."

"Um, well, okay, I remember that my father had dark eyes, and my mother was warm and used to hold me while I fell asleep." The memories felt so distant that they didn't feel real anymore. "I shared a bedroom with Henry. I had wooden boats on a mobile above my bed. That is all I remember."

"Would you go back if you could?"

"No, not now."

"Why?" Pan asked sadly.

"I might feel unsure of how long it has actually been since I was last home, but I do know it has been a very long time. I don't know if my parents would remember me, they might not even be alive anymore. And if they did remember and they were not dead I would have to tell them about Henry and I can't do that." They continued to walk in silence for a while, Pan mulling over what Nathaniel had said while Nat was busy fighting back tears. They eventually came to a small dirt track that led up to a dense part of the forest which Pan stopped in front of and pointed up at it with a smile.

"If we go up that trail it brings us out onto a high edge, the strangers are camped below," he explained. "We can hide ourselves in the low branches, it will be even easier to hide now the trees aren't as bare."

Pan led the way up the trail, which was incredibly wet and muddy even though the sun was now high in the sky and beating down onto the island with force. Nathaniel struggled in some areas, the mud holding onto his boots with such a tight grip that they were almost ripped off of his feet. He wasn't used to the heat either. It had been years since he had seen the sun like that, he regretted wearing such thick clothes. Pan fared a little better, he was much lighter on his feet than the younger man, but he did slip a few times and instinctively reached out to Nathaniel for support.

By the time they had reached the top of the trail they were both out of breath, their faces damp with sweat to compliment their blotchy red cheeks. Once they had taken a few minutes to even out their breathing Pan took Nathaniel by the hand and pulled him over to an unstable looking edge then yanked him down roughly to crouch beside him.

"Shh." Pan put his finger to his lips to emphasise the need to be quiet and pointed over the edge so Nathaniel could look down. He was taken aback at how big the camp was; he was expecting material tents and primitive living conditions, but these people had built a small town. The houses were sturdy and made of wood and they had even rounded up some wild pigs and built a pen for them. It was all surprisingly functioning and domestic, even better than the village The Lost Boys had built.

"How long have they been here?" Nathaniel whispered.

"I'm not sure, but definitely over a year." Pan narrowed his eyes as he looked down at the scene then looked back at Nathaniel with a mischievous expression. "Can you see what I see?"

"What?" Nathaniel asked anxiously and peered back down at the village.

"How many people do you see?"

"I don't see anyone."

"Exactly, this place is usually full of people. There is no one here. I can't hear a sound." He looked at Mildew, who was still finding things to argue with Tippy-toe about, and he pulled her quickly away to his face by her dainty wings. She squealed in surprise and looked back at Pan with a deathly glare. "I need you to fly down there and tell me if there is anyone in the village," he told her but she shook her head in response. "Mildew, if you don't do this for me then I won't let you sleep in the ship tonight. I will tell all of the other fairies that you are banished." Mildew started to glow red—a complete danger sign for anyone who was talking with a fairy. "Don't look at me like that," Pan said seriously. "I mean it, Mildew, you don't want to be banished again, do you? You hated it last time didn't you? So, get down there and do this for me." Mildew spoke quickly back at him, so quickly that Nathaniel couldn't understand her, but she caused Pan to pout. "Okay, okay, I'm sorry. Mildew, *please* can you do that for me?" Mildew took a few seconds to return back to her normal coloured glow and as soon as Pan released her wings she flew at great speed down to the village. Tippy-toe perched himself on Nathaniel's shoulder, he could feel the fairy vibrating with anger.

"Oh, come on Tips, she's not that bad," he said to him but Tippy-toe didn't reply.

"She *is* bad," Pan said and Tippy-toe smiled at him. "But, I would be lost without her." Within seconds Mildew had returned and she whispered animatedly in Pan's ear before flying off again in the direction of the ship that Pan called home. "No one is there." Pan said happily to Nathaniel.

"This is perfect, let's go and explore." Before Nathaniel could react, Pan had started to climb down off of the ledge with Tippy-toe flying after him.

There was an eerie feeling in the village, like it had been abandoned suddenly for some grave reason that they might never discover. There were fires still burning outside the houses with food left half eaten on the floor. This didn't seem to bother Pan, who ran from house to house trying to find anything that was of any value to him. Nathaniel walked around with more caution, peering into the empty homes while expecting someone to jump out at him and attack. It was too quiet, and no obvious explanation for why it had been abandoned so suddenly.

"Do you think that they will come back?" he called out to Pan as he crouched down to pick up a discarded journal from the muddy floor.

"Of course!" Pan's voice came from one of the buildings but Nathaniel couldn't tell which one. He flicked through some of the pages but then put the journal back where he found it. "Look at this." Pan appeared in one of the wooden doorways, a large black hat adorned with an enormous red feather stuck out of the top of it on his head. Nathaniel laughed as Pan posed elegantly then started to saunter around haughtily.

"What a magnificent hat," Nathaniel giggled which only spurred Pan on with his jaunty movements.

"You will call me Lord Pan from now on thank you Nathaniel."

"That is not the hat of a Lord," Nathaniel snorted.

"No?" Pan frowned and took the hat off to look at it. "What kind of hat is it then? Looks pretty fancy to me."

"I don't know who would wear that hat, but a Lord certainly wouldn't."

"How would you know?" Pan scoffed.

"Um, well, I don't I guess." He took the hat from him and turned it around in his hands as he studied it. "Why would anyone want to wear a hat this big though? What is the purpose?"

"To keep the sun off of your face," Pan said rather logically.

"Okay, but why the feather?"

"Because feathers are fancy." Pan tutted at him like he was some kind of ruffian and snatched the hat back. "It is my hat now."

"You're not going to start wearing it all the time are you?"

"Of course I am, I am very refined and this hat suits me perfectly."

"Refined is not how I would describe you." Nathaniel turned away from him and began to walk further into the town, he heard Pan following behind him.

He still didn't feel right about being there, like he was treading on sacred land and was bound to end up being cursed because of it. "I think we should probably go."

"What? Why?" Pan asked as he placed the hat back on his head.

"They could come back at any time, right? What if they aren't friendly and they kill us?"

"Well, at least we would die together," Pan said simply. "What an amazing adventure that would be."

"I don't think dying would be an adventure for us. We would just die, that would be it. We wouldn't even know we were dead. Everything would just be black and empty."

"Who told you that?" Pan asked with a worried tone and Nathaniel was sure he could see fear in his eyes.

"Nobody," he responded quietly. "I just don't think that anything happens after you die."

"You don't think that we would go somewhere magical?"

"We are already somewhere magical." The moment was disturbed by a loud crash in the distance. It was loud enough that it could have been a tree tumbling down, or some kind of explosion. Either way, it was too close for comfort. Tippy-toe flew high into the air to get a better look of the area but came down quickly shaking his head.

"What was that?" Pan asked as his eyes darted around their surroundings to see if they were being watched.

"It sounded like something blew up." Nathaniel felt the fear as well; he had never heard anything so loud before, it had to have been nearby.

"Let's go." Pan grasped Nathaniel's hand in his and began to guide them back to the forest.

"We can't get back that way, we jumped down, there is no way we can get back up there."

"I can give you a boost," Pan said and let go of his hand to kneel down so he could help Nathaniel climb.

"What? What about you?" Nathaniel shook his head. "No, we need to get out together, there must be another way. You can't fly any more Pan."

"We might not have time to find another way." Pan spoke with fear in his tone, Nathaniel hadn't heard him speak like that since the day he saw his grown reflection in that awful washed up mirror many years before.

"I'm not leaving here without you." Nathaniel grasped Pan's bicep and pulled him up from his crouched position. "Come on." Pan didn't object this time and allowed Nathaniel to pull him back through the village, both of them on high alert for any new or unfamiliar sounds that could be heard.

They eventually came to the edge of the space, where the buildings thinned out onto grassland. It was strange to see an area that wasn't densely populated with trees and it dawned on Nathaniel that he had never been to that area before.

"If we follow the lake over there we will eventually reach the sea," Pan said as he pointed to some water in the distance.

"It's so open," Nathaniel said, not wanting to step out any further into the empty space where there was no where to hide.

"We can get into the water if anyone comes." Pan squeezed his hand reassuringly. "They won't see us. You can hold your breath can't you?"

"Sure but I don't know for how long." This answer seemed good enough for Pan who started to jog out into the clearing and Nathaniel instinctively followed him.

Tippy-toe kept flying ahead of them as they walked to see if there was anything that they needed to be aware of in the distance. Every time he returned with a smile that told them everything was okay until he didn't return at all. He could have encountered something or simply got distracted and not returned, but it left Nathaniel with an uneasy feeling that Pan picked up on.

"He is okay, you know what fairies are like."

"What if he saw someone and they did something to him?"

"To Tippy-toe? No one would hurt him, and if someone captured him they would soon let him go. He would whine at them until they couldn't take it anymore." Nathaniel tried to smile at the comment but it was clearly forced. He noticed then that Pan was no longer wearing the hat he had found, it had vanished without either of them realising it. He looked back over his shoulder but couldn't see it anywhere behind them.

"Wait–" Pan stopped dead in his tracks and raised his arm in front of Nathaniel to stop him walking as well.

"What is–"

"Shh!" Pan hissed and it only took a second before he was pulling Nathaniel towards the water and they splashed in less than elegantly. Nathaniel didn't have time to think before Pan was holding his head under the water and he thought how much of a fool he was. *This* was Pan's plan all along, to get him away from everyone and then drown him. He couldn't focus on anything other than the fact that he hadn't been able to take a deep breath before being plunged under and he was painfully aware of the water in his mouth as he tried to gasp for air. He stretched his hands out in front of himself until he grasped the front of Pan's top and pulled and hit at him as hard as he could. He felt himself being dragged to the surface and he was able to take a much needed gulp of air before being plunged under again. He was sure that he was screaming, his voice eaten up by the water surrounding him but he suddenly stopped when Pan's face became clear in front of him. The other man's eyes were wide and he shook his head slowly before allowing Nathaniel to break the surface of the water again. He took in the air as quickly as he could, coughing as he did so and flailed in the water. He couldn't see Pan, but in the moment he could only think about getting back on land and he managed to swim to the edge of the lake. He stopped still when he saw a line of men and women walking towards the village that they had left in the distance. His breath caught again but for an entirely different reason.

"Stay still," Pan whispered from behind him and he felt him place his hands on his shoulders. He braced himself to be pushed down into the water again but it didn't happen, Pan stilled him and the only sound that could be heard was of footsteps in the distance and Pan's breath against his wet skin.

"What are you two doing?" came a voice from the left which caused them both to turn their heads suddenly towards the sound. A woman stood to the edge of the water, looking at them with an amused smile on her lips. Nathaniel wanted to smack Pan in annoyance; if he hadn't have been trying to keep him hidden under the water maybe this woman wouldn't have noticed them.

"Swimming," Pan said petulantly which made her laugh then wave over to some of the other people who were walking.

"No wait!" Nathaniel hissed, but it was too late, three or four men were starting to make their way over, followed by another woman.

"What have you found over there Daisy?" One of the men asked as they drew closer. Nathaniel looked to Pan with wide eyes, there was apparently no plan if they got caught. He supposed he could set them on fire, but really that would make him no better than Raesh.

"You boys fancy getting out of the water and saying hi?" the woman, who Nathaniel took to be Daisy, said in a friendly tone.

"We are fine where we are," Pan retorted stubbornly which made Nathaniel roll his eyes.

"Whatever you say darlin'." Daisy shrugged her shoulders then grinned as her companions joined her by her side.

"Fine day for a swim lads!" A man with dark brown hair and a bushy beard beamed down at them, he was holding an ax in his hand which he swung to rest on his shoulder. "Bet that water is still a bit nippy though, huh?" Nathaniel hadn't thought about the temperature of the water until the man mentioned it, and now he had he realised just how freezing he was.

"A bit." Nathaniel shivered.

"Hows about you boys join us for some lunch?" Daisy suggested. "We can light a fire and get you both warmed up, we caught some rabbits, should be real tasty."

"Like I said, we are fine where we are," Pan said again, but this time another man reached down to pull Nathaniel out of the water which caused Pan to shout angrily. "Don't touch him!"

"Calm down mate, the kid is freezing," the man who was pulling Nathaniel out of the water said and Nathaniel let him get him out of the river despite Pan's protests. From the water they seemed huge, *adults*, but being stood next to them Nathaniel realised he wasn't as small as he thought he was. He knew he was no longer a child. But a grown up? Surely not.

"Here," the lady who had not spoke said and draped a shawl around Nathaniel's shoulders. Nathaniel locked eyes with Pan who was still in the water, this really was not how he was expecting his day to go. *Bloody Pan.*

Intruders were not supposed to be so hospitable. Pan didn't trust them. He didn't like the way they were so laid back and comfortable on *his* island. He didn't like their stupid rabbit stew. And he really didn't like the way Daisy was being with Nathaniel. Every chance she got she had her hand on him, on his thigh, arm, she even had the audacity to touch his hair. What was worse is that he didn't stop it, he didn't push her away or tell her to back off. If anything, he seemed to be enjoying it.

"So, you going to report back to your village about where we are?" The man with the bushy beard said to Pan and handed him a small mug of drink. Pan eyed the liquid suspiciously before taking a sip. He coughed at how strong it was–it burned the back of his throat and made his eyes water. Whatever it was, it definitely had a kick to it.

"My village?" Pan huffed. "No, it's not mine. I don't live there. Nothing to do with me."

"You didn't come from there?"

"No." He shook his head and took another sip of the drink. "Like I said, nothing to do with me."

"Strange, we have scouted almost every part of this island and not discovered anyone else, we must have missed you."

"Must have." Pan looked over at Nathaniel again who was speaking to Daisy with a smile. "Besides, I doubt you have managed to look everywhere, even I haven't been everywhere."

"My name is Drake, by the way, Drake Therault." The bearded man said warmly.

"Drake Therault?" Pan looked away from Nathaniel to look at the man to his side. "That is the most stupid name I have ever heard."

"It is?" he laughed. "Well, I got my fair share of stick over my name when I was a kid, but, sticks and stones and all that. It really isn't an unusual name."

"Sticks and stones?"

"You know, sticks and bones may break by bones, but calling names won't hurt me?" Drake poured himself out some drink and downed it in one mouthful without flinching. Pan scowled at him.

"What a weird thing to say," he commented after a moment.

"What's your name then?" Drake asked.

"Pan."

"Oh? Like Peter Pan?"

"Yes, exactly like Peter Pan," Pan scoffed and straightened his posture.

"Like, as in, flying with fairies Pan Pan?" Drake let out a laugh. "I think I've been drinking too much."

"What's so funny?" Pan asked as he started to get angry, the tips of his ears turning red as a tell tale sign.

"My mum used to tell me stories about Peter Pan when I was a lad, nothing more than a fairy tale though." Pan sucked his tongue on his teeth as he looked at him.

"Well, I am not a fairy tale, I am here. And *you* are trespassing on my island."

"Your island?" Drake laughed again. "Didn't think anyone was in charge here. The place is like a giant free for all. Everyone just racing around with no worries in the world. You need a bit more order around here."

"I think that you should shut your mouth." Pan raised his voice as he spoke which made Nathaniel and Daisy look over with concern.

"Are you okay?" Nathaniel asked, directing his question to Pan with a soft tone to his voice.

"No, I think that we should leave." Pan stood from the log where he had been sitting and shoved the mug he had been drinking from back to Drake.

"Hey, now, no need to be rude lad," Drake frowned. "We are trying to be friendly is all."

"You can't come here and start telling me how Neverland should be run, you are visitors here, and you are not welcome."

"Pan–" Nathaniel said as he stood up as well. "Come on they haven't done anything wrong."

"Yet," Pan retorted bitterly.

"We want to live here peacefully," Daisy said firmly. "If we didn't we could have killed you both down at that river. Would have been dead easy too. Sitting there like sittin' ducks." She flicked her black curly hair over her shoulder.

"Oh yeah? Shoot us with your guns would you?" Pan pointed a finger at her accusingly. "I've been watching you all, I know exactly how you all think!"

"I'm going to have to ask you to calm down," Drake said. "Pan, we don't take kindly to people being rude to us. Not nice is it?" He looked over to Daisy who shook her head. "Like Daisy here said, we could have killed you both if we wanted. But we don't want to. We want to live here and get on with you all."

"We have been watching you too you know. How you treat each other. The violence. Those kids are feral." Daisy looked at Nathaniel as she spoke.

"They are hardly kids are they? None of us are kids...not anymore" Nathaniel said quietly. "But we are nothing to do with Pan. The Lost Boys don't have a leader."

"Yeah, if you have a problem with the way the boys do things, you take it up with them," Pan snapped.

"Then, get us close enough to speak with them." Drake looked at Pan with dark eyes.

"No, we can't do that," Nathaniel spoke for Pan and stood up as well. "We may not have a leader, and I don't speak for the others, but I don't know you, I don't trust you, how do I know you won't hurt us?" Drake stood and took a step towards Nathaniel. He was taller than him, with a wide broad body that was practically double Nathaniel's size. He suddenly felt small again.

"We don't want to be your enemy."

"Then don't be."

"How can we live here in peace when there is so much animosity in the air?" Drake asked. Nathaniel's eyes flicked to Pan quickly.

"It will take time. But, for now, we are leaving." Pan reached for Nathaniel's hand and pulled him close, causing him to bump past Drake as he did.

"Now, there is no need to be actin' all defensive." Daisy sighed and stood up. "Can't we just enjoy a little dinner together? We want to be friends, you're making this hard."

"Because what you are suggesting is stupid!" Pan shouted at her. "I don't want to make plans and try and be friends." Nathaniel could see just how worked up he was getting. Pan was never diplomatic. That was never going to change. "Come on Nat." He pulled Nathaniel's hand again and started to drag him back to the entrance of the forest. Nathaniel looked over his shoulder; he was half expecting Drake to be following them, but he stayed by the fire with Daisy, eerily watching them as they left.

Four

Why did you get so angry?" Nathaniel asked when he was sure that they were out of view from the town. "We could have tried to get more information out of them."

"I didn't like that guy, he was arrogant." Nathaniel couldn't help but laugh. Peter calling someone else arrogant? That was new.

"Hurts to receive a taste of your own medicine huh?"

"What is that supposed to mean? No one gave me medicine," Peter tutted.

"That's not what I–don't worry," Nathaniel sighed. "I just don't know why you got so worked up so quickly."

"She was all over you!" Peter stopped in his tracks and swung himself round to look at Nathaniel with fire in his eyes. "And you sat there giggling and enjoying it!"

"What?" Nathaniel said in exasperation. "Is that what made you mad? That she was showing an interest in me and not in you?!"

"I–I–I...shut up Nathaniel!" Peter continued to shout and pushed Nathaniel back so he tumbled to the floor of the forest. "You're a liar. You always have been! You told them that there was no leader of The Lost Boys. I *know* that there is. I have been watching you." Nathaniel got up from where Pan had pushed him down and brushed off his clothes angrily.

"What difference does it make what I tell them? I don't owe them anything, and I assumed you knew who had taken your place."

"No one can take my place," Pan said darkly. "Especially Raesh."

"Oh? So you you do know then," Nathaniel said with an angry sounding laugh. "What is this all about, Pan? Jealousy?"

"Me? Jealous? Of *him*? He is nothing compared to me. Nothing."

"Then why haven't any of the boys come back to you? We all know that you have been back on the island and no one has left Raesh to join your side."

"*You* have. Why are you here with me right now and not with your new leader, hmm?" Nathaniel couldn't stand the look in Pan's brown eyes. He couldn't tell if it was betrayal or anger, or even hurt, but either way he couldn't bare it. "Go back to your leader, Nathaniel." Pan said and pushed him again, even harder this time. His back hit the trunk of a tree and he let out a pained gasp of air. He closed his eyes as he felt a wave of heat erupt in his chest, but it quickly subsided. When he opened his eyes again Pan had gone.

Nathaniel didn't make it back to his village the same day that he left it. He found himself in the forest wandering aimlessly, getting more and more confused with each minute that passed. His mind kept switching between Peter and Tippy-toe and then to the abyss that was the forest. He had got lost once before, back when Henry was still alive. He could hear his brother and the boys calling out to him yet no matter how hard he tried to follow their voices he couldn't find them.

That was when he met Tippy-toe for the first time. The fairy had been on his own too and was flying around in a craze as he tried to find the group of fairies he had been with. The found each other and stayed together ever since. It was Tippy-toe who managed to get Nathaniel back to his brother and friends and Nathaniel felt such a debt to the fairy that he promised he would return the favour one day. What if he had now missed the chance? What if Tippy-toe had flown head first into a trap and was now imprisoned or laying dead somewhere? The thought made him feel nauseous and more than once he hunched over at the base of a tree to be sick.

Then there was Peter, who had left him alone in a part of the forest he didn't know. Part of him knew that this was the childish way he dealt with things. But what if Pan was so angry that he never wanted to see him again? His mind was swirling with so many what if's that it was all consuming. He wasn't even concerned about being lost in the forest, his own well being the last of his worries. He was slightly concerned about the fire drumming through his veins, though. He was surprised that he hadn't yet set fire to the whole island.

He kept walking. Walking and walking until he was sure he was just going around in circles. Every time he looked up at the sky he expected to be greeted with a vast expanse of blue, but all he could see was leaves, dense thick branches that only made him more disorientated. He wasn't even sure when he fell to the ground, when it all became too much and he closed his eyes, not expecting to ever open them again.

When he did blink his eyes open he found himself in an unfamiliar room, he went to get out of the bed quickly but found that his body was beyond weak and he stumbled and fell to his knees on the hard wooden floor. He stayed there on his knees while he looked around his surroundings and his heart rate fell to a normal pace as he realised that he was in Raesh's room. He was back at the village. They had found him. The sense of calm didn't last long, his eyes fell to a white cloth on the table which had Pan's baby teeth spilling out of it.

"Ah, someone is finally awake. And just in time," Raesh spoke coldly and his voice floated around the room with an ominous flair. He stepped into the room from outside and gently closed the door behind him then sat himself in front of Nathaniel on the floor. "What are you doing down here little one?" He grinned as he spoke and Nathaniel could feel him taking in every inch of his body with a piercing stare.

"What happened?" Nathaniel asked, his voice weak and small.

"We found you out in the woods. We wondered where you had run away to. Bit strange to take a nap in the forest, Nathaniel. Aren't you grateful that we rescued you?"

"Yes...yes I am, thank you."

"Good." Raesh stood himself up and grabbed Nathaniel harshly by the arm to pull him to his feet as well. He couldn't help but let out a moan of protest and wobbled on his feet. Raesh let go of him and he stumbled back to sit on the edge of the bed. He couldn't place why his body felt so painful, why every movement hurt more than the last.

"I lost Tippy-toe." A sob escaped Nathaniel and he bit back the urge to cry.

"Too bad. There are plenty more fairies. And, to be honest, a missing fairy is the least of my concerns now. I'm guessing that your little camping session was something to do with the new people on the island. So, what do you have to say for yourself?"

"Why would you think that?"

"Where else would you have been?" Raesh went to a small cabinet in his room and got out a dark brown bottle. He pulled the cork from the top then took a swig of its contents. "Everyone was here and accounted for, apart from you. You were no where to be found." Nathaniel watched his every move intently, Raesh wasn't doing anything threatening physically, but the threat was evident in his voice. "Where were you?"

"The forest."

"With Peter Pan."

"What? No. I haven't seen him in years."

"You're lying." Raesh sat down beside him on the bed and offered him the bottle to drink but he shook his head no.

"Why would you think that?"

"When you were gone some of the boys thought that you might be working with these intruders. They demanded that we searched your room for any clues."

"You wouldn't have found any." Nathaniel pushed the bottle away that Raesh was now forcing against his lips. "Stop."

"Oh, come on, you don't want a drink? This is the rum we found in that cave by the sea, don't you remember?" Raesh laughed.

"I don't want any."

"Fine." Raesh placed the bottle down on the floor in defeat. "But, you're right. We didn't find anything that linked you to the intruders. But we found a great deal that linked you to Peter Pan." Nathaniel frowned, there was nothing in his room that could have tied him to Pan, apart from the teeth.

"That's impossible." Nathaniel scoffed then tensed as Raesh wrapped an arm around his shoulders. With his free hand the older man got something out of his pocket then laid it flat in his palm for Nathaniel to see what it was.

"A kiss." Raesh said as Nathaniel looked down at the silver thimble in his hand. "Why do you have a kiss from Peter Pan?"

"That is not a kiss, that is a thimble." Nathaniel stared down at the small object, he knew it belonged to Pan but he had no idea how it got into his room.

"Kiss, thimble, whatever you want to call it. Pan is the only person who has one of these. He guards it fiercely. We all know that." Raesh moved the thimble to hold it between his thumb and forefinger and held it up to the light. "Such a small little thing, but so much meaning behind it. Did Pan give it to you before he left?"

"No."

"Then, why was it under your pillow, Nathaniel? Such a meaningful object, and intimate place to keep it. Was Pan in the village?"

"No." Nathaniel felt the tears burning at the sides of his eyes again but he wasn't going to let himself start to cry. The thimble couldn't be explained, he would have noticed it there if Peter had left it that one time he visited before the winter. "I don't know where it came from. I swear, Raesh." Raesh put the thimble back in his pocket and looked at Nathaniel thoughtfully.

"Most of the men out there want me to sentence you to death, for clearly consorting with such a tyrant. But, I said no, you would be able to explain yourself. I'm bitterly disappointed that you can't."

"I just wanted to know who the new people were on the island, to see if they were a threat to us," Nathaniel said quickly. "I wasn't with Pan, he hasn't been here. I swear." He hated how he sounded, how his words came out too quickly and pathetically. "Please Raesh, you know that I wouldn't go against you."

"We will see," Raesh said as he stood up and looked down at him, looming a dark shadow across the room as he did so. "You stay here until I decide what to do with you. Don't try and escape either, you won't get out." Nathaniel watched him as he left the room and heard him locking the door behind him.

The only indication that Nathaniel had of what was going on in the village was the loud shouting coming from the center. He couldn't make out what was being said, or if there was any anger or if it was excited shouting, but something big was happening and he could only guess as to what.

He leaned out of Raesh's window as far as he could to catch a glimpse of the boys, but he was too high up and they were too far away. He wished that Tippy-toe was with him, and it brought on the same nauseous feeling he felt before knowing that he didn't know where the fairy was. He tried to open the door numerous times but it was pointless, no matter how much he tried to jimmy the lock it would not budge. He couldn't fit out of the window either, not that it was really an option as there was no where to jump to and if he tried to get to the ground he would die doing so. He did consider setting fire to the place, but he guessed he would only end up killing himself in the process.

Being stuck in a room only gave him time to think over what had happened out at the town. How Pan had filled himself with rage and stormed off before they could come to any conclusion with Daisy and Drake. It had happened so quickly, Pan was never good at controlling his tempter as a child, he didn't know why he thought he would be any different as an adult.

After a while he ended up laying on Raesh's bed and stared up at the ceiling for what felt like days, until he finally heard a key turning in the lock again one night. Raesh stepped into the room, dressed head to toe in worn black clothes that Nathaniel had never seen him wear before. He sat up on the bed and watched him as he moved towards him and took a place beside him on the bed silently.

"Can I have something to eat?" Nathaniel asked nervously which made Raesh laugh loudly, breaking the calm in the room.

"Later. I need you to pledge yourself to me first."

"What?"

"You want to prove that you are loyal to me? Well, show me, in front of everyone."

"Now?"

"Now. Come on." He held out his hand for Nathaniel to take, which he did, and he noted just how stone cold Raesh's grip was. Stepping outside of the room felt like a sudden rush of freedom, a warm night air swept over all of his features and he breathed in deeply to smell the heady scent of blooms on the breeze.

Five

All of the boys in the village had pledged themselves to Raesh at one point or another. Those that hadn't were deemed too young, but they all did it eventually. It wasn't usually something that the whole village would come out to see, but as they walked towards the middle of the village they passed the face of every person who lived there.

Nathaniel felt a sudden pang of fear as they reached the center and he saw a blazing fire and he couldn't help but think that his death had finally caught up with him. He wasn't sure if fire could actually kill him, not with the element basically living inside of him, but he sure as hell didn't want to find out.

Raesh shoved him towards the fire and stood back to take in his appearance. He hated how Raesh would give that judgemental stare; it shook him to the core and now, in front of his peers, he could only feel dread.

"Get on your knees," Raesh instructed and Nathaniel fell to his knees in front of him. This was a good start, everyone who pledged themselves did so on their knees. The first time Nathaniel had done this he was scared, but only because it was such a huge thing for him to be doing. The fear now was that no one had pledged themselves twice, he didn't know how this would go.

Raesh pulled a dagger out of a pocket, Nathaniel should have noticed it before, it was a good ten inches, not something you would usually miss. The older man stepped forward and grabbed Nathaniel's hair to pull his head back, their eyes locking immediately. Sweat was forming on Nathaniel's skin, the heat from the fire roaring at his back, simply calling for him to step inside of the flames.

Raesh pressed the tip of the blade to the center of Nathaniel's throat and pressed down enough to start drawing blood. A red droplet trickled down his neck and he felt Raesh press the blade in harder and he waited for the final movement, for Raesh to kill him.

"I pledge myself to you," Nathaniel managed to say, despite the drumming in his ears becoming deafening. Raesh looked down at him with a blank expression, seemingly trying to decide if he should kill him or not.

"You swear to stay loyal to me, to fight for me, to pledge yourself to this village and this village alone?" Raesh spoke in a hushed tone.

"Yes, I swear." Nathaniel let out a breath of relief when the blade was removed from his neck and Raesh pulled it quickly over the palm of his hand. He winced slightly then gestured for Nathaniel to hold out his hand as well, as soon as he did he cut along his palm swiftly. Nathaniel stood and Raesh clasped his bloody hand in his, which made the boys cheer. The ritual had been no different to how it normally was, but it felt like there was more depth, that Raesh really would kill him if he strayed from his word.

"I can't believe you did that." The voice woke Nathaniel with a start and he sat up in his bed and looked around the room to see who had spoke. There was no one, not even a shadow lurking in the corner to explain what he had heard.

"Hello?" he called out into the darkness but there was no response so he pulled his blanket around him protectively. "Henry?" It felt stupid to even think that Henry would respond, he was dead, the dead did not talk.

"No, not Henry," the voice snapped and Nathaniel got out of bed quickly, his legs tangling in the blankets as he tumbled to the floor. The voice laughed at him and as he lay on his back. He scrambled to get up before a face appeared above his suddenly. Pan, with his black hair and deep eyes, looked down at him with dimples in his cheeks from his wide smile.

"What are you doing?" Nathaniel hissed as he pushed Pan away and sat up to fumble about with the blanket so he could stand up. Pan let out a loud laugh which caused Nathaniel to quickly press his hand over the taller mans mouth in panic. "Shut up! Do you want to wake up everyone? They are keeping an eye on me now."

"Because you are Raesh's loyal little pet?" Pan flicked his hand away angrily. "I have been coming here every night to see if you are okay, I was worried you were lost somewhere.

Then I come back tonight and see you giving yourself to Raesh."

"It is a pledge, I have to pledge myself to him or they will kill me."

"Then, you are a coward." Pan gave him a look of disgust.

"And you're not? If you never left the village then no one would have to pledge themselves to him in the first place. I am only doing what I need to do to survive. And you leaving trinkets in my bedroom does not help."

"Trinkets?" Pan turned up his nose at the accusation.

"A thimble? Under my pillow? When did you put it in here? I know it was you."

"I left it in here for you to find for when you got home. I didn't think I would get here before you did, or that it would get you into any trouble. It is a good thing to be given."

"No, Pan, it isn't. They knew it belonged to you. I'm lucky that they didn't know the teeth were yours too."

"So, you do have my teeth!" he exclaimed. "I knew that you took them, why did you lie?"

"I didn't take them, Tippy-toe did. Have you seen him Pan?"

"Yes, he has been living with me on the ship, he was too scared to come back here if you weren't here," he explained. "You can come and get him, he is a pain."

"I can't. And you can't be here," Nathaniel said after enjoying the moment of relief knowing that Tippy-toe was okay.

"Because Raesh said that you can't?"

"Exactly, Pan, I don't have any reason to be hanging around with you anyway, look at the trouble you have put me in."

"No one forced you to come out to the ship, you came out because you were scared of me leaving Neverland. If you didn't care about me then why do you care if I leave or not?" Pan smirked, knowing full well that he had put Nathaniel in a position where he had no choice but to explain himself.

"I-I, I don't want to be here without you."

"And why is that?"

"Maybe for the same reason that you left a thimble under my pillow." Pan seemed startled at the answer and opened his mouth a couple of times to speak but couldn't find any words. "Why would you want to grow up anywhere else but here?"

"So that I can get a job, find a wife, be a real man. I am not real here."

"Yes, you are," Nathaniel said. "You don't want a job, a wife, you don't need those things to become a man. You are already a man."

"Did you mean what you said about death, Nathaniel?" Pan asked suddenly. "That there isn't anything after you die?"

"Why?"

"I can feel my body dying, every day it hurts more and more and the only way I can describe it is death. I don't want to die and be nothing, I couldn't stand a forever of darkness." Nathaniel eyes widened as he saw tears forming in Pan's eyes. "If I leave Neverland and find a family, then a part of me will live on, if someone thinks of me in a loving way then surely it can't be an eternity of darkness, not if someone still lives and thinks of me."

"I would think of you," Nathaniel said as he took the other mans hands into his. "I would never let anyone forget about you. I haven't forgotten about Henry, have I? I keep his memory alive. I would do the same for you, but you're not dying Pan, you do not need to fear death."

"Stay with me, Nathaniel, come back to the boat with me." There was a tremble in Pan's voice as he spoke. "We can be together like we were meant to be, then neither of us will forget or be forgotten. Don't stay here with Raesh, he has drained the sunshine out of you. You don't glow anymore, and I know it is because of him. Don't you want to be my sun anymore?" Nathaniel's breath caught in his throat.

Sunshine.

That is what Pan used to call him before he left. He had felt the warmth of the sun leave him when Pan ran away from Neverland, the fire in his veins dampening. Now, well, now he felt a jolt of heat that he never thought he would feel again. He wasn't going to let it go.

Leaving the village under the cover of darkness was the best chance that they had without being detected. Pan had clearly been in and out of the village more times than Nathaniel knew about though—as he moved around in the darkness like an expert, knowing every corner and extra shadowy areas. As they moved through the area all Nathaniel could think was if he was making the right decision. Raesh would be out for him, wanting his blood for betraying him, especially after re-pledging himself to him.

Everyone knew where Pan lived, it was no secret that he had made a home on the abandoned ship, so it would make sense that would be the first place that they would search for Nathaniel. He felt oddly safe, though, knowing that Pan would protect him at all costs. The question was—why? Why had Pan chosen him as the one he trusted the most, the one he wanted to spend time with over all of the others? Nathaniel didn't want to question it too much—scared at what the answer might mean.

The hours that it took to get to the ship didn't feel like they usually did when Nathaniel travelled there alone. They didn't have the light of Tippy-toe or Mildew to guide them, but the beautiful shimmer of the stars glowing down on them was more than enough to get them back to the ship safely. It felt surprising that no words were spoken between the two of them the whole time that they travelled, both too intent on getting to the ship without being followed to get involved with small talk.

The boat was eerie at night, even the glow from the fairies inside the cabin didn't put Nathaniel at ease. Sensing that Nathaniel was less than comfortable Pan gently took his hand in his and gave it a squeeze.

"Everything will be okay," he said seriously. "Tippy-toe is in there, waiting for you, he was sure that I could convince you to come back." He smiled.

"He knows me well," Nathaniel commented and gave a smile back to him. "I feel scared, though."

"Scared of me?"

"No, not of you. Of Raesh. Of the new people here. Raesh said that they had wanted to find the village, it was why he killed that man."

"Well, who knows what they really want. I can defeat them anyway," Pan said triumphantly.

"Yeah? How? Do they even need defeating?" Nathaniel laughed.

"I don't know yet, but we will think of something. And, as for Raesh, don't worry about him. He is not as brave as you think he is, he would never come out here." Nathaniel narrowed his eyes at him, he wanted to ask why Pan thought that, but the other man was already walking them towards the cabin.

"Will I sleep in here with you?" Nathaniel asked and Peter nodded.

"Some of the rooms below deck are damp, I don't think it would be very comfortable down there. Plus, we are safer together than apart, and the fairies keep a good look out at night." When they stepped into the cabin Nathaniel was accosted by a bright light which he identified as Tippy-toe after a moment.

"Tips!" he exclaimed and the fairy danced in the sky with happiness. "I was so worried about you, where did you get to when we were leaving the town?" Tippy-toe stopped moving and considered the question before shrugging. Ah, so he must have got distracted, it was better than the alternative. "I'm going to live here now with Pan, are you okay with that?" Nathaniel asked and Tippy-toe nodded then flew over to a small bed made from a coconut shell with a smug grin.

Mildew peeked her head out of a cotton blanket that covered the shell then pulled Tippy-toe under it with a tinkling giggle.

"Yeah, they fell in love," Pan laughed as he sat down at a large ornate chair in front of the wooden desk in the room. "I was surprised, but at least they are no longer arguing."

"That is an unexpected development," Nathaniel laughed as well and went to the desk then ran his fingers over a wooden box that was placed in the middle of it. "What is in here?" he asked and turned the box so that the gold clasp was facing him. "Can I look inside?" Pan nodded his approval and watched as Nathaniel's deft fingers unlocked the box and peered inside. He tentatively reached out and touched the contents, his fingers running over each cold metal object slowly. He eventually picked one up and brought it to his face to study it.

"I don't know what they are for," Pan said.

"They aren't for anything in the ship?" Nathaniel examined the hook in his hand and touched the tip of it. He guessed that it was once sharp, but it was now dull and blunt.

"No, not that I can tell. And parts for the ship wouldn't be kept in a box like that, they must be some kind of treasure but I am not sure what."

"They are strange," Nathaniel said as he placed the hook back in the box then looked at the other two that sat in there. "Maybe they are some kind of weapon?"

"Possibly, I had that thought too. Only good for close range though, not something that I would want to use."

"Me neither, but I bet that they could cause a lot of damage."

"Yeah, imagine one of those being stuck into your stomach," Pan grimaced. "It would completely rip your insides out."

"That's disgusting." Nathaniel scowled. "Remind me never to get on your bad side."

"You won't." Pan got up from the chair and went to his bed to pull off some blankets and animal pelts. "You can take the bed, I will set up camp over there." He pointed to the corner of the cabin where there was just enough space for someone to lay on the floor.

"You remember when we lived in the bunker below the trees?" Nathaniel smiled as he made his way to the bed and lay himself down on the soft materials. "The bed down there was huge and we all used to share."

"Was hardly comfortable though was it? Especially when some of the boys used to toss and turn in the night."

"It wasn't so bad, I felt safe down there, comfy. I wonder if it is still accessible."

"Not really. Not after the fire. I go out there sometimes."

"You do?" Nathaniel asked quietly.

"Lot's of memories in that place, I would have gone back and lived there if it was stable, but, it is empty there without the boys, it was too sad to try and salvage it."

"Take me back there?" Nathaniel asked with a yawn. "I know its not as it was before the fire, but I would love to see it again, I remember the stories you used to tell down there, how excited I used to feel every morning that I woke up. "

"I used to tell stories?"

"Yes, all about yourself usually." Nathaniel grinned as Pan arranged the blankets for himself on the floor. "Other times you told us about princesses and dragons, it was amazing."

"I'm sorry that all ended," Pan said as he lay down on his make-shift bed. "That things went the way that they did."

"I just wish that you could have embraced the changes within yourself, you were a better leader than Raesh."

"Why didn't you follow me? When I left?"

"I was scared, Pan, I had no idea what to even say to you. I remember the despair in your eyes, how could I do or say anything to fix that?"

"I don't know," Pan said softly. "I guess that doesn't matter anyway, you are here now." Nathaniel looked up at the ceiling as the light from the fairies started to dim as each of them drifted off to sleep. For the first time in a long time he felt safe, and that heavy feeling of sadness didn't feel like such a struggle in his chest anymore.

"Goodnight, Pan," he whispered.

"Goodnight, Nathaniel."

Six

Pan lifted a smooth wooden cup to his lips, the liquid inside was called wine and it tasted foul. Nathaniel had told him to be polite though, so he drank it and did his best to not pull a disgusted face. Daisy sat opposite him, her curly black hair hidden under a bright orange head scarf that contrasted beautifully with her dark brown skin. She watched him with amusement plucking at the corners of her lips and then raised her own glass to drink. Gold bangles clinked on her wrists as she moved, the sound reminding him of an angry fairy that he used to know. She put her cup down then reached forward to push forward a stone bowl full of grapes towards him with a smile.

"I promise you, they taste amazing," she said when she noticed the uneasy look Pan gave the fruit.

"You eat one first," he challenged which caused her to laugh.

She picked up a grape and popped it in her mouth. "See? Not poisoned," she said as she chewed. "I want to be an ally to you Pan, not kill you."

"Why?" Pan asked as he picked a grape for himself. He rolled it around in his palm before finally eating it.

"The leader of the others, we know he is plotting against us...we get the impression he isn't exactly fond of you either."

"Raesh is threatened by me."

"Did you know he killed one of our men?" Daisy asked, her expression turning serious. "He burned him to death."

Pan sucked in his bottom lip then nodded. "That was ages ago, though, don't dwell on it."

"Don't dwell on it?" Daisy frowned. "Pan, he will want to do the same to all of us. You and Nathaniel included. But, we won't allow it. We have strength that he cannot comprehend. We are offering you a chance to join with us."

Pan took a deep breath then narrowed his eyes at her. "What strength? None of you seem like you are fighters."

"You will find out with time."

"If you are talking about magic then you are not the first and won't be the last people here to have that power," Pan informed her flippantly. "So you can forget that being your advantage."

Daisy looked momentarily surprised before clearing her throat and puffing the air out of her cheeks. "Then. What?" she asked. "What can we do? We shouldn't have to live in fear of him and the mindless people that follow him. He won't let us live in peace. If you are more than the stories people tell about you, then you will help us."

"Why should I?" Pan snapped. "I am happy with Nathaniel on my boat. We aren't in any danger. Your problems are just that—yours."

"Stop acting like a child, it is obvious that you are a grown man now," Daisy said angrily. "We are asking you to join us. To stand with us. To potentially lead us, Pan."

Pan's eyes lit up at that. The chance to have people following him again was something that he would find hard to resist. "What about Drake?"

"You think that Drake calls the shots around here?" Daisy laughed. "Far from it. He is assertive, I will give him that. But it is me the people look to, it is *me*. I am willing to share that power with you if you can help us."

"But what is it you think I can actually do?" Pan asked. "I can't fly anymore."

"We don't need you to fly. We just need *you*."

Nathaniel couldn't help the pout that had formed on his lips as he listened to Pan talk in excitement. He couldn't get his head around the fact that only a few months before Pan had been adamant about never seeing Drake, Daisy or any of the other new settlers again. Sure, he had encouraged him to go meet with them after getting bored of their numerous requests, but he didn't think Pan would actually want to join them.

He had got comfortable being alone with Pan and the fairies, living in their cabin on the waves. He enjoyed having Pan to himself. Now, *now* Daisy wanted Pan to be by her side. To rule over a stupid town that they were calling Nova. Nova. It was a stupid name.

Not only that, but Pan was excited about it. He seemed thrilled at the thought of leaving their ship and going to make a home in the new settlement. The only good thing he could get from Pan's fast words was that it seemed they were planning to remove Raesh from the position of power he had given himself. That was the only good thing though.

"Well, what do you think?" Pan asked breathlessly and sat himself down next to Nathaniel on the bed. "We can leave right now!"

"But, Pan, this is our home," Nathaniel reasoned. "How do you know you can even trust them? I thought it was just going to be me and you...don't you want that?" Pan opened his mouth to speak but then thought better of it and gave Nathaniel an oddly thoughtful look.

"What are you worried about?"

Nathaniel looked down at his hands anxiously. He could feel embers starting to ignite. "What if you go there and forget about me?" Pan turned his body so he was sitting crossed legged on the bed directly in front of him and gently brought his hand up to brush the unruly curls away from his face softly. Nathaniel closed his eyes at the touch and allowed himself to get lost in the closeness of Pan for a perfect moment.

"You are the only reason that I am still here, Nathaniel. In every way. There were times when I was on my own that I felt so hopeless, so lost and confused. The only light in my life, the only thing that guided me was you...even when we were apart, it was always you.

"You were the same light for me," Nathaniel said. "I am glad that we are here together now."

"I am too." Pan closed the gap between them and pressed his lips against Nathaniel's gently. They kissed softly and slowly, neither one of them wanting to break that moment that felt like it had been years in the making. Nathaniel felt warm and the heavy feeling in his chest of anxiety had completely gone. When Pan broke the kiss Nathaniel pressed his hand to the other mans cheek and ran his thumb over the line of his cheek bone, tracing up to the small mole at the corner of his left eye.

"You know, that was my first kiss." Nathaniel smiled and pressed his forehead to Pan's.

"That's not true, I left you a kiss under your pillow," Pan said quietly.

"You know that a thimble is not a kiss, don't you?"

"It is to me, it means as much. I only had one thimble, one kiss, and I gave it to you."

"It makes me sad that Raesh has it."

"Let him have it, it was more of a promise than anything, that I would give you a real kiss one day." Nathaniel felt a flutter in his chest, like something was trying to set flight inside of him and it gave him an overwhelming surge of emotion that brought tears to his eyes.

"Why am I crying?" Nathaniel asked with a laugh as Pan wiped away a tear on his cheek that had escaped.

"I think, that, maybe, these might be happy tears?"

"They are." Pan pressed his lips to Nathaniel's cheeks in response, kissing him each time with purpose and care. "Sleep with me tonight." Nathaniel stated, but his voice sounded uncertain, like he was scared Pan would reject him.

"I was hoping you would say that, the truth is, the floor isn't particularly comfy."

"Then, share my space, always."

"Always."

Seven

Nathaniel laughed as he ran through the field of sunflowers. His feet hit the ground with such speed he was sure that he was almost flying. Maybe this is what it would feel like to fly with Pan, to feel weightless and filled with joy as they soared through the sky. He gasped as Pan ran at him from the left, pushing through the tall flowers with a loud laugh as he grabbed Nat in his arms, his weight tumbling them both to the floor. Nathaniel groaned before placing his hands over his stomach as he started to laugh again.

"Told you, I would find you," Pan panted as he lay beside him, dust covering the both of them from where they had fallen. Pan rolled onto his front and propped himself up on his forearms as he looked over at Nathaniel who was still laying on his back.

"It hurts!" Nathaniel giggled. "How can it hurt from laughing so much?" He brought his hands to his face to wipe away a few tears that were spilling out of the corners of his eyes.

"See? This is why you will be useless if we actually have to fight Raesh and The Lost Boys," Pan said as he leaned down to press a kiss to Nat's lips. "You can run fast, but you are noisy as hell."

Nathaniel smiled. "Well, I will hardly be laughing during a battle, will I?" He cupped the back of Pan's neck to pull him closer so they could kiss again. "We wouldn't be doing this either." After placing several more kisses to Nat's lips Pan pulled away from him and rested his head on his hand to look at him warmly.

"I can't believe you have never been here before," he commented thoughtfully. "This whole places just screams 'Nat' to me."

"There are plenty of places in Neverland I have never been to. The island is huge, Pan, I don't think I could ever discover all of it."

"You can, and you will," Pan said surely. "We could do it together."

Nathaniel pursed his lips together then sat himself up. "How would we do that? If you go ahead with this plan with Nova...you won't have time to have adventures."

"Are we going to talk about this again?" Pan frowned as he sighed heavily. He pushed himself up onto his knees then stood up. He held out his hand for Nat to take and when he did he helped him get to his feet. "Nat. I need you to trust me. The whole reason we came out here today was to get us both fitter in case we need to fight. You agreed to fight by my side."

"I..." Nat started but trailed off and focused his attention on the sunflower closest to him. He reached up and plucked one of the bright yellow petals off so he could fiddle with it as a distraction.

"Nat..." Pan said softly and took the petal from him. "I know I hurt you when I left before. But...that isn't going to happen again. You have me, you have my heart, nothing bad is going to happen," he said sincerely. "I love you."

Nathaniel's eyes snapped to Pan's in surprise. So many words had been spoken between them in the years they had known each other, but never those words.

Pan was looking at him expectantly, and the words were there on the tip of Nat's tongue, but they were stolen by the sound of something moving fast in the air. He turned his head just as something hit him. A sudden jolt that made the air escape his lungs.

Time stood still. He didn't move, neither did Pan, until everything started moving all at once and the world turned into a buzzing kaleidoscope of colours that was impossible to focus on.

Noise.

All he could hear was noise, loud shouting and swiping, air biting at his skin. He raised a hand, his natural instinct to let his power make decisions for him taking over before he felt another hand wrap around his.

"No." He heard Pan. He couldn't see him, but he knew it was his voice, his hand holding his, putting out the fire he was trying to let escape. He squeezed his eyes shut, the only reaction he could think of in the fog of confusion he was stuck in. The world was spinning, twirling at such a rate that he was sure he could feel the earth moving under his feet. The noise was unbearable, so loud that it became a roar where no single sound could be identified on its own.

When he opened his eyes again he was met with yellow. Yellow flecks falling from the sky all around him. For a split second he thought it was fire, tiny flames sprinkling down to set fire to the land. He reached out his hand, palm facing forward as he caught some of the confetti in his grip. He brought his trembling hand up to his face to inspect what he had caught.

Sunflower petals.

He loves me. He loves me not.

Thousands of them continued to fall from the sky, when he let his eyes adjust to his surroundings he found that the hundreds of flowers that had been around him only minutes before had been cut down. Streaks of red decorated the stalks, flicked out over the earth than held dozens upon dozens of footprints.

"Nat!" Pan appeared in his vision, worry etched across his features as he raced towards him. His head was bleeding, a steady stream of blood flowed down from a wound on his forehead. "Nat, Nat, can you hear me?" Although he could hear him, Nathaniel didn't respond. He looked back at Pan blankly; he had no idea what had happened, or if anything was still happening.

A memory came to him. Him and Pan together, in the grove by the lagoon that was filled with orange trees. They had picked the juiciest of the fruits from the branches, plucked them clean off of the trees in a hurry. They had pulled the peel away from the flesh of the fruit, bursts of zest erupting into the air as the skin tore, releasing a fresh and vibrant smell that attacked their senses. They bit into the fruit, not bothering to pull apart any segments, then spat out any seeds that they found. Juices spilled out of their mouths, ran down their chins, left their hands sticky and sweet. The sun was hot that day. After gorging themselves on the oranges they had fallen asleep under one of the trees, Nathaniel's head on Pan's shoulder. Their stomachs full. They woke to wasps crawling over their bodies; attracted to the orange juices and warmth of their skin. Pan panicked and swatted them away, only to anger them and cause them to start stinging him. The more he waved his arms around the more they were drawn to him—the reddening of his autumn skin irresistible to them.

Nathaniel had pressed bay leaves to the stings on Pan's skin that night. The coolness of the evening contrasted with the oppressive heat of the day. Pan cried as he pressed the leaf down onto each sore lump of skin. Nat didn't even know if a bay leaf would help, but it was the first and only thing that came to his mind to try and heal him.

He thought of those bay leaves now and wondered if they would do anything to help the deep throbbing in his chest. He finally looked down to see his blue cotton tunic blossoming with a deep crimson that he knew was blood. The arrow that stuck out from his torso confirmed that the blood belonged to him.

"Pan?" he whispered as he looked back up at him.

"It's okay, it's going to be okay." Despite Pan's words he knew that everything was far from okay.

"Peter!" Another voice flew in the air from the distance, then more footsteps pounded towards them. Nathaniel fell to his knees and let out a choked gasp. He placed his hand on the end of the arrow and started to pull, only for Pan to drop down in front of him and hold his wrist still.

"Don't pull it out," he warned. "Don't touch it. Let them help you." Them. Them? Nat could hear more voices, closer now, just like the sound of footsteps.

"You weren't meant to get caught up in this." A female voice. Daisy. Concern laced through every syllable. He didn't know what they weren't supposed to have been caught up in, he still didn't know what had happened. Petals still fell lazily from the air. Once tall, strong, full of sunshine. It was like they were never there.

Eight

Mildew pressed some kind of green tonic to Nathaniel's wound. She tutted to herself as she spread the medicine evenly over the area, the colour the same shade as her hair. Tippy-toe sat on the pillow next to Nathaniel's head and kept pressing his tiny hand to his forehead to check for any fever. Despite how selfish and volatile the fairies could be, they were there when they were really needed.

Nat watched Pan who was sitting at the end of the bed picking dirt out from under his nails with a knife. He had never seen him so solemn, so very quiet. Mildew wiped her hands on her black dress then flitted her wings to take her over to Peter.

"He will be okay," she said softly, but not quiet enough so that Nathaniel couldn't hear. "But he can't fight, he will do more damage to himself."

"Pan?" Nathaniel asked which made the other man look away from the fairy and at him. "When are you going to tell me what is going on?"

Pan sighed and gestured for Mildew and Tippy-toe to leave. They both made an unhappy sound but eventually complied and left them alone. "Nova attacked The Lost Boys. But, I swear, I didn't know anything about it."

"In the sunflower field?"

"Yes. Someone there has a power, like you, but they can control the air."

Nathaniel held his breath for a moment. "That's what knocked down the flowers?"

"Yeah," Pan nodded. "But, they weren't expecting The Lost Boys to be ready to attack back. The bows and arrows, that was them, it was one of them who shot you."

"Why did you take me there, Pan?" Nat asked uneasily. "Of all the places in Neverland for them to attack, they had a fight right where we were? That...seems like a little more than coincidence."

"I didn't know about it," Pan said again but averted his eyes away from him.

"So...it was just a coincidence?"

"Look," Pan said with a clipped tone. "What difference does it make if it was or it wasn't?"

"It makes a *huge* difference. You could have warned me, we didn't even have to be there!"

"I didn't know," Pan said again, but the doubt had now been firmly planted in Nathaniel's mind. He wished he could storm out of the room, just get away from Pan and go out onto the deck for fresh air. He thought better of it though, the pain in his ribs was enough to stop his dramatic exit.

"So what now? Nova and The Lost Boys are officially at war with each other?"

"We have a plan," Pan said defensively. "And we will win."

"A plan?" Nat laughed bitterly. "Like their last plan? Because I kinda don't think that went down very well did it?"

"Why can't you be supportive?" Pan hissed at him. "Why are you so negative? This is the only way to get rid of Raesh."

"You never cared about him! You never cared about what he was doing until these new people showed up. Now it is all you think about. I just...don't get it Pan. I support you, but I'm scared for you."

"Scared for me?" Pan raised an eyebrow and scoffed. "I am *Peter Pan,* I can do anything, no one can hurt me Nathaniel."

Nat looked at him in disbelief. The growth he had seen in him was squashed in seconds. "Listen to yourself, Pan, you sound like you did as a child. I thought you had grown up." Pan slammed his hands down on the bed and stood up angrily.

"Shut up!" he shouted, his face full of anger, a rage that had clearly been waiting to erupt for a while. "You know nothing, Nathaniel. You will never be able to understand. Never." He stormed out of the cabin before Nathaniel could make any further argument.

He wanted to cry, scream, throw things. He felt like everything he had ever wanted had been handed to him and then snatched away before he could enjoy it. The Pan he had known, had grown up with, was fighting the man he had become. A childlike sense of authority at war with an adult weight on his shoulders.

Pan walked with no real destination in mind. He pushed branches out of his way, kicked at stones and swatted fairies away who tried to talk to him. Nathaniel just didn't get it. He wanted to turn his back on all of the problems in Neverland and just run away like Pan had done years before. But, he couldn't, he couldn't run away like Nat wanted them to; he had things to do, scores to settle.

He didn't feel alive unless he had an enemy to fight. He knew that there had been plenty before, there would be plenty more after Raesh; it was his job to make sure that they were put back in their place. The reason Nathaniel didn't understand that was because he was still a Lost Boy, his loyalty was still with them despite everything that had happened between them. He wanted to trust Nat...he *did* trust him...but he had to have a reason for why he was acting the way he was. It couldn't have been concern as the sole reason. He knew that Nat loved him; he saw it in the way he looked at him, in the way he kissed him. He loved him too, he meant it when he said it.

He had never understood love before. He had heard The Lost Boys talking about love years ago, about how they loved their parents...siblings, even their friends. Pan didn't love anyone. He had proclaimed that proudly. He never thought he would experience the feeling, the overwhelming emotion of caring about someone so much. He wasn't even sure when he acknowledged that the feeling was love. He just knew that he was in love with Nathaniel. He still did. He always would. But Nat was being *stupid*.

A hand pulled at his ankle suddenly, causing him to stumble and then splash into water he didn't know he was walking beside. He instinctively tried to push his head up over the surface but found that he was stuck, the motions of his arms making no difference to where he was submerged in the lagoon. He looked down, and through the glassy bubbles that floated around him he saw dark eyes looking back at him. The merfolk.

He kicked his leg out as hard as he could, which made the sea creature recoil in surprise so he grasped the moment of freedom and threw his head up over the surface. He gasped, he had only been under a few seconds, but when you are being pulled down those seconds feel like hours. He grabbed the cool white rocks at the side of the lagoon and hoisted himself out of the water to relative safety.

He shook his head, cold droplets of water splattering onto the ground around him. Priya peeked out from the lagoon, deep black eyes focused on him like he was prey. Which, he guessed he was.

"Don't. Don't do that again," he warned as he wiped his hand over his face. "You could have killed me."

Priya swam closer to him then rested her forearms on the rocks beside him. "That was the idea."

Pan scowled. "Why would you want to kill me? I thought we were friends."

Priya blinked slowly at him then let out a laugh. "I would rather eat you than be your friend."

Pan stared at her before rolling his eyes. "Food comes first, huh?" he mumbled as he got himself up and looked down at his soaking wet clothes.

"What are you even doing out here Peter? Where is Nathaniel?"

"He's back on the ship. I needed a walk."

"Why?" Priya licked her tongue over her sharp teeth as she watched him. "I thought that you flew."

"Is that meant to be a joke?"

"I don't know what you mean." she replied innocently.

"Everyone knows that I can't fly. Not anymore."

"Why? Are you terribly miserable?"

Pan cocked his head to the side as he looked at her. "What do you mean?"

"It can't be because you have no fairy dust. There are fairies everywhere. So it must mean that you have no happy thoughts. So. In conclusion. You are miserable." Pan hadn't thought of it like that. Losing the ability to fly was a direct consequence of him facing the fact that he had grown up. He was at peace with that now, so...maybe he could fly again.

"I am not miserable. I have plenty of things to be happy about," he retorted.

"Like what?"

"Like...Nathaniel."

Priya sucked in her cheeks and made a clicking sound with her tongue before answering. "What else? Surely one person can't make you *that* happy. I know you, Peter Pan, there has to be more."

"Well..." Pan sat back down and pushed his wet hair back from his face. He couldn't think of anything else straight away, his brain just screamed Nathaniel to him over and over again. He chewed his bottom lip until he finally thought of something else to say. "I guess...I am happy that I am going to be in charge again."

"Oh?" Priya raised her eyebrows in interest. "How so?"

"The new people...in Nova...I am joining with them to kill Raesh and rule The Lost Boys again."

"I see..." Priya smiled. "How do you plan on doing that?"

"An ambush," Pan replied cockily. "We will do it right before winter sets in, when they are getting ready to get all cosy...great timing huh?"

"Absolutely. You will win for sure," she said while Pan missed the sarcasm in her voice. "Well, then, you should be able to fly, why don't you try now, over the lagoon?"

"I am not falling for that, you just want me to fall in," he laughed. "Thanks, though, Priya, you've been a big help."

"Anytime." She let her hands slide off of the rocks back into the water, her head sunk down slowly, leaving one small ripple twinkling on the surface.

Pan raced back through the trees, a new found energy capturing his every movement. He crowed, a loud triumphant noise that Neverland had almost forgot. As he moved he jumped in the air, his feet lingering on the breeze as he laughed. He felt like he was dancing with the trees, using their magic given to them by the fairies to lift himself up.

Up. Up. Up.

He was so close to touching the sky. Fingers reaching, reaching, but just not close enough to grasp. He closed his eyes. A happy thought. He started to run through the plan to take down Raesh, to rule over The Lost Boys once more, but the thought didn't take him any higher. Then he thought of

Nathaniel, the happy thought he should have let take over his mind first, but he was still scared to let himself believe that he was the thing that now mattered to him most.

He opened his eyes and found himself above the canopy of the trees. Nathaniel. He should have believed, he should have admitted it to himself years ago, the feeling was there all along. He laughed. A jubilant sound that cascaded back down to the trees and woke any slumbering fairies that were beneath him. How could he have thought that power was what defined him? Power. It was nothing if he wasn't actually happy.

He swooped down, the wind brushing his face as he went, grasping him like a long lost friend. As he flew near the ground he grabbed flowers, pulled them up from the soil and bundled them together in his hands. Bright, beautiful blooms, exploding with sunshine from each precious petal that flowed out of his palms, their colours vibrant against his dark coloured clothes.

He circled the ship when he got to the dock. Fairies came out of the cabin to look at him, many started to exclaim excitedly and burst up into the sky to meet him, little twinkling lights guiding his way back to the deck. As soon as his feet hit the deck he ran to the cabin door and burst through, causing Nathaniel to flinch in surprise.

"Nat–" Pan beamed and went to the side of the bed and knelt down beside him. "Here!" He held out the absurdly large bouquet of flowers, which Nathaniel took gingerly. He held them back slightly so that the soil from the roots still attached to them didn't get over the bed covers.

"Wow, Pan, these are beautiful."

"I had to pick them for you, to make you smile...I'm sorry, so so sorry about earlier," he said quickly. "I realised...I finally realised how much of an idiot I am."

Nathaniel couldn't help but laugh. "Yeah? What made you come to that realisation?"

"*You*. You're my happy thought, Nat, I never...I never thought I would find something that would fill me with happiness again. But I did, I found you."

"What...what made you think that?"

"Priya asked me, she said what made me happy, and I didn't even have to think, Nat, the answer was you." Pan smiled at the other man then took the flowers away from him and put them on the large wooden desk to the side of the room. "Are you well enough to get out of bed?"

Nathaniel frowned then shifted his torso about a little bit to see if he was comfortable. "I mean...kinda? Why? Do I have to?"

"Come with me."

Nathaniel stepped onto the deck carefully as he held onto Pan for support. His chest ached, the medicine Mildew had given him was good, but it didn't do much to dull the pain. Pan was surprisingly gentle with him; he held his arm like he was made of glass, a precious piece of treasure.

"I want to show you...I want you to come with me," Pan said once they were fully out in the open.

"Come with you?"

"I can fly again, Nat."

"What?" Nat gasped softly.

"It was so natural, like I never lost it, you know? Because of you."

Nat smiled brightly at him. "I am so happy for you, it's what you wanted."

"You don't think you can come for a little fly with me?" Pan asked hopefully.

"I...not right now," Nat sighed regretfully. "When I am better? You can take me?"

Pan nodded. "Yes. As soon as you are better," he agreed. "And once I have helped Nova, I am going to take us away from here?"

"What? To where?"

"There is a place called London."

"London?"

"It will be us, no more fights, no more Raesh or Daisy, we will be safe there, we can be happy. Just me and you." Pan cupped Nathaniel's cheek as he looked at him. "I am sorry for losing sight of what is really important."

"But, Neverland is important to you, Peter, I know it is. I am not asking you to leave this all behind for me."

"It isn't for you," Pan said with a smile and a shake of his head. "It is for us. I will be happy knowing that I have left Neverland in safe hands. Besides, I want to have new adventures, in new places, and in all of those adventures I need you by my side." Nathaniel felt a swelling in his chest. At first he thought it was fire, but he quickly identified it as an overwhelming sense of belonging. He belonged with Pan. Neverland, London, an undiscovered star, it didn't matter where.

"I can't wait to be your next adventure."

"Me neither."

Part Three

One

R ica pulled her curled black hair into a tight knot at the back of her head, then covered her locks with a navy headscarf that used to belong to her mother. She looked at herself in the mirror and drew in a deep breath before dabbing ruby red berry juice onto her cheeks. She moved her fingers over her skin smoothly, making sure that the colour blended in perfectly. Once she had finished she looked over her shoulder to Pan who was looking out of the window with a concerned expression over his face.

When she had first met Pan she was just a child, though, in the grand scheme of things she guessed she would still be considered as that. Compared to Pan, who had lived countless years, she must have still appeared as a mere baby. She wondered what he looked like as a child, if his cheeks were rounder, hair wilder. He stood now as a tall man, curls slicked back away from his face and a sadness in his expression that never seemed to really lift. He must have felt her eyes on him as he pulled his attention away from the window and to her. A small smile crept over his lips and he gestured for her to stand. She smiled back at him and stood from her seat and twirled around in a circle. She rarely wore dresses, and this was one that her mother had made for her.

It was navy like her head scarf, but scattered with precious pearls that had been sewn so perfectly they resembled a night sky. It was sleeveless, showing off her toned arms and wrists that were adorned with gold bracelets. Pan had never seen her look so...powerful.

"My goodness, Rica, if only your parents were here to see you." Pan stepped forward and took her hand into his. He leaned forward slightly and kissed her knuckles. "Your mother always told me it was polite to kiss a lady's hand."

"Did she?" Rica laughed then tugged her hand away from him. "Such a strange sign of respect. Nathaniel and Raesh never kissed my hand."

"Raesh is hardly one to show any respect for others," Pan sneered.

"What about Nathaniel?"

"What about him?" Pan stepped away from her. "He is no one of importance."

"I think I would have to disagree with you on that," she said as she watched him pick up his cloak and wrap it around his shoulders. "Are you sure it will be safe for you to join me tonight?"

"They are announcing the competitors tonight. I need to see who I will be facing up close. Besides, Kaz is already passed out drunk in his room, someone needs to be there, it won't be him."

Rica tutted and sucked on her teeth. "For God's sake. He is impossible. How that man was blessed with magic is beyond me." She threw her hands in the air in exasperation. "I guess we have no choice then. But, Pan, if you feel that someone is starting to figure out who you are, you will slip away won't you? We are so close to ending Raesh's reign. We can't afford to mess up now."

"Princess," Pan said and placed his hand over his chest. "You have my word."

Rica raised an eyebrow. "I would be a fool to trust you on your word, but, hey, like I said, I don't have much choice do I?"

"I feel like I should be offended by that," Pan admitted. "But, you have a good head on your shoulders, Rica. You are going to be a wonderful ruler one day."

"I know." She smirked in response. "Now, let us go check out our competition."

Nathaniel could feel his hands starting to sweat, Raesh was standing at the front of the hall with the parchment containing the competitors names and with every second that passed he felt more and more nervous. The room fell silent as Raesh raised his hands to signify that he was ready to speak. There was an excitement buzzing through the air, but all Nathaniel could focus on was the hot fire that was burning in his veins.

"Welcome, everyone, this is such an important evening and I am sure you are all eager to find out who will be competing for each settlement in the games. So, let me begin." He started to announce competitors, names that Nathaniel had learned off by heart since they were told to him. As each name was called the competitor made their way to the front of the room to stand behind Raesh proudly. Seeing each person lined up made it feel all the more real, especially as most of those who were standing would not live to see the actual crowning at the end of the games.

When Kaz was called he moved through the crowd silently as others whispered, he brushed past Nathaniel, his fingers grazing his wrist in a move that could have been a mistake or deliberate. Nathaniel felt a lump forming in his throat as Kaz took his position, there was something not right about him, it didn't help that his damn hood was pulled up over his head like usual, casting his features into darkness. He was too busy staring at the man to hear his name called, but the collective gasp from around the room brought him back to his senses.

"Cheat!" a voice cried out which caused Raesh to squint his eyes in the direction it came from.

"Cheat?" he responded but gestured for Nathaniel to come and take his place with the rest of the competitors. He walked through the crowd, feeling every set of eyes on him, it took every ounce of control for him not to burst into flames. "How is my choice of competitor cheating in any way?"

"He has known all our competitors!" Char shouted and stepped angrily towards the King. Raesh didn't move, just looked at him with such disinterest Nathaniel wasn't sure how he managed it. "He has an advantage over us all, he has been plotting this whole time."

"Nathaniel is not smart enough to plot anything," Raesh said bitterly. It took him a moment to really register the insult and he felt Kaz bristle beside him. Not smart enough to plot? There was a few laughs from people in the room which did nothing to aid the deep red colour Nathaniel's cheeks were turning. He could feel his skin starting to heat up, the familiar feeling in his chest of panic rising up in his throat. "If anyone here thinks that I am a cheat then we need to have a very serious discussion. There are consequences for speaking about your King in such a way," Raesh continued. "But, for now, that is the end of the competitor announcement–"

"Wait!" an unfamiliar voice shouted from the back of the hall and thankfully the eyes that were locked on Nathaniel turned to the new voice. It came from a man who was leaning against the back wall, arms folded across his chest. His hair was pitch black and fell in loose ringlets to his shoulders, contrasted beautifully with a deep emerald green jacket that fitted him perfectly. Gold buttons adorned the material, fastened over his chest right down to his hips where the jacket parted into two tails at his back. His boots were black, shining so much that the light from the candles reflected off of them. He was too far away for Nathaniel to see what colour his eyes were, but they were intense, he could tell that much.

He stood from his leaning position and stretched his arms out over his head. It was then that the light caught an object other than his shoes. In place of a hand on his right side there was a hook.

Nathaniel felt a chill roll through his body, he could picture the wooden box back on the ship he shared with Pan all those years ago. The box, that was so beautiful, so well kept, that homed hooks. He gasped softly and Kaz edged closer to him, only a slight move, but it was enough for him to notice. It was as if the whole room was collectively holding it's breath–no one dared move, speak or even blink. They all knew who he was from some shared nightmare that was nestled deep in their memories, a monster. A shadow.

"Who are you?" Raesh finally spoke, but his voice had a faint tremble to it.

"I am merely here to register for the games," the man chuckled, his voice deep, smooth, like the water of the lagoon. "Anyone can register, am I correct?"

"Only settlements of the island," Raesh retorted with a sneer. "I have never seen you before."

"Just because you do not see something that does not mean it does not exist." The man took a step forward, the crowd parting for him. "We arrived. We settled. We wish to enter the games."

"We?" Raesh narrowed his eyes at him. "What is the name of your settlement?"

"I suppose we should just call it...Jolly Roger," he laughed. "When I say 'we' I refer to me and my men. I am going to compete, I register myself."

Raesh swallowed thickly. "And what is your name?"

"Captain James Hook."

The air was sucked out of the room. Nathaniel felt Kaz grasp his hand and he turned his head to look at the other man. His features were still covered by his hood, but there was *something* that rang so familiar to Nathaniel, he wished he could figure out what it was.

"Guards!" Raesh shouted, but those he had to protect him did not move from their spots. It was as if the whole room had been stuck in time. A photograph blur of a moment. Raesh turned his head and gestured for Nathaniel to move. He stepped forward, but Kaz gripped his hand tighter and pulled him back. "Nathaniel!" Raesh practically roared, causing him to shake Kaz's hand off of his and make his way forward.

He raised his hand in front of him, a flame already dancing in his palm as a warning to the pirate. *Pirate*. It didn't seem possible, that a fairy tale had walked right into their palace.

"Stand down," Nathaniel heard himself say, and to his surprise there was no tremble to his voice.

"I am hardly threatening anyone," Hook chuckled and gestured to his own body. "I am not even carrying any weapons boy, stand down? Are you an imbecile?" The fire crackled in Nathaniel's hand, daring to leap forward and engulf the man in front of him. "Silly little boy who likes to play with fire," Hook mocked. "You will only end up hurting yourself."

"Hey!" Nathaniel's head snapped to the new voice that had entered the situation. Rica stepped forward from the crowd, head held high, such a beautiful strength about her that Nathaniel wished he possessed. "What is the commotion here?" she asked. "Anyone can enter the games, it is written in the rules. Why are you acting so hostile?" She looked to Raesh with a raised eyebrow. "Well? Your Majesty?"

"You stupid girl," Raesh said sharply. "Have you not heard of Captain Hook? This man in front of you is a villain."

"I believe this room is full of villains," she countered which encouraged the crowd to start murmuring among themselves again. "What is one more? Does anyone else object to this man being added to the roster?" she asked and looked around the room. The murmuring turned into grumbles, but no one spoke out. "Well, then, I guess we should welcome you to the games, James Hook." She held out her hand to him. Hook seemed to be considering her, a thin smile on his lips, before he stepped forward and lowered himself to kiss her hand.

When he rose again he cocked his head as he looked at her. "I believe that you will be a wonderful opponent."

"Oh, I look forward to my competitor facing you in the games, Captain." She gave him a wink then clapped her hands together a couple of times loudly. "Now, enough drama, this is meant to be a party, let us have some fun."

"We need to pull the names," Char announced. "If this *pirate* really thinks he can waltz in here and declare himself a worthy competitor, then fair enough," he said with a smirk. "I would love to see him face my competitor."

Raesh gestured for Nathaniel to move back and stand beside him, which he did obediently. He could practically feel the tension rolling off of the King, he liked to be in control, this must have been driving him crazy.

"Fine," Raesh said after several seconds of silence. "Nathaniel, add his name, let us decide the order of the battles."

There was an excitement vibrating around the room as Raesh dipped his hand into a large wooden bowl to pull out the first name. Nathaniel kept his eyes on Kaz who was now standing with Rica again opposite him. He knew him. He knew that he wasn't the man he met in the hallway that night. His attention was pulled back to the task at hand when Raesh cleared his throat and held up a piece of paper with the first name on it.

"Nova," he said and focused on Rica who gave a stern nod. "And..." He reached into the bowl and pulled another settlement. "Hemmingstone." There was silence before a small round of applause. Raesh continued with a few more names until he finally pulled Spire out of the bowl. "And Spire will be competing against Thelan." Nathaniel couldn't help the drop in his stomach. He would be facing Yulia's competitor, the woman who was easily twice his size and looked like she could crush him with her finger. He could only hope that she didn't have any magic, if she didn't he might be able to overpower her with his. "And finally, the new Jolly Roger settlement," Raesh said with a mocking tone and rolled his eyes. "They will be facing the last settlement, which is Amberlan...which is what you wanted, isn't it, Char?" He looked over at the usually boastful leader to see that he had gone rather pale.

"Wonderful," Hook said with a deep chuckle. "I look forward to it. But, for now, I must return to my men. It really was an pleasure meeting you all." His eyes rested on Nathaniel. "Especially you, boy, I have heard many stories of you...you did what I never could. You defeated Pan." Nathaniel's head snapped to Raesh at the mention of the name, but for once Raesh didn't seem to be reacting. "I would love to talk to you, properly, one day, just me and you." The pirate smirked at him then dipped his head in acknowledgment at Raesh.

The room fell into silence yet again as he left, either from nerves or relief, Nathaniel wasn't even sure what he was feeling in that moment. Fear? Maybe. Either way, the games had just got a lot more interesting.

Two

Pan was drowning. At least, that is what he thought it would feel like to drown. As soon as he could he made his way out into the dark garden of the palace. His hands were tingling, his head swimming in a sea that he could not float in. This is what it must have felt for Nat when he couldn't control his magic. He hated it. He hated feeling confused, and more than anything he hated feeling scared.

Hook.

As soon as he had seen him the memories came hurtling at him at full force. Every angry word, every swipe of a sword. A ticking. A sickening ticking noise that was now stuck in his brain and only got louder. He pushed his hood down, not caring in that moment if anyone saw him. He placed his hands over his ears and shook his head, wanting the sound to stop but it just drummed louder in his ears to the point that he wanted to scream. He dropped his hands and looked up at the sky. He couldn't see any stars. A new panic spread in his chest as he started to walk, his eyes focused on the sky, feet moving in time with the ticking in his head. The sound got so loud he didn't hear the small twinkling of bells, he didn't hear the tiny voice in his ear or acknowledge the petite weight on his shoulder.

Mildew pinched at his ear lobe as she shouted his name, but there was no response from Pan at all. She looked behind her at Tippy-toe who was flying behind them and gestured for him to get help. He stopped and fluttered in mid-air before darting in the opposite direction back to the palace.

Pan didn't stop. He had no idea where he was going, he just knew he had to get away. A part of him was telling him to stop; he had left Rica back there with only Kaz, who was roaring drunk, and the less than adequate guards to protect her. If her parents found out he had left they would have him killed. Rica was the future. But Hook was his past, and he didn't expect to have him staring him in the face.

Hook couldn't have known who he was, surely? His face was covered, he was just a child the last time he saw him, even if he did see his face would he have even recognised him? What would he even say to the man after all these years? "Oh, super sorry for chopping your hand off and feeding it to a crocodile? Think we can put it behind us?" He somehow didn't think the pirate would go for that.

Then there was Nathaniel. He could still feel his palm pressed against his. The warmth of his skin, that tingling heat that was always there with Nat, he hadn't changed. His first instinct was to hold him, to get him away from Hook and that whole palace and just get him somewhere safe. But, Nat had walked up to Hook with no fear, none that was visible at least. He had matured in so many ways, even if it was an order to stand off against Hook he still did it without flinching. Now, though, not only was he going to have to face Hook in the games, he was also going to have to face Nat. That is if Hook didn't kill him first.

He didn't think he could stand to watch Nat fight. He was powerful, he wielded fire with ease and grace when he wanted to, yet there were so many hidden elements to the games. Competitors could have been holding back on revealing their powers–what if they were stronger than Nat? What if they were even stronger than Pan? Not once had he considered losing the games up until now; he was sure he would win. He could fly again. That had to be the biggest advantage, being able to soar out of an opponents reach?

He could remember the day he lost his ability to take flight. The crushing feeling in his whole body as he realised he had lost the one thing that had made him special. Getting that back was a feeling of euphoria. Fairy dust was an easy thing to obtain, but a happy thought was like trying to find hidden treasure back when he was a child. After all these years Nathaniel was still his happy thought. Even after everything that had happened between them, he was the one and only thing that made his feet lift off of the floor and reunite him with the stars.

Nathaniel.

It was always going to be him.

Crickets could be heard in the long grass that circled the graveyard on the outskirts of Spire. It would have been silent if not for their chirping, the sound weaving through the air with such vigor that it became a constant thrumming buzz. The sound summed up exactly what Nathaniel was feeling, a mixture of pins and needles and numbness that left his entire body feeling irritated.

Pan was alive. At least that was what Tippy-toe had told him. The truth had yet to be determined. The young fairy had burst in through the window in such a panic it took Nathaniel a good ten minutes to get him calm enough to make any sense out of him. The gist of the story was that Pan was alive and needed his help.

Of course, Tippy-toe didn't actually know where Pan was at that point, which resulted in Nathaniel wandering around Spire for a couple of hours without finding any clue of where he could be. He did ponder the possibility that this was some weird joke that Tippy-toe was playing on him, yet he didn't quite believe that the fairy would be that cruel.

Having a pirate show up and Pan in one evening seemed a bit far-fetched. It was as if there was a line of people at the palace waiting to come in and throw a spanner in the works. If Pan was back it was good that Raesh didn't know about him. Yet. He dreaded to think what was going to be next on the infinite list of things that could go wrong. Maybe, if he found him, Pan would just kill him and he wouldn't have to worry about any of the numerous stresses he was adding up in his head.

He eventually found himself on the outskirts of the city at the entrance to the graveyard. If he ever went out of the palace for a walk this is where he always eventually ended up. It was like he knew he would be there himself one day, deep in the ground, under a pile of rocks. Just like Henry. He looked down at his brother's grave and wondered how long it would be before he was buried there too. He knelt down and ran his hand over the pile of rocks that marked where Henry was buried and frowned at how some of the painted colours had begun to fade. He pressed his fingers into the soil and took a deep breath as he closed his eyes. Henry. He was the opposite to Nathaniel in so many ways. Where Nat was relatively short, Henry towered over the other boys. He had straight bright blonde hair that contrasted with the unruly brown mess that Nathaniel possessed and eyes the colour of the ocean. Nathaniel let out an involuntary sob as he thought about him. The image of him alive and well never stayed for long. That perfect memory of how his brother used to be would always morph into how he looked when they found his body. He didn't recognise him. His features had been scorched away.

"You still come out here?" Nathaniel opened his eyes but didn't turn his head when he heard who spoke. He felt his heart start to race faster in his chest but he didn't dare look behind him. "I know it is a graveyard but it is bloody depressing here. Nothing nice about it." He felt a hand on his shoulder but he still didn't dare move. He could see the man's fingers on his shoulder out of the corner of his eye. Walnut coloured skin with bitten nails. A dark brown mole at the base of his index finger. It really was him. "I'm sorry I have been gone so long." Nathaniel closed his eyes again and felt a tear roll down his cheek.

"Pan," he whispered and he felt the hand lift away from him.

"This wasn't how I planned to speak with you," Pan said quietly and sat himself down beside his old companion. "Please, Nat, open your eyes." He did as Pan asked and when he laid his eyes on the other man he felt a painful pull in his chest.

"I am meant to kill you on sight," Nathaniel choked. Pan looked the same as he did when he vanished forty years ago. His skin still looked like it had been speckled with gold dust, his eyes held a million stars. Lips, God, his lips that he had kissed a thousand times were that same dusky pink colour that used to darken when he chewed them, a bad habit that only Nathaniel used to notice. Just the sight of him made him want to turn back time and be on the old ship with him again. The days seemed so long, so full of carefree adventure and promise. Now he felt a detachment that he knew was never going to be repaired.

"Are you going to kill me Nat?" Pan asked, he was too close, Nathaniel could feel his breath on his skin. "I know you could kill me in a second if you wanted to."

He shook his head. "I could never harm you."

"Not physically at least," Pan mumbled and looked down at the pile of rocks. Nathaniel felt his stomach turn, the comment hurting more than any weapon could, but that was Pan's intention.

"You are mad at me for being in Spire?"

"I am mad at you for standing with that tyrant." Nathaniel sighed as Pan sucked his bottom lip between his teeth anxiously.

"If I didn't he would have killed me."

"That isn't true. You went to him after the battle. You could have gone to Nova. You had a choice." Pan said seriously.

"No. Peter. I didn't." Pan's eyes flicked back to Nathaniel's face at the mention of his first name. "I made a mistake. A huge mistake. The people of Nova thought that I had betrayed them."

"You did betray them. And you betrayed me."

Nathaniel shook his head slightly. "No. It wasn't like that. I was trying to help. I thought I was helping."

"How on earth was telling our enemies our plan of attack helping?" Peter asked.

"Because..." Nathaniel frowned. He had thought of what he would say to Pan if he ever saw him again, how he would explain himself to him, but now all those plans had drifted away from him. "You were no longer a child but you still acted so impulsively without thinking of the consequences."

"The consequences?" Pan narrowed his eyes at him. "The aim was to get rid of Raesh, he was literally killing anyone who didn't agree with him. It was going to be *easy* but then you went and told The Lost Boys what we were going to do!"

"They already knew, Pan!" he said angrily. "You were so full of yourself you were telling every fairy you saw what you and the people of Nova were going to do. Even the merfolk knew. Raesh and the boys were ready for you."

"What?" Pan said with a small laugh in disbelief. "Don't be stupid."

"Priya told me that you told her about the plans. They knew everything right down to the last detail. You know what the merfolk are like, they will give up any information that they have for a stupid trinket."

Pan pursed his lips together as he listened then scoffed indignantly. "So, everything that happened was my fault?"

"That isn't what I am saying."

"You gave them ammunition against us. They were there and waiting for us when we were planning to ambush them. And where were you, Nat? Hiding off somewhere?"

"I was in a tree house."

"So you *were* hiding?" Pan said angrily. "All these years I had hoped that wasn't true. That you were not a coward."

"I wasn't hiding, Pan." Nathaniel whispered again. "They had me chained up in there. They had removed the ladder too. Even if I could move I wouldn't have been able to get down." He waited for Pan to say something, but when he didn't he continued. "I was just outside of the village. I could hear everything that was happening Pan, I could hear the screaming and the violence. But there was nothing I could do."

"You're lying," Pan said. "You have magic inside of you Nat. You could have got yourself out of that tree."

"By setting fire to it?" Nathaniel laughed. "I would have just ended up killing myself. Probably would have set the whole forest on fire while I was at it too. Pan...I was up there for days. Tippy-toe and the fairies found me in the end...you had gone by then...I didn't know if you were dead or alive. I was terrified."

"Why did you go to Raesh though? Why didn't you come and find me?"

"He promised me that he wouldn't fight you. He said that he would have peace talks with you and Daisy. That didn't happen, did it? He used everything I said against you. How could I come and find you?" he asked. "How could I come and expect you to forgive me? You are right. I did betray you. I betrayed everyone in Nova, betrayed everyone who was killed. It wasn't my intention but that is what I ended up doing. Then...then everyone said you had gone. Left Neverland, it was better than the thought of you dying...but you were still gone."

"So you decided to be his right hand man? Decided to live a life of luxury? Pretty nice life you have in Spire, Nathaniel. While everyone else had to start from scratch and build up settlements to only have to answer to Spire and Raesh? Then, to add insult to injury, he dangles the crown in front of everyone with these stupid games. And now, you are competing for him." Every word that Pan said felt like a knife being slowly inched into his chest. He couldn't argue with him. He was right.

"I am sorry," he said and he was fully aware of how pathetic he sounded. "It hasn't been easy for me, Pan."

"If you say so, Nathaniel." Pan stood up from where he had been sitting and brushed off his clothes. "I fully expect you to tell Raesh that I am here. But given that Hook is back I think I am actually the least of his concerns." Nathaniel looked up at him for a moment before standing as well.

"Pirates are real."

"Yes."

"Why did you tell me they were shadows when we were children?"

"I forgot, Nat, I forgot what they were." Nathaniel could tell that what Pan was saying pained him. "I was a child, my imagination was bigger than anything else. Hook was around long before you were."

"You remember him now?"

"I remember everything."

"You do?" Nathaniel asked quietly. "Everything?"

"Hook isn't a good person, Nat," Pan warned. "Which is why I am talking to you now. To warn you."

"I know he isn't a good person. Raesh has told me stories about him. But, I didn't think he was actually real."

"He is real. And he is here. He wants to kill us all."

"So, you risked being exposed just to warn me? I am competing in the games. I am facing death anyway. You would know...you are Kaz Bresis aren't you?"

"No," Pan laughed, a genuine laugh this time that made butterflies explode in Nathaniel's stomach. "Kaz Bresis is a real person. I am pretending to be him though, you got that right."

"I knew you were back."

"I knew you would figure it out." Pan said softly and reached his hand out to cup the other mans cheek. His touch was something that Nathaniel had been yearning for, it had been missing in his life for so long it almost didn't feel real now that it was happening.

Pan's touch used to be as natural to him as breathing. He knew every inch of his body, as Pan knew his, had slept in his arms and woke to the steady rise and fall of his chest.

"I'm not going to tell Raesh that you are back."

"Why?" Pan dropped his hand back down to his side.

"Pan, I don't want him to win these games. You don't know what I have seen over these years. I am going to stop him."

"Then why fight for him?" Pan asked.

"I guess it is the only way I have some control over what could happen. I don't have a plan like you clearly do."

"Whatever happens, Nat, Raesh will not be King at the end of it. I don't want you to get caught in the crossfire."

"I think it is a little too late for that," Nathaniel said regretfully. "Kinda got stuck in the crossfire the moment I met you I think."

"Do you wish you never came to Neverland?"

"No. I would never have met you if I didn't come here."

Pan smiled. "Am I really that special?"

"I never stopped loving you, Peter," Nathaniel said. "I never will."

Pan hesitated then took a deep breath. "I can't talk about this right now, Nat."

"I know." Nathaniel nodded. "Just...be careful. In the games. I am on your side."

"Are you?"

"I always have been."

Three

I have decided against marrying Rica." Raesh said as he took his seat on a wooden stage to the edge of the games arena. He was wearing his usual black ensemble, topped off with emerald jewels on his fingers and crown. He wore no velvet cape, much to Nathaniel's relief, the sun was high in the sky and threw down an intense heat that rendered the garment useless. Still, Raesh must have been boiling all in black, but the King didn't have a single bead of sweat on his forehead. "She is far too unruly for me. I need a woman who actually listens and shows me the respect I deserve." Nathaniel was grateful his seat was placed slightly back from the King's so that that the man didn't see him roll his eyes.

"A wise decision," he commented then brushed his hair back away from his face and fastened it at the back of his head with a leather band. "It is warm today," he continued with lack of anything better to say. The arena was now full of spectators, mainly from Spire, but some had travelled from other parts of the island and were wearing colours to represent their settlements.

"Yes, it is rather," Raesh turned his head to the right to look at him. "You look lovely today." Nathaniel was surprised at how sincere the King sounded but offered him a soft smile.

"Thank you, they are the clothes you picked out for me."

"Obviously," Raesh said, a bitterness back to his tone.

When Nathaniel had woke that morning he had been met with an array of servants bustling about his bedroom. Tippy-toe and Mildew were no where to be seen and he guessed that they had been told to leave. Once he had been pulled out of bed and practically pushed into a tub of freezing cold water by hands that were too hasty to care about his comfort, he was presented with a uniform he had never seen before. The material of the top was the softest thing he had ever touched and the colour of rain kissed grass. It fit him snugly, with a black leather harness fastened across his chest and over his shoulders. He didn't really know what the purpose of that was for, if it served any purpose at all.

The trousers were of a similar material, but jet black in colour, when he held them up his mouth turned into a frown. They looked tight. When he put them on they were snug, just like the tunic, but he was amazed at how easily he was able to move in them. The boots came up to his knees, a black leather that was stiff, if he had time he would have taken them for a run in the forest, broken them in a bit, but time was not something he had a lot of.

He did wonder if Raesh had always intended for him to fight in the games, if he was waiting patiently for Nathaniel to volunteer himself. It seemed a little suspicious that the King was able to have clothes made that fit his form so perfectly, they were clearly made just for him.

"I have something else for you," Raesh said as he snapped his fingers at a guard to the edge of the stage. The man jolted in surprise then hurried forward with a wooden box. Raesh took it from him and gestured for him to return to his post. He handed the box to Nathaniel nonchalantly. "Open it."

Nathaniel ran his hands over the lid then slowly opened it to reveal a thin band of gold that was shaped into a circle. He picked it up from the box and turned it around in his hands before looking at Raesh in confusion.

The king huffed and got up from his seat and snatched the gold from Nathaniel's hands. "For God's sake. It is a crown you imbecile," he said as he placed the band on Nathaniel's head. "It would look better if that stupid hair of yours looked tidier, but it will do."

"I cannot accept this," Nathaniel said quietly. Despite the band being light as air in his fingers, it now felt like a heavy stone pushing down on his head.

Raesh raised an eyebrow. "You can, and you will. I cannot have my competitor going out there looking a mess." Raesh cupped Nathaniel's chin with his thumb and forefinger as he looked down at him. "I think it is time to start these games."

The crowd erupted in cheers as Raesh walked to the front of the stage. The leaders from the other settlements sat on a stage on the opposite side of the arena, all of them clapped politely but none of them stood for their King. Raesh raised his hand in the air to quiet the crowd. It took several minutes for the roar of voices and clapping to die down, Nathaniel could see the King's fingers twitching in annoyance.

"Welcome, everyone, to Spire and the Crowning Games," he bellowed. Half of the people there couldn't hear him, but they all look enthralled as their King spoke. "I am pleased to see so many wonderful competitors this year, it will be a very close competition. I am sure you are all familiar with the rules but I will explain for any...newcomers..." He directed his gaze at Hook who sat between Rica and Char with an amused expression plastered across his face.

"The first round knocks out the weakest," Raesh warned. "Those that win their fight will progress into the next rounds. Of course, a competitor can surrender, if that happens the game will end and that competitor will lose their round. Competitors will be eliminated until there are just two standing. Those two will face off in a final battle, which, as you all know, is a battle to the death. There will be no surrender in this final match—the winner takes the crown for their city." There was a jolt of excitement throughout the crowd, no matter how civilised they made themselves out to be, no one could resist seeing a death played out in front of them.

Nathaniel looked over to where the competitors were sitting—an area that he should have been but Raesh had insisted he stay by his side. Kaz Bresis was sitting with his hood down, a cocky smirk on his face as he listened to Raesh speak. He wished he had tried to get more out of Pan, he would have liked to have some idea of what he was planning with Rica. Clearly there was a switch going to happen, goodness knows when though, and he *needed* to know. If Kaz was going to fight with his hood down, then it would be easy, but if he didn't, well, that would make things a lot more complicated.

He didn't want to fight Pan. He would happily face any of the others, Hook included, before facing Pan. He hadn't seen him fight in years, but with his fire he was sure that they would be pretty evenly matched. He didn't want to hurt him.

He never wanted to hurt Pan. He was positive that Pan didn't want to hurt him either. Kaz Bresis on the other hand, he could fight him. Fire against water. An elemental battle. No feelings involved. He could handle that.

"Without further ado, I would like to announce our first battle. Nova versus Hemmingstone. Good luck." Raesh clapped his hands together and the crowd followed suit, applauding as Kaz and the competitor from Hemmingstone walked to the center of the arena.

The woman from Hemmingstone, Kendra, was petite, if anything a little pathetic looking. Her features reminded Nathaniel of a mouse, sharp, twitching, timid but fast. She shook hands with Kaz in the center of the arena then both of them stepped back. Raesh raised his right hand in the air, and when he lowered it the games officially started.

Four

Kaz fell backwards, his body creating a cloud of dust as it hit the floor. He dragged his hand over his face, smearing the blood that was trickling from his nose over his cheeks. Kendra panted as she stepped over him, a rock held tightly in her hand. She dropped to her knees, straddling Kaz's waist then raised the rock above her head. She brought it down quickly, with a force that made Nathaniel's stomach turn. The sound it made as it crashed against Kaz's head even made Raesh flinch.

Rica stood from her seat, panic written across her features as her competitor let out a gurgling gasp. He coughed, blood spluttering past his lips and somehow managed to conjure up the strength to push the blonde girl off of him.

"How is he still alive after that?" Raesh leaned over slightly to talk quietly to Nathaniel. "She's practically caved his head in. Why doesn't he just surrender while he still can?"

"I suppose he would rather fight to the death than have Nova surrender. No one expected this." Nathaniel couldn't help but keep looking around the arena for any sign of Pan. He must have been watching, he must have had a plan in case something like this happened. But, he was no where to be seen. The panic on Rica's face also didn't sit right with Nathaniel, she looked like she was going to faint or be sick, or maybe even both.

Kaz moved onto his hands and knees as he coughed up more blood. Kendra stood, she looked like she was deliberating on if she should attack him again, but stepped back and crossed her arms over her chest. Kaz tried to stand, but stumbled and fell back to the ground. His eyes didn't seem to be focusing on anything, just gazing aimlessly into the air. Nathaniel couldn't pinpoint the moment he took his last breath, but after several silent and still seconds one of the games masters stepped forward to check his pulse.

After an agonising thirty seconds the man confirmed that Kaz was dead and declared Hemmingstone as the winner. Kendra looked up at the stage where Raesh was sat and bowed deeply at him, a smirk on her face, eyes not leaving the King the entire time. Raesh took a deep breath and signaled for her to leave the arena then got up to announce the next battle.

It was undignified, the way Kaz's body was dragged out of the arena. No care was given to him, not an ounce of respect. Rica did her best not to run to the cabin assigned to Nova, she didn't let a single tear fall until she was safe behind the closed door of the cabin.

Pan rose from his seat and walked up to the body that had been dumped in the middle of the floor. He looked down at Kaz, his face covered with blood, a nasty dent in his skull that would have killed him even if he did surrender after it happened. He glanced at Rica who covered her face with her hands and started to cry.

This was not the plan.

Kaz had magic running through his veins, just like Nathaniel. He should have won that fight easily. Kendra didn't possess any kind of magic–none that she had demonstrated–and had defeated him with complete ease. It didn't make sense. Pan wasn't sure if he was upset or furious.

This was not the plan.

"Stop crying," Pan said and gently pulled Rica's hands away from her face. "He wouldn't want you to stand here crying over his body."

"How am I not meant to cry?" she asked and wiped at her cheeks. "Pan. He has been part of the guard for as long as I can remember. I just watched him get killed in front of me."

"He knew that there was a risk going into this. Hell, he knew there was a risk by even joining the Nova guard. I'm not saying that this is okay, it isn't, but Rica, we don't have time to mourn."

Rica closed her eyes and inhaled deeply before clearing her throat and looking back down at Kaz's body. "Help me get his body onto the bed. We can't just leave him on the floor like this." Pan nodded at her and between them they managed to get Kaz onto the bed with relative ease. Rica pulled a blanket up over him and covered his head gently.

"We will take his body back home to Nova, make sure he has a proper burial," Pan assured her. "His death will not have been for nothing."

"How can you say that? How can you say with such confidence that his death will have meant something?" she sneered. "What happens now, Pan? We cannot win the games. Raesh will continue to rule while everyone else remains oppressed by him. This whole thing has been a waste of time and life."

"I am going to speak to Nathaniel," Pan said defensively.

"Yeah? And what the hell will that achieve Pan? He will probably kill you the moment he sees you."

"He told me that he is on our side."

"What?" Rica narrowed her eyes at him. "When? When did he tell you that? Wait–he knows you are here?"

"I saw him."

"When?" Rica glowered at him. "Why didn't you tell me? How *dare* you keep this from me Pan?"

"After Hook showed up. I had to talk to him, Rica, seeing Hook again threw me off course."

"You talked to me about Hook," she snapped. "You didn't need to talk to anyone else."

"This was before I spoke to you. My head was all over the place," he explained. "He was there, Rica, he was there in the moment I needed him to be."

"And you think that we can trust the right hand man of the King? Are you stupid, Pan?"

"I can trust Nat."

"Why?"

"Because I love him."

Rica's eyes widened slightly and she swallowed thickly. "You love him? You have not seen him in years...he...he works for the King."

"Rica. I will love him forever. It doesn't even matter what happened all of those years ago...I could never lose those feelings for him. Trust me, I have tried. I even thought that maybe I had lost them. But I knew, the moment I saw him again back at the lagoon the day we got here, he is it for me. My heart always has and always will belong to him."

"I've never heard you talk like that," Rica said quietly. "Not sincerely, anyway. I knew...of course I knew that you had something with *someone* once. I never knew it was him...I never knew that those feelings were still there."

"Regardless of my feelings, I do know we can trust him. And right now he is the only chance we have left of taking down Raesh." Pan looked to the door. "I need to go and find Nat before his round in the games."

"You won't be able to get close to him. He is sitting on the royal stage with Raesh."

"I wasn't planning on just walking up there," Pan scoffed. "I will get Mildew to go there."

"And who is Mildew?"

"My fairy, of course," Pan said bluntly.

"Why have I never seen you with a fairy?" Rica moved away from the bed and pushed open the wooden door to the back of the cabin to get some air. "I thought your fairy died years ago."

"That was Tink," Pan explained. "Mildew just kinda...turned up one day. She didn't come with me when I went to Nova. I actually think she thought that I was dead," he continued as he moved to stand in the doorway beside her and looked out at the trees.

"Well, you were in hiding," Rica reasoned then took a deep, steady breath. "So. You get Mildew to talk to Nathaniel. And then...what? He kills Raesh?"

Pan pursed his lips together tightly. "I don't know. I really don't know how this is going to end. But it will. Neverland cannot belong to him any longer, I am going to win it for you Princess."

Five

Nathaniel stepped out into the arena. It felt like as soon as his feet touched the earth the sound of the crowd was drowned out into complete silence. He stood opposite the competitor of Thelan, Luger. Her long black hair was tied back into a tight knot on the top of her head, sharp cheek bones jutted out the side of her face as she stared down at him. He was terrified. He looked over at Raesh as he lowered his hand, signaling the start of the battle, and within seconds Luger was lunging at him.

Before he had the chance to muster any magic, the strong woman had knocked him to the floor with a thud.

"I'm going to surrender," she said, intense eyes staring down at him as he scrabbled on he floor. He looked up at her, still winded, in complete confusion.

"What?" he managed to choke out just as she raised her right hand in the air. There was a collective gasp in the arena at her action. Surrender. "What are you doing?" he hissed as he got to his feet and pulled her hand down. "You will win this," he whispered.

She narrowed her eyes at him then shook his head defiantly. "I surrender!" she shouted, which earned her a wave of unhappiness from those in the crowd. Nathaniel looked over at Raesh, who had an expression of amusement settled on his face.

"Why?" Nathaniel asked, ignoring the booing crowd and smug King who was overlooking them. "You could have beaten me, you are throwing away the chance of glory."

Luger frowned at him. "You really have no idea what is going on here, do you?" she said quietly as one of the games masters approached them. "This is bigger than you."

"You are surrendering?" The games master asked when he was close enough. "You do realise that you will be out of the games, you won't be in any further rounds."

"I cannot win against fire," she said strongly and turned away from them both to head back to her seat. Nat watched after her in disbelief then pulled his attention back to Raesh. He bowed at him, like all the winners did, then left the arena to sneering laughter from the crowd.

Pan watched from the back of the arena. Thelan was out of the competition. Nat didn't even have to do anything. He was sure that Luger was going to put up a fight, especially with the way she had knocked the man to the ground within seconds, but then to surrender? It was incomprehensible. Mildew frowned as she sat on his shoulder then let out a small huff.

"That was pointless," she said. "Do you still want to me to go and talk to him? After that?"

"Yes, go, you know what to tell him." The fairy floated up off of his shoulder then pecked a kiss onto his cheek. "Be careful, okay, Mildew?"

"When am I ever not careful?" she laughed. "See ya, Pan."

Nathaniel could feel his heart pounding against his chest. He was confused, he felt that there was a plan but he had no idea what it was or how to play by the rules. Did the other competitors want him to win? Were they scared of him? Or was it some kind of protest against Raesh? He was plagued by a myriad of thoughts plummeting through his mind, none of them made any sense and none of them gave him any answers to his many questions. He wondered what Raesh must have been thinking as he watched the rest of the first rounds play out. He seemed smug, confident, not worried that Luger has surrendered without a fight.

He loosened the harness around his chest and found that he was able to breathe slightly easier. The reprieve was only momentary before someone was stepping into his space. Yulia, the leader of Thelan stepped through the doorway, her large frame taking up most of the space, but behind her he could see another figure. As she made her way into the room he could see who the figure was behind her. He moved in front of the woman and stood boldly in front of Nathaniel.

The man, who he knew now to be Hook, smelt of warm cinnamon and cloves. He had expected him to smell like rum and sea water, not warm and somewhat comforting. Up close he was surprised to see that he didn't look as old as he should have done, he did have wrinkles around his eyes and a few frown lines, but other than that his skin was smooth.

"Nathaniel," he said, his voice rich, deep, full of self-worth. "Congratulations."

"This is the Spire cabin, you are not supposed to be in here."

"I have never been one for following rules," Hook smirked. "I haven't even been given a cabin to rest in, rather rude, don't you think? Yulia here was kind enough to let me use hers," he said as he gestured to the woman.

"You entered the games last minute," Nat sneered. "We didn't have time to prepare for you like we did the others."

"Fair enough," Hook said and took a step back from him. His eyes went down to his hook, it was different to the one he was wearing the other night, it shone, looked sharper. Deadly. "I am due to fight in a few minutes and wanted to run something by you." The pirate walked around the cabin slowly, raking his hook over the wooden walls as he went. "I have....a proposition for you."

Nathaniel raised an eyebrow as he watched him then looked to Yulia. "Are you working with him? Is this why Luger gave up in the arena?"

"Listen to him," she said, her eyes wide like she was pleading with him. "Please, we have had no other opportunity to talk to you, just hear him out."

"I am meant to stand here and listen to a proposition from a pirate?"

"Will you?" Yulia asked. Nathaniel looked back at the man then gave a quick nod.

"I have heard whispers, much like everyone else, that Pan is back." Hook stopped walking and looked back at Nathaniel. "These games are simply a childish distraction from the fact that the real ruler of Neverland is waiting to take back what once was his. Your King is a fool if he thinks he can hold onto power if Peter Pan has returned. And, Pan is a fool if he thinks he can exist without me."

"Pan doesn't need you to function. He forgot you even existed."

"Is that so?" Hook laughed. "Regardless of what you say, I know Pan better than anyone else on this island. I know how he thinks, what motivates him. Raesh is...an inconvenience right now. I would like for you to do the right thing...and remove him."

Nathaniel swallowed thickly. "Why do you think I would go against my King?"

"I have heard about you, Nathaniel, the boy who can control fire. How you broke Pan's little heart," he said with a grin. "This is your chance to change things, to show Pan that you really are on his side."

"You know nothing of what happened," Nat scowled. "And it is absurd that you are in here, asking me to kill Raesh, for what? To allow you to bring harm to Pan?"

"I am offering you a chance of a lifetime, boy," Hook said seriously. "To get rid of a useless King, to give Pan the power he so desperately wants. Tell me, do you want Raesh to rule Neverland, honestly?"

"I cannot talk against my King."

Hook's eyes squinted at him. "You are afraid."

"You do not know what he is capable of," he said by way of explanation.

"But I do," Hook said sincerely. "This land is not how I left it. I have listened to the leaders here, they have seen me as...a savior somewhat, a way to restore order."

"Nathaniel," Yulia said sternly and placed a strong hand on his arm. "The games this year are rigged. By us. Not by Raesh. Coming to you now is a huge risk, we know that you are fighting for him, that you are his right hand man. But, I am hoping, that as you have seen his cruelty up close you will know that this is the right thing to do."

"If the games are rigged how come Kaz Bresis was killed so horrendously earlier?" Nat asked as he looked between them.

"That was...*he* was an unfortunate casualty. We didn't feel that we could approach Nova. Rica, she is clearly here to disrupt the peace, but...I don't know I just didn't think she would go along with this. This is her first time here, taking over from her Father."

"So, everyone apart from Nova is planning on...what exactly?"

"We didn't ask the leader of Amberlan either," Yulia admitted.

"Char?" Nathaniel frowned.

"A complete knuckle-head." Hook scowled. "There is no point in wasting time on people like that."

"So. Everyone apart from Rica and Char, then?" Nathaniel pressed. "But what is the plan?"

"We could simply kill you in the games," Hook said nonchalantly. "It wouldn't be difficult, no offence intended of course." He smiled. "Or, you could join with us. The people of Neverland have had enough. The uprising is starting. You could be a hero."

"And who would lead? The Games are the only way to decide who can rule."

"Why should only one person rule?" Yulia asked seriously. "Nathaniel. The island is made up of strong cities and settlements, we do not need one ruler. We can come together, the leaders of each settlement can speak for their people. We can be stronger together."

Nathaniel looked at Hook suspiciously. "As lovely as that sounds how can I trust you?" he asked him. "How can anyone trust you, Hook?"

"I guess I am the lesser of two evils," he said with a laugh. "All I want is to be able to have my ship docked and my men happily drinking rum to their hearts content."

"And what has any of this have to do with Pan?"

"I am so glad you asked," Hook said triumphantly. "When I heard what had happened to poor Pan all those years ago my cold dark heart simply broke for him."

"Pan needs to return," Yulia said and shot Hook a dirty look before looking back at Nathaniel. "He is the balance in Neverland. You must know that. If the rumours are true and he has returned...we need to let him know he is welcome." Nathaniel took in a sharp breath. Her admission was not what he was expecting to hear.

"You don't see Pan as the enemy?"

"*I* don't," she said and gestured to Hook. "I don't know about him."

"He is my life-long sworn enemy, he always will be."

"I'm not going to do anything that could bring Pan any harm," Nat said with a sense of finality. "I have hurt him before, I can't do that again."

"I do not wish to harm Peter Pan," Hook said and sounded remarkably sincere. "I just want to restore order to Neverland...kill the King, Nathaniel, you are the only one who can get close enough to him." He dipped his hand into the pocket of his overcoat and pulled out a small glass vial filled with clear liquid. "This wonderful little potion is the answer to our problems," he said as he held it up for Nathaniel to look at. "You just have to slip it into the King's drink."

"We have the banquet tonight," Yulia explained. "After that, when he returns, you could do it then." Nathaniel looked at the vial that was being offered to him before reaching out a timid hand to take it.

"If I do this...how do I know you won't turn against me?" he asked as wrapped his fingers around the glass. "How can I know this isn't a ruse to work against me?"

"The word of a pirate might not mean much," Hook said as he stepped backwards to the door. "But, my dear Nathaniel, I *promise* that this is for the greater good."

Mildew flew away from the cabin at speed. Nathaniel was plotting with Captain Hook. She had only heard a snippet of their conversation, but it was enough. Nathaniel. The traitor.

As she flew she turned a deep shade of purple, anger sweeping through her tiny body as she made her way through the air. Pan was with Rica in the Nova cabin, preparing Kaz's body to take back to their village. The fairy burst in through the window, causing Pan to jump in surprise.

"Bloody hell Mildew!" he seethed. "I thought you were an intruder."

Rica looked over at the fairy with a small smile on her face. "Ah, so you are Mildew," she said. "What's wrong? Why are you so angry?" Mildew turned up her nose as she looked at the Princess. She didn't like the idea of Pan having another companion, especially one so...pretty, but now wasn't the time for her to let jealousy take over.

"Nathaniel is working with the pirate," she stated as she set herself down on a small wooden chest of drawers. "He is going to kill the King and then join with Hook to kill you."

Pan glanced at Rica before focusing on the fairy. "Did you hit your head or something?"

"No!" Mildew fumed. "I heard them talking, just you wait, the King will be poisoned. Then, they will come for you."

"Hook doesn't even know that I am here," Pan said with a disbelieving laugh. "Nat wouldn't have told him. You must have heard wrong."

"I did not."

"I don't believe you then."

"Fine!" Mildew shouted and stamped her foot down, causing dairy dust to glitter down onto the dresser. "Don't say I didn't warn you!" Her face resembled thunder as she looked at him, Pan was surprised she wasn't flaming red in colour.

When the fairy had left the room as quickly as she had entered Rica sat herself down with a heavy sigh. She looked at Pan with tired eyes and shrugged her shoulders.

"So, what now?" she asked.

"What do you mean?"

"Mildew clearly didn't tell Nathaniel any plan, and now he is apparently plotting against you with a pirate who was hell bent on killing you as a child. Seems like a bit of a shit storm to me."

"She doesn't know what she is talking about," Pan said dismissively. "Nathaniel wouldn't plot against me...he would never..." he trailed off as he thought of what happened forty years ago. How Nat definitely did go against him and told Raesh his exact plan of attack. An unsettling feeling started to take over him and he ran his hand through his curly hair to push it back away from his face. "We need to get you back to Nova."

"What?" Rica stood up from where she was sitting and went to stand in front of Pan. "We cannot go home without the crown, Pan, you promised my parents that we would win."

"I was stupid," Pan said as he looked at her. "This is so much bigger than us. I didn't think of all the players...I thought it would be easy...but if Mildew is right and Hook is now working with Nat...then we have a bigger enemy than Raesh and the only safe place for you is back home."

"I can look after myself, Pan."

"I don't doubt your courage and strength, Rica, but, we need to re-group, we need Nova behind us. We cannot do this alone. We need to go back."

"You want us to run away?" Rica asked in disbelief.

Pan rubbed a hand over his forehead in frustration. "I don't know what to do," he admitted. "But, you are my priority, please, let me keep you safe."

Rica shook her head. "I am not going back home until I see this through. No matter what happens I am going to be here to make sure that I made a difference. It starts now, Pan, everything leading up to this has just been a game. We will take out the King, and Hook too if we have to. But we *will* do it." She spoke with such certainty that Pan almost believed that she knew what she was doing. He looked over to the covered body of Kaz, which had been cleaned and re-dressed to return to Nova. He couldn't let his Princess go back to her people in the same way. If she was staying, then so was he.

Hook stepped out into the arena. The rumours about the mysterious pirate, who was back from the dead to compete, had been spreading through Spire like wildfire. The black haired man raised his hook into the air smugly as the crowd booed him, the louder they protested the happier he seemed. It took three minutes for the competitor for Amberlan to fall to his knees after his stomach was split open. It had been a swift movement, but the strength behind it was abundant. The hook inserted into the other man's abdomen with such ease it made Nathaniel feel nauseous. The crowd fell silent.

"What? No cheering for the winner?" the pirate laughed as he wiped the blood off of his hook with a white handkerchief he had taken from his breast pocket. "And now, I bow to you?" he asked as he looked at Raesh. The King raised his eyebrow as he looked at him, his eyes scanning the bloody scene before letting his mouth twitch into a small grin.

"Who knew that the Jolly Roger settlement would make it past the first round eh?" he laughed. Hook cocked his head to the left as he looked up at him before drawing himself into a bow. He twirled his hook as he stood and let his gaze fall to Nathaniel who was sitting beside the King again.

"I look forward to the next round, my King."

Six

The palace was quiet. Nathaniel had never really noticed just how much noise there was normally. There was usually clanking and chattering coming from the kitchen on the lower levels, footsteps of guards patrolling, the sound of Raesh's breath on his skin.

He shivered as he looked out of his bedroom window. After the first rounds were over it was custom for the King to attend a banquet in the city with the winning settlements. They would ascend on a poor tavern that would have to deal with snobbish demands and outlandish patrons without being paid anything for their hosting. Nat should have been there too, but Raesh had told him to stay behind. He didn't mind being excused from the event, but he failed to see a reason why the King wouldn't want to show off his competitor. Then he remembered how he had won that first round, completely by default, which most likely embarrassed Raesh to some extent. The quiet did give him time to think, though, and given the events of the day he needed a lifetime to mull over what had happened.

Nova had lost. He had expected Pan to come to him, to tell him what was going to happen next, but he had seen nothing of him. He was so out of the loop with whatever Rica and Pan were planning that he didn't know if his absence was a good or bad thing. Maybe they even planned to lose, though that seemed unlikely.

Hook had won his round, of course. That was one thing Nathaniel didn't doubt would happen, especially against Amberlan. The pirate was determined that was for sure. The previous games had shown brutality, but never before in the opening rounds. To see Kaz Bresis get killed and then Hook disembowel another competitor was a shock.

Nat wasn't sure what his next move was. He had volunteered to fight for Raesh on a whim, he didn't actually consider how it was going to play out or how he was going to *lose*. That was the aim after all. The power was in his hands. The moment he tapped out of the games would be the moment that Raesh would lose his crown. He should have surrendered before Luger had the chance to. He would have been killed for it by the King, but at least it would have been done. He would have played his part. Now, his grand exit was hanging over him like a scythe.

He could use the potion. The tiny vial was a heavy weight in his pocket and he slipped his hand into his jacket to wrap his fingers around the glass. Something so tiny could solve all of his problems. Poison was something Tippy-toe had wanted to use years ago, maybe the fairy was right all along. But, if he did what Hook asked, what would that imply?

He lifted the poison from his pocket and raised it to his face to look at it. He blinked a couple of times before squinting at it accusingly. The vial was empty. He patted down his jacket to see if it had somehow spilled out, but the material was bone dry. He looked back at the bottle. The lid had been put back on properly, there were no cracks to be seen, but the bottle was definitely empty. He felt a surge of panic erupt in his chest, which soared down his arms and caused the glass to shatter from the heat.

"Where is it?" he exclaimed as he looked down at the shards of glass in his hand. "Shit...shit!" he dropped the glass onto his desk and squeezed his eyes shut. Breathe. Breathe. He let out a shout, not knowing how else to form his confusion and anger in any other way. He thought back to when Hook had given it to him, the liquid was clearly in the vial then. The only person who had been able to access it was...was Tippy-toe.

Nat let out a soft gasp as he tried to think of when he last saw the fairy. It had been in the Spire cabin, he had been there listening to what Hook was saying. He had put the poison in the pocket that Tippy-toe liked to sleep in. Tippy-toe had either taken the poison himself, or had gone to deal with the King. The thought of Tippy-toe putting himself in danger made Nathaniel feel ill, but at the same time it wasn't an unexpected thing for the fairy to do. He was flippant, had no regard for consequences. He just hoped that he hadn't paid for his actions with his life this time.

Pan watched Raesh from the corner of the tavern in the shadows. It had been a last minute decision to watch the King and actually get another plan together seeing as Rica refused to return home. He remembered when he first met Raesh, many many years ago. He was a child, probably around five or six years old. He cried for his parents every night before he went to sleep. He also cried every time he fell over and scraped his knees. It wasn't unusual for some of The

Lost Boys to be that way; it took some of them a long time to adjust to life in Neverland, even longer to forget their families altogether. He never would have thought that Raesh would ever be any kind of threat, would ever hold any power. Then again, that was before Pan had started to grow up, no one was a threat to him back then.

Watching him now, under the secrecy of his cloak, he could still see the scared little boy he once knew. Sure, he was older, potentially wiser and with a crown on his head, but Pan couldn't sense any inner strength or belief from him. His power was built from fear. Nothing more, nothing less. But, fear was an incredibly powerful thing, and he harnessed the emotion like a fine-tuned weapon.

Pan hated himself for letting it get to this point. He remembered leaving, the first time, when The Lost Boys were still his men. All because of a stupid washed-up mirror. He had taken one look in it and panicked. He knew, of course, that he had been changing; his body was not like it used to be, his limbs were stretching and forming into something new and strange. It was seeing it that frightened him. He didn't recognise the person looking back at him in that shiny object. He had left, flown away to escape from what he needed to face. He wasn't sure how many years he had been gone, but it was long enough for Raesh to take over and make some kind of domestic settlement with The Lost Boys.

When he returned to Neverland he lost his ability to fly. It was like the island was punishing him for abandoning it in the cruelest way it knew how. It rewarded him with the gift of flight again when he showed love for not only himself and Neverland, but for someone else as well.

If he had of been braver...if he had of stayed and looked at the man he had become then this situation he was in now wouldn't exist. He went into hiding in Nova for the past forty years to work up the courage to redeem himself. After losing what should have been an easy battle against Raesh four decades ago he didn't know how to react.

He could have returned and made amends with Nathaniel if nothing else. Despite the betrayal he felt he knew it could have been fixed back then, it should never have turned into whatever it was now. Seeing him again made him realise just how much he missed him. He had to not only repair the damage he had inflicted on the people of Neverland he also had to repair his relationship with Nat.

The tavern fell quiet when another figure entered the room, Pan shouldn't have been surprised to see Hook walk in, but he was. The man had guts, that was for sure. All eyes were on the pirate, who was dressed in a rather beautiful deep blue waist coat, with billowing white sleeves underneath. His black trousers hugged his thighs and led down to long black boots with a small heel. Pan let the thought that the man was handsome flutter through his mind, but quickly squashed it when he remembered how much he actually hated him.

Hook smirked at the table where the King and winning settlement leaders and competitors sat and pulled up a wooden chair of his own so he could wedge himself in between Raesh and Hamish, the ruler of Hemmingstone. His competitor, Kendra, gave the pirate a sly smile.

"You know," Hook said as he fished a wooden pipe out of his pocket. "I am starting to think that you lot don't like me very much." He didn't look at them as he spoke, instead he retrieved tobacco out of another pocket and started to stuff it into the end of the pipe.

"We don't usually socialise with pirates," Raesh said and turned his nose up at the man beside him.

"No?" Hook placed the pipe in his mouth then lit the end with a match he had produced from somewhere Pan hadn't seen. "Well, it is about time you changed that, don't you think?"

"I don't plan on making it a habit," Raesh said curtly. "But, as you won your first round, you do have every right to be here."

"Shouldn't your competitor be here?" Hook asked. "I was rather looking forward to having a chat with him. It isn't like he has to recover from a tough battle is it?" he laughed, which made Kendra grin beside him.

"Nathaniel has things to attend to back at the palace. He may be my competitor, but that doesn't mean he cannot perform his normal duties."

"Normal duties? Like keeping your bed warm?" Hook blew out a cloud of smoke from between his lips. Pan stiffened at the comment.

"What are you trying to imply?" Raesh scowled.

"Oh, nothing, I thought it was common knowledge that he is used by you in *all* ways. I suppose that you just demand whatever you want, being King and all."

"I hardly think this is a topic you should discuss with a King." Raesh waved some of the smoke away. "I guess you pirates have a lot to learn about manners."

"And I guess you have a lot to learn about consent," Hook countered which made Raesh turn a dark shade of ted.

"W-what?" Raesh spluttered while Hook took another deep inhale from his pipe.

"You heard me, boy." He looked at the King with contempt. Raesh looked to be considering what his next words would be. He knew that everyone around the table was watching him, the distaste had moved from Hook onto him.

He cleared his throat and gestured to the goblets of wine on the table. "We are here to drink and celebrate. Let us leave this heavy and rather distasteful conversation for another time." He reached for the goblet in front of him. "Well done to you all for making it past the first round. This wine that you are about to drink is from my private collection, reserved for those who truly deserve it," he said as he raised his drink to his lips. "To the Crowning Games." He took a large sip while the rest of the people around the table followed suit. Hook frowned when he realised that there was not a goblet for him but covered his disappointment with another puff of his pipe.

The tavern fell into forced and awkward conversation as the patrons tried to move past the interaction between Hook and Raesh. The pirate didn't speak again, but sat back in his chair and gave his full attention to his tobacco. Raesh sat uncomfortably next to him, sipping at his wine and avoiding eye contact with the rest of his guests.

Pan felt strangely grateful that Hook had decided to show up. He hadn't known of the rumours that circulated about Nat and Raesh; he had tried to stay away from idle gossip over the years, but if it was true he was glad Hook had put

Raesh in his place in a public way. The mention of consent had left Pan feeling uneasy, he wanted Raesh to feel as uncomfortable as possible now.

The King cleared his throat loudly and placed his now empty goblet back down on the table. He raised his hand to signal to one of his guards who came to his side immediately.

"Your Highness, are you okay?" she asked as Raesh settled his attention on the cloaked Pan.

"Who is that?" he asked and pointed at Pan, which startled him. He stood from his seat in the corner of the tavern and started to make his way towards the door. "You there!" Raesh shouted and stood up. "Stop him!" The guards near the door blocked his exit, he could have pushed past them, but he knew it was already too late.

"Go to the King," one of the guards hissed at him. He resisted the urge to punch him in the nose and turned back to the table. Everyone was looking at him and the tavern had fallen into silence.

Pan took a step towards the table and balled his hands into fists to stop them from trembling.

Scared? Peter Pan didn't get scared.

"It appears we have had a shadow watching us tonight," Raesh said as he narrowed his eyes at him.

Kendra looked over her shoulder at him. "Who are you?" she asked as she pulled a knife out of her waistband defensively. Pan didn't move, having everyone's eyes on him was more intense than he could have ever imagined.

"Ah," Hook said with an understanding nod of his head. "I think we have a legend in our midst." He grinned. "It is good to see you...where have you been, Pan?"

"Pan?" Raesh practically growled as a guard stood in front of him protectively. The King rolled his eyes and gestured for them to back down.

"Well, show your face, boy," Hook sneered at him. The game was up, Pan knew he had no reason to remain hidden, so he lowered the hood of his cloak as Hook stood from his seat.

The pirate looked at him with something that Pan couldn't identify behind his eyes. They stood now, looking at each other, like long lost friends. Hook stepped forward towards him and raised his hand in the air before closing it in a fist as if he was grasping for something. He bit down on his bottom lip as he looked at his long lost enemy then broke out into a smile.

"I must say, Pan, you have turned into a rather fine young man," he said, which caught Pan by surprise. "Never thought I would be able to have a conversation with you where I wasn't breaking my back to stoop down to your height."

Pan huffed a laugh. "And what now, Hook? Do we battle like we used to?"

"My darling boy, I have no interest in fighting you right now." Pan didn't know why he felt insulted by the comment; before, when he was a child, Hook seemed to only live to fight him. "Oh, don't look so upset, we have moved on from that haven't we? We are all adults here, squabbling over a crown."

"Have you poisoned him yet?" Pan asked, figuring Hook was the bigger threat to him in that moment and he needed Raesh and his guards on side.

"Poison?" Hook laughed. "It is good to know your child-like imagination is still alive, Pan."

"Excuse me but what the bloody hell is everyone talking about poison for?!" Raesh shouted above them. "You are plotting to kill me?"

"Oh calm down Raesh no one is trying to poison you." Hook rolled his eyes. "Clearly Pan here is trying to cause trouble, as usual. I am surprised you haven't had him arrested yet."

Raesh stuttered before he spoke. "Um, well, yes," he said and clicked his fingers. "Arrest him." His guards swarmed around Pan within seconds. He could have flown, soared up out of their grasp, but even then there was no clear way out of the tavern. He could tell Raesh that Nathaniel was planning on killing him, turn the tables and get Raesh to turn on Hook. But he couldn't. He just couldn't.

Seven

Tippy-toe sat on the window sill looking down at his hands. Mildew scowled at him before smacking him around the ear angrily. Nathaniel didn't think that violence was the answer, but he also couldn't blame her sudden burst of anger at the other fairy. Tippy-toe shot her a rage filled look before rubbing at his ear sadly.

"Are you sure you can't remember where you put the poison?" Nathaniel asked as he pinched the bridge of his nose in frustration. "In what glass or drink?"

"No..." Tippy-toe replied quietly. "I just...wanted to kill him."

"You should never have taken poison from him!" Mildew shouted as she directed her anger towards Nathaniel. "I thought that you were working with him! Why else would you take the poison if you didn't plan on using it?"

"I...I don't know, I didn't know what I was thinking. I just...took it. I didn't think Tippy-toe would actually go and use it!"

"Oh, don't be ridiculous," Mildew said as she threw her hands in the air in exasperation. "Of *course* Tips used it! He has been waiting for a chance to do Raesh harm, you handed him the opportunity on a plate."

"That's true. You did." Tippy-toe nodded.

"I am not taking the blame for this," Nathaniel sighed. "Hopefully no one has come across it and we don't have to be worried about anything."

"Well..." Mildew hummed. "We might have to be worried about something."

"What now?"

"So. I might have told Pan that you were working with Hook," she admitted.

"You did what?" Nat snapped.

"I thought you were going to work with Hook and kill Peter! I couldn't let that happen could I?" she said innocently. "So...Pan might now think you are working against him. Just...be prepared for him to kill you or something."

"Kill me or something?!" he exclaimed. "I have had it with the both of you!" He turned away from them and started pacing his room as various thoughts swam through his head. He only stopped when a loud drumming noise started from outside and he went back to the window to look out.

The gate to the palace garden was opening slowly. It couldn't have been Raesh returning, the gates were only used for the delivery of goods or other large objects, never for people. The King would have used a side entrance, something more discreet. As the gates inched open Nathaniel could see a glow, at first he thought it was fairies—a ridiculous thought in hindsight; they could have gone over the gate if they wanted. It took him a few seconds to recognise the glow as fire, fire that was being carried as torches by dozens upon dozens of people.

It was the people of Spire. That could have been the only answer. They were going to storm the palace and remove

Raesh, no more silly games, they wanted it over and done with.

"Hide, get as far away from the palace as possible," he said to the fairies who looked at him with concern.

"What about you Natty?" Tippy-toe asked as he wrapped his arms around himself protectively. "I want to stay with you."

"I need to get everyone out of the palace, I will find you both, just go, now." Mildew took Tippy-toe's hand into hers and gave him a reassuring smile. They spoke quietly for a moment before she flew out of the window, leaving Tippy-toe to stay with Nathaniel. "Tips, it could be dangerous here," he warned but the fairy flew up and got himself into his pocket.

Nathaniel left his room and started to make his way down one of the hallways, trying hard not to let his panic get the better of him. Now was not the time to lose control.

As he made his way through the building he stopped at each window he passed to survey the scene outside. There was more people that he had originally anticipated, hundreds of them flooding into the gardens, shouting and angry. He finally stopped at the window on the east side of the palace that looked out over the gardens he had accidentally set alight to several days before. A small gasp escaped the back of his throat as he looked down at the people. Hook was there. With Raesh. As was Pan. Seeing the three of them together was unsettling in itself, but then he looked closer and his stomach dropped. Pan wasn't just standing with them. His hands were tied behind his back and a gag was wrapped around his mouth. He couldn't tell from where he was but he looked like he had a cut above his left eye with a stream of blood falling down his face.

He stepped away from the window in shock. They had caught Pan. Hook had said he didn't want to cause Pan any harm, but there he was, with Raesh, with Pan as their prisoner. He heard the doors to the palace open and he ran down to the entrance as fast as he could. When he got to the grand hall Raesh was already inside with Hook and Pan, his guards had lined themselves along the walls while more were going outside to settle the crowd.

"What is going on?" Nathaniel asked as he slowed his pace to a walk and tried not to look too alarmed.

"Pan was found spying on the King," Hook said as he stepped towards him and gave him a discreet wink. He leaned forward, his mouth close to his ear. "Go along with it boy."

"Pan. You have returned," Nat stated as he stepped away from the pirate and approached Pan who was kneeling on the floor in front of Raesh.

"He came to kill me," Raesh stated as he looked down at the figure on the floor. "Tomorrow we will kill him, in front of everyone. It will be a true display of my power." Pan looked up at them, the cut on his head more obvious now he was close. He wanted to drop to his knees beside him and kiss every angry wound away. "Nathaniel?" Raesh said and he managed to drag his eyes away from Pan to look at the King. "Go to my bed chambers. Wait for me in bed." He placed his hand on Nathaniel's cheek and held him still as he kissed his lips. Pan let out a sound that could have been a whimper as Raesh broke the kiss and looked down at him. "*Everything* that was once yours is now mine Pan, including him." He knelt down in front of his prisoner. "And tonight, I am going to make sure that every moment is agony."

Nathaniel stood by the window as Raesh entered the room. The King didn't say a word as he took off his crown and cloak then went to the side of his bed and picked up a jug of water that had been left there by one of his servants. He poured himself out a cup and raised it to his lips before stopping.

"Nathaniel," he said sternly and held out the cup for him to take. "You look thirsty. Drink." Nathaniel saw the challenge in his eyes, he thought of the poison, Raesh couldn't have known...unless...Hook...

"No!" Tippy-toe squealed from his pocket as he took the cup from Raesh and the King raised an eyebrow at him.

"Was that a fairy?" he asked, and before he could respond the King had grasped the front of his shirt and yanked Tippy-toe out of his pocket by his wings.

"Let go!" Tippy-toe shouted, his glow turning red as he thrashed his arms and legs angrily.

"Nathaniel. Why would this little fairy say no to you taking that water?" Raesh asked as he held Tippy-toe up to his face. "Is there something wrong with the water in my room?"

"No, Raesh," Nat gulped. "Please, don't hurt him."

"Maybe, he should be the one to drink the water." He looked at the fairy. "Unless, little fairy, you can tell me why you shouldn't?"

"It is poisoned!" Tips groaned.

Raesh looked at Nathaniel angrily. "So, there is a plot to poison me? Pan just accused the wrong person. It was you. You all along."

"No, no, Raesh, why would I poison you?"

"Because you are pathetic." Raesh wrapped his fingers around Tippy-toe and held him tightly in his fist which made the fairy cry out in pain. "Did you think that if you killed me you would get my crown, hmm?" he asked as he started to squeeze his hand tighter.

"Raesh, stop," Nat pleaded and grabbed his fist desperately. "You're killing him!"

"Then do something about it!" Raesh shouted, closing his fist completely around Tippy-toe, crushing his tiny body in his palm. Nathaniel let out an anguished cry. He instinctively raised fire in his palms, but within seconds he was being dragged to the ground, the life being beaten out of him. Guards? When were there guards in the room? He could feel the flames flickering his fingers, heat growing around him, but it mounted to nothing. It went dark. Then. There was nothing.

The Jolly Roger was spotlessly clean. It was not at all what Pan had been expecting, especially as he knew he used to live on the ship that Hook used to have. When he made himself home there he remembered how untidy it was, the main cabin cluttered and dirty. Hook had clearly got himself and his crew into shape and was now enforcing a rather strict cleaning regime.

Pan turned his head and looked at Nathaniel who was still sleeping soundly beside him. They had dragged him out of the palace covered in blood and unconscious, a sight that had terrified Pan. He only felt some relief now as he could see and hear Nathaniel breathing. He knew he should have been trying to escape. If he got out of the cabin he could easily fly, even with his hands bound, it would be dangerous but he could do it. There was no way he was going to leave Nat though, not when he knew the fate that awaited him. Nat had once said that when you died there was nothing...he didn't want the other man to face that alone. If he was to die he would at least be by Nat's side. Pan and Nathaniel. Inseparable. Just like old times.

His thoughts sometimes drifted to Rica. He had left her alone in Spire, not technically alone as her guards were with her, but to Pan that was as good as being alone. She must have heard by now what had happened; everyone knew. He hoped that she wouldn't try and save him; he hoped that she had started her journey back to Nova, possibly the only safe place for her.

When the guards dragged Nathaniel into the hall Hook had done something unexpected. He lunged at the guards, he tried to help Nathaniel. Pan wasn't sure what happened, or why it happened. The pirate was against Raesh, but whose side was he on really? He was now being held captive with the other leaders on his own ship. Pan could just imagine the pirate's humiliation.

Nathaniel made a quiet noise beside him and Pan turned his head to look at him. Even now, with his face bloodied and bruised he was the most beautiful thing Pan had ever seen. He remembered waking up next to him every morning. Pan was always the first one to wake and he would simply look at the man who slept beside him. He thought he appreciated him then, but looking back he didn't grasp those moments as tightly as he should have done. He didn't kiss his lips enough, he didn't feel Nathaniel's breath in his lungs or acknowledge the soft touch of his skin enough. He wanted to reach out and touch the small curve of his nose, run his fingers through his permanently messy hair and feel his eyelashes against his cheek.

"Nat?" he whispered as the brunette opened his eyes. He blinked several times, taking in the unfamiliar surroundings, then turned his head slightly to focus on Pan.

"You're hurt," Nat said, his voice barely a whisper as he looked at Pan in anguish.

"I'm hurt?"

"Your head. It's been cut..." Nathaniel tried to move before realising that his hands were bound behind his back.

"I think I got off lightly compared to you," Pan frowned as he watched him try to get comfortable. An impossible task when your arms were numb from being tied so tightly in an unnatural position. "Don't struggle."

"I can't feel my hands," Nathaniel whimpered.

"Why didn't you use your magic against them?" Pan asked, needing to know the answer. He couldn't understand

228

why Nathaniel didn't just set fire to everyone who attacked him, why he didn't try and defend himself.

Nathaniel stilled and took a deep breath. "I can't," he said with a shake of his head. "I couldn't. I tried...I don't know. I didn't want to hurt anyone."

"But they hurt you."

"I know."

"You could have stopped them, Nat."

"And what would that have done?" he asked. "He killed Tippy-toe. Tips..he...he put the poison in the water...and Raesh, Raesh knew...he knew about the poison."

"So, you were going to kill him?"

"What?" Nathaniel narrowed his eyes at him.

"Mildew told me that you were given poison from Hook. That you were to kill Raesh...and hurt me."

"I didn't do it, and I would never hurt you." Nathaniel replied quietly. "He gave me the poison but I didn't use it. I don't think I had any intention to. I have never had any intention to hurt anyone." There was a huge empty silence in the room that both of them were too scared to fill. Words danced on the tip of Pan's tongue but he couldn't find the courage to let them go. "I know what I did...to Henry."

Pan took a heavy breath. He didn't expect Nathaniel to address what had been unspoken for decades. "You do?"

"I blamed you because I didn't want to face what I had done."

"It wasn't your fault, Nat."

"It was my fire that killed him."

"You didn't know he was in the bunker. I didn't know either...if we had of known I would have gone back for him,"

Pan said sincerely. "You didn't create that fire to do harm, Nat, you were just a child, you were scared, you didn't know what was happening."

Nathaniel took a shaky breath and let his tears start to fall down his cheeks. "Raesh wanted me to use this magic as a powerful force. To see it as a gift," he cried. "But, it's been nothing but a curse. It killed my brother. People see me as a weapon. I'm not a weapon, Pan. I don't want to be used anymore."

Pan felt a lump form in his throat as he listened to Nathaniel talk. "I'm sorry. I should never have thought that you would hurt me."

"You have no reason to trust me."

"I do, Nat, you know I do...please don't cry."

"Because boys don't cry? Isn't that your rule?" Nathaniel sniffed.

"No, because I hate seeing you cry. Especially when I can't do anything about it. I'm sorry for ever making you feel like you can't express yourself though...I used to be a jerk."

Nat couldn't help but laugh sadly. "Yeah, you were."

Pan smiled. "It is nice to hear you laugh. I missed that sound."

"Bit sad that this will be the last time we get to talk and try and laugh together though isn't it?"

"You think this is the last time? Do you even know where we are?"

"I'm assuming we are on Hook's ship," Nathaniel said correctly. "Which means we are likely to die soon."

"Maybe...are you ready to die?"

"No. Are you?"

"I'm Peter Pan," he smiled. "I don't die. And if you aren't ready then I suggest we escape this rather ridiculous situation. Good plan?"

"Escape on its own is not a plan."

"No, but it is a pretty good place to start."

Rica ran a hand through her curly hair then pulled on the spider-silk trousers she had worn the day she arrived in Spire. No doubt by the end of the day they would have more holes in, and she didn't care. She was still unsure what had happened exactly, but she knew it involved Raesh, poison and Nathaniel. Just like Mildew had said. How Pan had got himself caught up in the commotion she was not sure, but now everyone knew he was back, not just back, he was *alive* and at the mercy of Raesh.

She blamed herself. Some of her earliest memories as a child were hearing stories of Peter Pan and the adventures he used to have. As she became older she spent time with him, was taught by him, admired him. But, she knew how deeply flawed he was. She never saw the kinks in his armor as a bad thing, every little scar on his skin or sad tales from his past wove the intricate tapestry of Peter Pan and made him the hero that she knew he was. Despite believing him to be a hero he was also pretty damn stupid. Maybe stupid wasn't really fair...he was like the fairies in that he let emotions make decisions for him, anger one minute could turn into happiness the next, but the bad decision had already been made. She guessed that his fleeting and volatile emotions and hasty decisions had got him into the mess he was in now.

She was going to try and save him. Obviously. Pan would never leave her behind in danger so she wasn't going to leave him either. The main problem was that Raesh and his guards had taken him out to the docks to where Hook's ship, the Jolly Roger, sat proudly on the water. It appeared that the only boats allowed to sail out to it had to be approved by Raesh himself, and Rica highly doubted that she would be authorised to go out there. Her only saving grace was that she could swim. She had never attempted to swim out to a pirate ship and board it, but really, how hard could it be?

The crowd at the dock was bigger than the crowd that had turned out to watch the first round of the Crowning Games. There was anger in the air. As she walked through the crowd she caught snippets of conversations. Hook was working with the other settlements, now that sounded absurd. Raesh had gone to the boat to protect himself from the angry people of Neverland who were now going to remove him with force. That sounded more realistic. There was so much uncertainty about what was happening next she couldn't quite understand any of it.

She made her way through the crowd, head down, not that anyone was paying any attention to her, until she got to the edge of the dock where the crowd thinned out. The boat didn't look that far away, but she knew that it was likely further than she thought. She debated taking her clothes off to swim, the material would weigh her down and make her pace slower, but then she didn't want to creep around a pirate ship naked. She settled on removing her boots but as she dipped her foot into the water she let out a gasp. Despite the sun plummeting heat down on to the island the water was freezing cold.

She started to shiver as she put her other foot in, teeth chattering almost immediately. It didn't make sense for it to be so cold. She took a deep breath and submerged herself entirely, the pain was like nothing she had ever felt before. She surfaced, struggling to breath from the sensation of hundreds of knives cutting into her body. She looked over her shoulder at the shore, she could get out, get warm and dry, but then what? She looked back at the ship, it now seemed so impossibly far away, her limbs were heavy and the energy it took for her simply to stay afloat was exhausting. She couldn't do it. There was no way she would make it out to the boat, she would die trying.

"What's wrong?" Her head snapped to the unfamiliar voice as a body emerged out of the water in front of her. "Cold?"

Rica stared at the person in front of her, dark eyes staring into hers with wonder. "Y-yes..." she whispered as the creature moved closer to her.

"You are very beautiful." A webbed hand came up to caress her cheek. "Let me keep you warm." Cold lips pressed against hers, in one moment she thought that all life was being pulled out of her, the next she felt a burst of warmth creep its way over her skin.

"Who are you?" Rica asked, her voice no longer shaking.

"My name is Priya," the mermaid said, her voice steady like the tide. "Why are you in the water?"

"I...I'm trying to get to the ship." Priya looked over to where the pirate ship sat eerily still on the waves.

"That is a pirate ship," she said and drew her attention back to Rica. "You don't want to go there. Pirates are bad. Stay here, in the water, with me." Rica knew better than to do anything the merfolk asked of her, but being so close to a mermaid for the first time she felt utterly enchanted.

"Stay in the water..." she said softly which made Priya smile. "But...I need to help someone."

The smile dropped from the mermaid's face. "You are friends with pirates?"

"No...but the pirates have my friend."

"Who is your friend?"

"Peter Pan."

Priya's eyebrows shot up. "So the rumours are true. Peter has returned, and with him he has brought pirates. I think that maybe you should leave Pan to play his games, stay with me, here, in the water." She grabbed Rica's wrist, a grasp that was going to be difficult to break. She tried to remember everything that Pan had told her about the merfolk. They were dangerous, that was the main thing, they feasted on human flesh. But, like magpies, they liked treasure, anything shiny, anything that could have a value to someone.

"Help me to the ship and I will give you something," Rica said, her voice trembling now from fear. "I am a Princess, I have gold, jewels, beautiful things."

"I have enough gold and jewels," Priya said smoothly and wrapped her other hand around Rica's forearm. "I don't need anymore."

"What about something that no one else has?" Rica said, her voice rising as she felt Priya start to slowly pull her under the water.

Priya stopped, her interest piqued. "Like what?"

"A thimble," she said, knowing that there was only one on the island, according to Pan.

"A thimble?" Priya frowned, her fangs poking out over her bottom lip. "No one knows where the thimble is."

"I do," she lied. "I know where it is and I will bring it to you, if you help me."

Priya looked conflicted. She gave Rica's arm a harsh tug before letting go of her completely. "You must bring it to me tonight. If you bring it to me then I will help you."

"I will bring it to you," Rica said, she didn't know how she was going to keep her end of the deal but she would worry about that later.

"Fine..." Priya seemed skeptical but clasped Rica's hand in hers. "Let's get you to the ship."

Eight

Nathaniel managed to sit up and hunched himself forward. Pan sat beside him and leaned against him for support. He didn't know how long they had before Raesh or God knows who else came to check on them, time was of the essence and everything felt like it was taking a lifetime to do.

"Just...make a small fire," Pan said like it was an easy thing to do. It should have been easy in all fairness, but under such pressure Nathaniel wasn't sure he was able to conjure any magic at all. "Just hold it in your palm to burn the rope on your wrists."

"Yes, Pan, I know that the bloody plan is," Nat snapped at him. "I can't just make a little bit at the click of a finger, I need to focus or I will end up burning down the ship."

Pan rolled his eyes. "Okay, okay, sorry..." He knew that Pan didn't want to pressure him, especially after their earlier conversation, but he also knew why the other man was getting frustrated.

"What if we just sit back to back and try to untie each others wrists?" Nat suggested after another minute of trying to create a spark to no avail.

"That is a ridiculous idea," Pan said, though he looked to be considering it. "I might as well stand in front of you and you try biting the rope with your teeth."

"I mean...we could try it?"

"No!" Pan huffed. "Just...take your time okay? You can do it, I know you can."

Nathaniel closed his eyes and focused on what he had to do. Why was it that his magic would erupt whenever it felt like it but when he actually needed to use it it was no where to be found. He thought about Henry, about what his first outburst of magic had done to his brother. He could burn down the whole of Neverland if he wanted to, he had it in him, he just needed to harness it.

"Pan, I can't," he whimpered. Hearing the sadness in the other man's voice made Pan shuffle round to sit in front of him.

"It's okay. It doesn't matter. We will try something else," he said surely. "Don't worry, it's fine." He wriggled his wrists as much as he could behind his back, the rope wasn't getting any looser.

He looked around the room in desperation before his eyes settled on a hook that had been displayed over the door to the cabin. It must have once belonged to the captain, maybe one he used to wear, he must have had some kind of sentimentality to it to have kept it out on display.

"If we can get that hook down we can use it," Pan said. Nat looked to where he had gestured with his head and frowned slightly.

"We won't be able to get it down from there."

"I am assuming that you are forgetting that I can fly," Pan commented smugly.

Nat blinked at him then allowed himself to smile. "You've waited this long before reminding me? Couldn't you have just flown out of the window?"

"And leave you alone? Never." Pan shuffled to the edge of the bed and managed to get himself to stand. Flying wasn't easy without the use of his arms to balance himself out, but he somehow managed to get himself to the same level as the hook without smacking his head on the ceiling.

"Very graceful," Nathaniel stated from behind him.

"Shut up, do you want me to get us out of here or not?" Pan shot him a dirty look and then got back to inspecting the hook. It had been secured to the wall with string and nails, there was no way he was going to be able to get it off of the wall without using his hands. He somehow managed to get himself into a position where his back was pressed against the side of the cabin and he could maneuver his wrists to catch on the tip of the hook.

"Who knew you were that flexible," Nat remarked which earned him another less than impressed look from Pan.

"Seriously, you are distracting me," he said and kept adjusting himself until he felt the hook slide under the rope and press cool against the skin of his wrist.

It took a lot of moving, running his hands up and down the sharp curve of the hook before the rope started to fray. He felt it loosening strand by strand until he felt the pressure of it release from his wrists completely. He brought his hands round to his front and held them in front of his face with a triumphant smile.

"My arms feel real again!" he exclaimed and let his feet touch the ground before running over to the bed. "Turn around," he instructed and Nathaniel did was he was told.

Pan crouched down beside the bed and started to tug at the knot of the rope on the other man's wrists. Nathaniel's were definitely tied tighter than what his was, he suspected that he couldn't do any magic because his blood supply had effectively been cut off to his hands.

"How adorable." Pan stood up immediately when he heard the voice come from behind him. He turned to see Raesh standing in the doorway, an amused smile set on his lips. "Were you planning on escaping together? Running off and living happily ever after? You should know by now that you don't get a fairy tale ending Peter."

"Why are you doing this? Nat has done nothing but protect you for all these years," Pan said angrily. He stood in front of Nathaniel protectively. "Let him go."

"The people are turning on me...I know all about the plot that Hook and the other leaders cooked up. I know all about the poison. It is amazing what you can get out of people with a little light torture," Raesh laughed. "And now I need to make an example of the two of you."

"What are you getting out of this, huh? You think that you can rule Neverland forever through fear? The people are stronger than you, Raesh."

"I just want order restored," Raesh said as he took another step into the room. As he moved further in members of his royal guard followed behind him. "I always knew that you would come back, Pan. I also always knew that Nathaniel's loyalty would always lay with you, what is the saying? Keep your friends close but keep your enemies closer?" he gestured for two of his guards to start approaching Pan and Nathaniel.

"Why keep me close?" Nat asked from behind Pan. "You know I could have killed you easily."

"Yes, you could have," Raesh admitted. "But you never did, did you? You always have and always will be a coward." He made another small gesture and one of the guards reached out to grab Pan, but he was too quick, he avoided him easily then pulled Nat up off of the bed to stand in front of him with even more anger inside of him.

"You are the real coward!" Pan shouted at the King. "You use others to fight for you, you kill those who pose any threat. What kind of King does that?"

"I picked up where you failed. I turned your pathetic Neverland into a functioning society. I took it out of the shadows and infancy it was stuck in. I let it shine."

"You're wrong," Pan had an arm out to protect Nathaniel from the guards who were now backing them into a corner. If only he had managed to get his hands untied in time Nat could have used his fire to defend them. They were weaponless and outnumbered.

"Am I?" Raesh asked and seemed almost giddy in anticipation for Pan's answer. "You left Neverland when you realised you were no longer a boy. Tell me Peter, why did you return? Be honest for once in your life."

"I didn't want to grow old and be forgotten."

"Who would ever forget Peter Pan?"

"Everyone," Pan said quietly.

"Peter, don't let him drag you down into sadness," Nat said from behind him.

"Who is everyone?"

"The Lost Boys...the fairies, the person I loved."

"And they moved on without you, didn't they Pan?" Raesh said as he watched his men close in on Pan and Nathaniel. "No one mourned you, no one cared that you were gone."

"I did," Nat whispered, his breath tickling the back of his neck. "I missed you. I never forgot you."

"Don't listen to what that traitor has to say," Raesh sneered. "You returned to him, didn't you? And he betrayed you, sold you out to me, your enemy." Pan knew what Raesh was doing. Pan could fly, it was one thing that Raesh had never managed to do, and he knew it was an important advantage that Pan had over him. Without happiness Pan couldn't fly. Pan *knew* that, but it didn't stop him from listening to his every word. "Even the people you thought loved you turned against you. You will be forgotten, Peter."

"Don't listen to him," Nathaniel pleaded, but Pan was stuck to the spot, the words that Raesh said were spinning around in his head and refusing to leave. "Peter..."

Hands were grabbing him, pulling him forward to drag Nathaniel away from him. He turned his head to see the guards manhandling him, calloused hands bruising his already tender skin. He didn't do anything to stop them. He felt like his feet were completely stuck to the ground, like the pull of the earth was holding him so strongly that there was no way he could move. But he did. Not of his own volition, but by more members of the guard handling him like they had Nathaniel and hurled him out onto the deck.

The sun was high in the sky, but there was a chill on the air. Pan squinted as his eyes adjusted to the brightness and his focus fell onto those who were standing on the deck. The various leaders who had come for the Crowning Games stood in a row, all of them, hands bound behind their backs, even Char who he was sure was actually on Raesh's side. Hook stood on the end of the row, his posture tall and proud despite being bound like the others.

It was not like Pan to be still. He was a constant movement, even when he was in deep contemplation he was tapping at a surface or bouncing his knees. He stood now, in front of the leaders of Neverland like a statue.

"It is time for us to vote," Raesh said from behind him, his black boots making the wooden boards beneath them creak with each step. "After all, isn't that what you all want? Democracy?" he laughed bitterly. "So. Let us be democratic. In the case of Nathaniel, the right hand man of the King, who votes for death?" Pan blinked as he watched the leaders. No one spoke. Yulia, the Regent of Thelan, stepped forward and cocked her chin in the air.

"You cannot vote when there has been no evidence brought forward of his involvement in any crime. And, is death really the example we want to be setting here? Is this not the time for us to be more civilised?" she asked.

Raesh took a confident step towards her. "My dear-"

"Don't dear me," she snarled.

"Apologies," he laughed again and held his hand up in surrender. "What I was going to say, was, we have time to re-build, to make Neverland the glorious place you all want it to be. But justice must be served. So, come on, you have what you want, *vote*."

Yulia looked over to Nathaniel, her expression difficult to read. "I don't believe that this is the right thing to do," she told him. "I will not be voting for your death." The others stayed silent.

"Despite your valiant speech *dear*, and the lack of votes, I do get the final say." Raesh gestured for one of his men to escort her back to her place in line. "I have decided that he will walk the plank."

"No one walks the plank on my ship without *me* saying so!" Hook's voice boomed over them.

"Oh, you pathetic, dirty, old pirate," Raesh tutted. "The moment you docked on my island this ship was no longer yours."

Drowning was not the way Nathaniel thought he would die. Over the years he had thought about how he would go, the most likely outcome was that he could somehow burn himself to death. Water never came into the equation. Yet, there he was, standing on the end of a plank with his hands bound tightly behind his back. He was still trying to make a spark, but it seemed that his magic had well and truly left him.

He felt a tear roll down his cheek as he looked up to the sky. It was impossibly blue, not a cloud to be seen. He had imagined that one day he might have been able to touch that crisp blue expanse that sat above them, feel the air hold him as he flew with the breeze...Pan's hand in his.

"Keep movin'!" a rough sounding voice shouted out and he took another step forward. His feet were right on the edge of the wood, another step and he would be gone. He looked down at the water. It was beautifully calm, almost inviting.

"Nat!" He heard Pan's voice call out to him, he turned his head to see the other man lurching forward, breaking the grasp of the men that were holding him.

The last thing he saw was Raesh slamming his boot down on the end of the plank that was still on the boat. The movement caused the whole piece of wood to wobble and with it Nathaniel lost his balance. He wasn't sure how long he fell for, it could have only been a few seconds, but it happened in a blur of colour that seemed to last for hours. He saw his mother, a pale thin woman who looked at him with large chestnut eyes filled with tears. A hand pulled her back as she screamed and her image was tainted with blood. Then he saw a light, a bright blinding light accentuated with the sound of twinkling bells that he knew must have been a fairy. Then a shadow. A voice that was all too familiar yet strange. He saw Henry, his bright smile and loud voice, he was speaking but the words were so far away he couldn't decipher them. Then he saw Pan, but as the boy he once knew. He saw his deep dimples in his cheeks, he heard his sobs as his body morphed into that of the man he knew today. Pan...Peter...the beautiful person who owned every inch of his heart. He wanted to kiss him. He wanted to run his fingers over all of his skin so he could memorise every part of him. He needed to tell him that he loved him. He opened his mouth in a gasp, bubbles escaping his lips as his lungs started to fill with water.

Peter...Peter...all he could see was Peter.

Until he saw Rica.

Nine

Mildew scowled at Priya. She had never trusted her, especially after she had tried to drown Pan many years ago. Now Rica was in her debt. She didn't like that either. Priya licked her lips at the fairy and let out a cold sounding laugh.

"I've heard that fairies have the most delicious taste," she said as she glided through the water to the small rock that Mildew was sitting on.

"You try and eat me and I will slice your insides," the fairy said viciously which made the mermaid back off slightly.

"Stop it you two," Nathaniel warned as Rica rubbed some more ointment onto his wrists that had been chaffed from the harsh rope that bound them.

"I don't think I can do anything to help your face..." Rica said regretfully as she looked at the bruises that had already formed. "Mostly superficial though, you will be your pretty self again in a few weeks."

Nathaniel frowned. "I thought I was going to die."

"You say that like you are disappointed, did you want me to let you drown?"

"No. I mean...I guess I just want to say thank you."

"Go on then?"

"Go on?"

"Say thank you, what you did just then, that wasn't a thank you." She smiled.

"Thank you," he said sincerely. "All of you." He looked to Priya and Mildew. "But Pan is still on that ship. We need to help him."

"Peter knows what he has to do," Mildew said flippantly with a dismissive wave of her hand. "He always knew how he was going to kill Raesh. He will bring him here."

"What?" Rica asked. "Bring Raesh to the lagoon? Why? Why do I not know anything of this plan."

"Because he doesn't have to tell you everything. And because the crocodile is here." Mildew looked at them like they were stupid. "The crocodile? You know, the one that ate Hook's hand? That thing hasn't had a proper meal in years, one whiff of Raesh and...bye-bye Raesh."

"That crocodile died decades ago," Rica said.

Nathaniel's eyes widened. "Pan told me once that it wasn't dead. It was hibernating."

"Crocodiles don't hibernate for, what, hundreds of years!" Rica laughed.

"Rica, anything can happen in Neverland, a crocodile hibernating for that long really isn't the weirdest thing to have happened here."

The Princess looked unsure. "Okay, so *if* this crocodile is still alive, we just have to hope that it comes out and eats Raesh when we need it to?"

"You need to go in there and wake it up. But don't die, I need that thimble," Priya warned.

Nathaniel glanced at Rica with a frown. "Thimble?"

"Priya said she would help me if I gave her Peter's thimble," she said nonchalantly with a one shouldered shrug. Nathaniel hadn't seen that thimble since Raesh had confronted him about it years ago, he decided to ignore the uneasy feeling in the pit of his stomach.

"So, back to the plan," he said as he cleared his throat. "We just go into an ominous looking cave and wake up a crocodile that likes the taste of human flesh?"

"Yes," Mildew said with a nod. "And if I were you, I would hurry up, no doubt Pan will be here soon."

"You think he can get Raesh here?" Rica asked.

"Oh, goodness, no, not on his own," Mildew laughed. "I have called in a few favours. You will see."

"Your quarrel is with me, Raesh!" Pan shouted, his voice trembling with anger. "Face *m e*, that's what you want, isn't it? Huh? Ever since you were one of my Lost Boys, you have wanted to face off against me!" he screamed at him as he wrestled the other guards off of him. He snapped his head at the leaders, disgust written over his features. "Fight! You have it in you, fight! Nathaniel didn't deserve to die, you could have helped, you could have helped to stop him from getting killed!"

"Even his power didn't save him in the end, did it? You think these idiots could have helped if his own power couldn't?" Raesh chuckled low in his throat. "If he is lucky, the God's of the sea will take pity on him and let him live on forever as foam in the waves. Poetic ending for a monster."

"You are the monster," Pan seethed.

"Maybe I am, but you have lost to me now."

Pan shook his head. "No. No. You think that your words can defeat me?"

"They already have. You didn't fight for him back in the cabin. It was like taking candy from a baby, as they say. And now he is dead."

"Nothing stays dead forever in Neverland."

Raesh jerked his head back at the comment. "What is that supposed to mean?"

"Fight me. At the lagoon. Let them-" he said with a wave of his hand to the leaders, "decide what is best for Neverland. This bad blood between us is between *us*. It is time it finally ended."

"You are weak," Raesh boasted. "Why would I bother fighting you?"

"You want glory? You want to be the hero? Then be the hero, Raesh, show everyone, every person out in Spire just how strong you are. Let this be the game that they wanted to see. You versus me. You kill me and no one will ever think about challenging you again."

"No," Raesh said bluntly and before Pan could register what was happening Hook was moving towards the King. His hands were no longer bound and he raised his hook forcefully in the air then brought it down to impale into the King's shoulder. Raesh let out a sharp cry, a cry that only got louder as the pirate dug his hook even deeper under his skin then began to lift him up off of the floor with it.

"Stupid boy," Hook hissed as he lifted Raesh to his face. "You are insufferable. Worse than Pan!" Raesh gasped as his skin ripped from around the hook and he tumbled to the ground. The royal guards and settlement leaders let out various gasps, some in shock, others in awe of what Hook was doing. Raesh scrambled on the floor, crawling to the edge of the ship, but Hook was following him, kicking at the back of his legs with a laugh.

"Help me!" Raesh cried out to his guards, but none of them came to his aid.

"Coward," Hook spat down at him. "Crawling away?. You think that you can get away from me, boy?" Raesh managed to get to his feet, Pan wasn't sure how he managed it. Blood was pouring down his arm from the wound that the hook had inflicted, his clothes damp with warm sticky blood.

"I am not a coward," Raesh said with a trembling voice. "I will fight Pan, here or at the lagoon, wherever he wants."

Pan raised an eyebrow at him. "Oh? You think you fair a better chance with me than you do with Hook?"

"You are the easier foe to defeat," Hook commented smugly.

Pan turned up his nose at him. "Easy? That's why you failed every time you tried to kill me, huh?"

"Pan!" Yulia shouted to bring his attention back to the task at hand.

"I will deal with you later," Pan said to Hook then looked back at Raesh. "You can fight me. Now." He stepped closer to the King until he was almost nose to nose with him. It was the closest he had ever been to Raesh. He had a distinct smell of death.

Pan clutched the front of the King's shirt and grinned at him. A flicker of fear passed over the man's face before Peter launched them both into the air. He was relieved that he was flying and not plummeting into the cold water. He still had happiness. It was not over yet.

Raesh screamed as they climbed higher and higher into the air. Pan deliberately kept a loose grip on him; he wanted him to think he could be dropped at any moment.

"What's wrong Raesh, you always wanted to fly, didn't you? Not as you imagined?" Peter laughed loudly as they soared through the sky. Raesh didn't answer, but let out more screams and gasps as Pan pulled him through the sky.

Without really thinking of where he needed to go he still found himself at the lagoon, he reached the calm nook of water and allowed himself to take a breath as he landed. He dropped Raesh to the floor with a loud thud and smirked to himself as the King scrambled to his feet.

"He did it!" Mildew said triumphantly. "You got him here! You are not useless after all. Natty is in the cave, ready for you," she continued with a whisper into Pan's ear

Pan narrowed his eyes at the fairy. "Nathaniel is alive?" he whispered back to her.

"Yes," Mildew said and rolled her eyes. "The girl too. They are in the cave probably getting eaten by a crocodile."

"You let them go in there without me?!"

Priya yawned. "Can we hurry this up?" she said then realised that Raesh was looking at her with wide eyes. "Don't worry, I don't eat idiots," she told him which caused his initial look of shock turn into disgust.

"You look like you're going to bleed to death," Mildew said as she looked at the wound Hook had inflicted on Raesh.

"Shut your mouth," Raesh snarled. "Come on Pan, let's get this fight over with."

"You are wounded," Pan said seriously. "Why don't we make this a little more fair. You like games, don't you Raesh, why don't we play a little game of hide and seek? Like when we were kids?"

"Hide and seek?"

"Yeah." Pan grinned. "I will hide. If you find me, before...before Mildew does, then you win. I will let you execute me in front of as many people as you like."

"And if she finds you first?"

"Well, then, I guess I get to kill you."

Raesh pressed his hand to the wound on his shoulder. He knew he didn't have much choice. "Fine," he said reluctantly. "I will count to ten...but Pan, no cheating."

"No cheating."

The cave where the crocodile lived was eerily quiet. It was damp and dark and it seemed that it went back for miles. Parts of the cave had low ceilings, where other parts opened up into large spaces that echoed with each footstep that they took. Every now and then they came across an animal carcass or a pile of bones that Nathaniel was sure once belonged to a human. Maybe the crocodile was already awake. People went missing sometimes, but he never thought that they ended up in a hidden cave like this. Yet, there was no crocodile to be seen.

The main issue that they had was that neither of them actually knew what a crocodile looked like. The only stories that Nathaniel had heard of the creature had originated from Peter which meant that they really were clueless in knowing its appearance. No one had ever seen a crocodile in Neverland since it disappeared, for all they knew Pan had made it up.

Nat imagined a creature a little like a bear, but with a much larger mouth, something that could swallow a man whole. Rica, on the other hand, imagined some kind of large slimy sea creature that moved fast like a spider.

Of course the reality was nothing like either of them could have imagined. Nathaniel held his breath and pulled Rica back from the wall of the cave when he saw something that resembled a pile of rocks–though he knew that it certainly was not a pile of rocks.

"What?" Rica whispered quickly to him. "We don't have time to wait around, Pan will be here soon with Raesh, we need to find the crocodile."

"I think we might have found it," Nat replied quietly and pointed to the area that Rica was about to step in.

"Rocks?" she scoffed. "That isn't a croco-" Rica let out a shout of surprise before she could finish her sentence when the large pile of rocks made a sudden lunge at them. Yellow crooked teeth snapped at them in a frenzy, the noise was what startled them most–angry, sharp teeth crashing together in rage. The creature was huge, its mouth even bigger than the bear like mouth he had imagined. Then there was its body, long, heavy and dangerous–especially with the way it used its torso to whip its tail around aggressively. Nathaniel climbed up some rocks at the side of the cave and pulled Rica with him as the beast snapped at their heels.

"It can't climb," Rica said breathlessly as they looked down at the crocodile that was leering up at them. "Its legs are too small."

"How do we know it can't jump?" Nathaniel pressed himself to the wall of the cave the best that he could and pulled Rica with him, fearing that the animal would lunge up at them still.

"No, look at the size of it, there is no way it could jump. Let's just...stay where we are."

"What? And wait to see if it figures out how to get up here?" Nathaniel said in a fluster. "Why didn't Pan ever tell me how big a crocodile was?"

"He probably didn't remember what it looked like," Rica reasoned and pressed herself flat against the wall like Nathaniel. "Better to be safe than sorry and stay away from the edge yeah?" Nathaniel glanced back to where they had come from in the cave, he thought he could see a small glimmer of light approaching, but it seemed far away.

"I swear it is going to jump up here," he said as he looked back down at the crocodile again, not trusting that its small legs gave it any disadvantage. The crocodile was looking back at them with pitch black eyes, it looked like it should have been licking its lips at them.

"They don't jump," Rica groaned and kicked a small rock down at the beast which landed right onto its back. It didn't move, just kept looking up at them expectantly. "I never thought I would be facing death like this," Nathaniel tore his eyes away from the animal for a moment to look at Rica and saw her looking back at him in fear. "We walked right into this."

"What do you mean?" Nathaniel asked as he observed the change in Rica's eyes from fear to something else—something he could not place.

"Well, what did we think was going to happen? We would wake up the crocodile and it would say 'oh good morning thanks for waking me up!'" she groaned. "I feel like a fool. Pan's plan for the Crowning Games...no back-up plan, everything that has happened since...all of it comes down to really bad planning. *This* is just the icing on the cake isn't it? Standing in a cave with a massive crocodile with an angry King on his way."

"I will admit that planning is not Pan's strong point. It isn't my strong point either to be fair," he said as he drew his attention back to the crocodile. "Maybe I can...I don't know...distract it and we can get somewhere safer."

"You literally just told me that planning wasn't a strong point and in the same breath came out with a new plan." Rica glared at him. "Look. Don't try anything, I am just going to move a bit further along to the wider ridge." She pointed to where she was going to go and took an over-confident step. The rock beneath her foot crumbled and Nathaniel reached out to grab her. He held onto her wrist as he pulled her closer but his breath caught in his throat when he felt his own foot slip off the edge of the rocks, he pushed Rica back onto the ledge as he felt himself fall.

It felt like he was falling off of the plank of the ship again. When his back hit the floor all the air was knocked out of him and he lay still until he heard a deafening crunch then felt a burning pain sear through his arm. This was it. Forget drowning. *This* was how he was going to die.

Ten

The cool feeling of paint being brushed over his skin tickled down his spine until he let out a soft sigh. He looked over his shoulder and smiled at Pan who was sitting behind him, drawing long strokes onto his skin. They hadn't spoke since he had started, but Nathaniel felt no awkwardness between them in their silence. There was a look of concentration on Pan's face as he bit down on his bottom lip as he dipped his brush into more of the paint. Nat turned his head away from him and looked over to the space where Mildew and Tippy-toe were sitting on top of their bed, speaking together happily while pressing kisses to each others cheeks. He smiled. There was a warmth in the cabin of their ship that felt like...well..it felt like home. The sun was setting, creating a glow that was only accentuated by the lights of the fairies. He felt like he should have felt some embarrassment at sitting naked in front of them, but Pan was without clothes too, there was no shame in their home.

"I think I'm finished," Pan said softly, far too aware of being loud and breaking the tranquility in the room. Nat tried to look over his shoulder at his own back but gave a laugh when he couldn't see anything.

"I'm going to trust that you haven't drawn anything horrible on my back Peter Pan." Pan leaned forward and pressed a kiss to his bare shoulder.

"Never." He smiled and blew out his breath over Nathaniel's skin to help dry the paint. He shivered and looked at Peter with half lidded eyes. Pan was stunning; his features beautifully outlined by the late afternoon light. He wanted to capture that image of him, he wanted to be able to look at it any time he wanted then wrap it up and keep it in a pocket close to his heart. Peter Pan, the boy, had grown into an incredible man. He had blossomed with kindness, bravery, beauty and love. He was still that same cocky Peter Pan, but if he lost that, then he wouldn't really be Peter.

"I love you," Nathaniel said as he watched Pan stop blowing at his skin. "More than anything."

"Are you getting all soppy on me now, Nat?"

"Yes, do you hate it?" He grinned.

"No." Pan shook his head. "I like it when you are like this. You get this look about you, a warm one, kind of makes my heart burst a little bit."

"Your heart burst?"

"Like a sudden jolt of happiness." He gently gestured for Nathaniel to turn so that he was sitting facing him. "You make me happy," he said as he dipped his brush back into the paint then pressed it to Nat's chest.

"When you said you wanted to paint me I didn't think that you meant you wanted to use me as a canvas."

"What else would I mean?"

"Paint a picture *of* me, not on me."

"I always thought you would look perfect covered in colours like this." He slowly painted a yellow circle in the center of his chest. "Always said you were the sun. Now you have it on you." Nathaniel looked down to where Pan was filling in the shape with a mixture of yellow and orange. When he looked back up he cupped the other man's face in his and pressed his body against his gently. Pan made a small sound of protest when he felt the paint press against his skin and pulled back to see the colours smeared onto his chest as well. Nathaniel pressed his fingers to the wet paint on Pan and smoothed them round in a circle to blend the colours together with a smile.

"You have always said that I am the sun, *your* sun. But you are the one who lights up Neverland, the one who brings life and joy. If I am the sun, then I get all of that power and energy from you, Peter." Pan's eyes were brimming with tears as Nathaniel spoke, which made the younger man press another kiss to his lips lovingly. "Why are you crying?"

"I never knew that I could feel this way. I used to think that I was the happiest person in the world, being carefree, without any worries. But, no, I had no idea what I was missing out on. We might never know what caused me to start aging, but I no longer fear it, Nat, because if I didn't grow up I would never have found this with you. You are my new adventure."

"And you are mine."

"And you are mine," Nathaniel whispered to himself. There was darkness all around him, deep shadows that loomed out of every corner. He looked to his left to see the floor covered in red. Water?

No.

Blood. He didn't know if it was his, he was aware that he was bleeding, but surely that amount of blood couldn't have come from him. He wished he could see properly, that the cave wasn't a blur that kept erupting into a blinding white light every few seconds. He could hear screaming which was muffled by the loud ringing in his ears. He strained his neck to look further into the cave, squinted his eyes to focus. Left, right, more to the left, central, then he saw her. Rica was raising her hand, ice pouring out of her palms like fire once did for him. She was crying; he could see the tears rolling down her cheeks even though his vision was blurred.

He tried to sit himself up but slumped back to a laying position with each try, his head felt like it weighed a tonne and his vision only got worse with each movement.

"I'm sorry..." he whispered again and turned his head to the light that shone again for a moment. He swore he could see a slender figure in the light, the outline of Pan, he didn't want to let himself believe it was him.

He flinched when he felt something drop beside him and let out a barely audible gasp when he saw Raesh looking directly at him from where he landed. His face was red, most likely covered in blood as he plunged his fingers into the ground beneath him and dragged himself the small distance to where Nathaniel was laying. He had a dagger in his hand. Ah, so it would be death by Raesh. Bad luck crocodile.

Raesh didn't strike. He made no further movements and the breath that Nathaniel had been holding creeped out of his lips when he realised that he was safe to breathe. He felt hands behind his head, a voice calling out to him but it was so far away. So far away. Hands grasped at him, pulled him, but he was numb, he wasn't able to help whoever it was helping him to get himself up. Part of him wondered why they were even bothering, he knew he was going to die, dying inside of the cave or outside of it made no difference.

"Leave me," he rasped. There was a reply and more movement. Then there was light. This time it didn't stay for a split second, it lit up and didn't fade. He expected to open his eyes and see Henry in front of him, greeting him to take him to wherever they needed to go next. He could almost hear his voice, his laughter, Henry calling to him to play a game. He reached out into the white space, hand open so that Henry could reach out and pull him up. Any moment now. "I'm here, I'm ready, come and get me!" he shouted out as he felt a cool air wrap around him. "Henry!" He stretched his arm out further but no one reached back, no one clasped his hand and pulled him into a warm embrace. He let out a sob as he brought his arm back to his side and stood looking out into the white canvas.

Nothing.

There really was nothing.

Raesh wasn't his real name. It had been so long since his real name had been muttered that he wouldn't know it if someone said it to him. His name was long gone. Long gone were his carefree days of his youth. He didn't know what he was now. Old. Young. Dead? Not that it mattered. Not now.

Revenge is a funny thing. For Raesh, it had consumed him; his very purpose in life was revenge and nothing else. He didn't even know if revenge was the right word. All he knew was he wanted Pan dead. Pan who had not been the hero he had imagined as a child. He had run away to live with Pan and the Lost Boys. The fairy tale was not as he had expected.

Pan. The boy who refused to grow up. He hoped it hurt when his youth finally betrayed him. He hoped that it tore his mind to shreds.

Of course what he hoped was clearly not the reality. Peter Pan had fallen in love. Love! What a ridiculous notion. With one of the Lost Boys none the less. Who knew Pan could love? And where did that leave the others? Pan had forgotten them. Raesh and the others had become shadows. Raesh knew he was more than that, he always would be. There was no Peter Pan without The Lost Boys. One didn't exist without the thought of the other, he knew they would live on forever in stories...but now...what now?

The man that Pan was in love with was bleeding out in front of him. A river of crimson trickled from his body and all Raesh could do was look at him. It struck him then that he had been just as close to Nathaniel as Pan had been, maybe even closer, physically at least. He didn't know the details of their relationship, he didn't want to know. He had taken

Nathaniel's body as his own and took pleasure in knowing he had something that Pan loved.

This would kill Pan. Seeing his lover die in front of him. Victory would be sweet. So sweet. He would relish every moment. He would make sure that no one remembered Peter Pan. He would be plunged into darkness where no one would know his name. Pan would become the shadow. Only...he could no longer feel his body...fading...fading...

As Pan stepped closer to the cave a lump in his throat started to form; there was an undeniable smell of blood in the air, the chances of Nathaniel or Rica being hurt was incredibly high. He took another step inside, it was dark, silent, the area smelled of iron but he kept going forward. His friends were in there. He needed Raesh in there. This had to end.

The cave was somewhere Peter had never been before; something about it had always frightened him, he knew now it was because he must have been aware of the crocodile living inside—a warning that had stuck in the back of his mind despite forgetting the reason for it. As he went further in he became of aware of footsteps and Mildew's light behind him, he didn't have a lot of time.

The lack of evidence of Nat and Rica kept a feeling of unease in his gut, but as he got deeper and deeper into the cave he could hear voices that gave him hope.

Only, the voices turned to screams, horrifying sounds of pain that bolted a panic in Pan that made him sprint to where they were coming from. The cave went on and on, the screams got louder and louder until he came across a scene that made him nauseous. Rica was screaming as she looked at Nathaniel who was laying on the floor of the cave in a pool of blood.

He didn't have time to help him. Raesh was in front of him. Mildew fluttered behind him in a panic, she was shouting, but her words were lost in the drumming of his ears. A sharp feeling of ice swept over his body as his breath became visible in the air. He had no idea what was happening, and for a moment neither did Raesh until he came to his senses and locked his eyes onto Pan.

"Pan!" Raesh shouted and swung a dagger at him which he was able to dodge easily. Raesh appeared disorientated; swaying as he stood and tried to focus on where Peter had moved to. Pan wanted to hate him, he wanted to feel such rage that he could tear him down in seconds. But all he felt was pity as he watched Raesh flail his arms about and stumbled over the rocks on the floor. The floor had turned to ice. He dared a glance up at Rica who had her back pressed against the wall of the cave, her whole body trembling as she looked back down at the scene.

"You cheated. No one agreed to have weapons," he said which made the other man still and focus in on him. "What are you trying to gain, Raesh?"

"I am going to destroy you." Raesh spat but made no attempt to move closer to him.

"To destroy me. But, why?"

"You want to ruin me!" he roared. "You took away every happy thing in my life! I ran away to be one of your men! You abandoned me! I was meant to be eternal!"

"You *are* eternal; children are told stories of you and the Lost Boys all around the world, you and me, we will live on forever. But, I will always be the hero." Pan started to step backwards as he talked, to the area he had seen Nat laying. There was a pile of rocks near him, a pile of rocks that he knew was anything but a pile of rocks.

"I will not be second rate to you!" Raesh started to run, finding an energy inside of him that surprised Pan. He turned on his heel and ran from him, leaping over rocks until he stopped, his breath being torn out of his lungs as he looked at Nathaniel's body. He stopped only for a second before jumping and launching himself into the air as the crocodile lunged at him from the darkness.

Pan didn't watch what happened next; he didn't need to. He couldn't have done even if he wanted to. His attention then was fully on Nathaniel. Brown curls were wet with blood. His feet touched the ground beside his body, he couldn't stop himself from letting out a shaky cry as he looked at him. His skin was white, which made the blood that covered him even more vibrant. His eyes took in his body, his leg was at an unnatural angle—broken, but it was his arm that made Peter make a painful wail. His forearm and hand had been ripped from his body.

Rica let out a gasp as the crocodile missed Pan by mere millimeters, its teeth slicing through the air. Almost crashing down onto nothing, until it landed on Raesh. The man let out a scream, a sound that she was sure she would never forget. The ice that had escaped from her was slowly beginning to melt as she watched the crocodile treat Raesh like he was a rag doll. She clasped her hands together in an attempt to stop them from trembling. Before she had travelled to Spire she had never seen death. Being exposed to it in such a spectacular fashion from the Crowning Games to this, she felt her fear turn into a strong determination to not let it happen again. Raesh was dying.

Neverland was for the taking. She was going to take it. She had finally come into her power, she knew her role, and she was going to redeem all those who had had their lives snubbed out too soon on the island where you never had to fear death.

"Nat, Nathaniel, love, it is going to be okay," Pan cried and gently lifted his head to see if he was breathing.

"Leave me," Nathaniel whispered and just hearing his voice made Pan believe that there was still a chance he could save him.

"Come on, I'm getting you out of here, you are not dying here tonight Nathaniel." He pulled the man into his arms and Nat let out a sigh of pain. He was losing too much blood, far too much. Pan managed to cradle him in his arms and stood, just as the crocodile started walking back towards him. He looked at the creature as it looked back at him. There was a serene moment between them, something that he didn't expect from an animal as deadly as that. He took a step towards it, but the crocodile didn't move so he took another step. He nodded at Rica, just a small gesture to let her know it was safe. She hesitated only for a moment before climbing down from the safety of the ledge. She went to the other side of Nathaniel and wrapped her arm around his waist. They kept waiting for the crocodile to attack, but it never happened and before long they didn't even look back. It had let them go, the damage had been done for the night and forever.

Eleven

an flew up to the crows nest on the ship and looked out to the boats that were making their way to join them at the docks. He decided that there were ten, though he would need to get someone else to check, or failing that, actually teach him how to count.

He could make out some of the faces of those who were coming to the island, most seemed to be excited while a few others had tears streaming down their cheeks. That was normal. Younger children usually cried; the island was daunting and Pan imagined that it must have been scary being away from their families for the first time. That was why he was there though–to make sure that they found a new family on the island. He climbed onto the edge of the nest then jumped up into the sky before soaring down towards the shore where several of the greeters from Spire had already gathered to help unload the boats.

"At least fifty out there today, Peter," Newt, one of the guards said as Pan landed beside him.

"Fifty? Yes that is exactly what I counted too." He nodded and placed his hands on his hips as he watched the boats draw closer. "Quite a lot isn't it? We might have to split some groups and send a few over to Ipsling."

"Most definitely," Newt agreed and gestured for one of the guards to come over. "Alert the fairies that we will be sending some newcomers over to Ipsling, on Peter's orders." The guard gave a curt nod then ran back up the sand dune towards the forest.

"Will you be able to do this alone today?" Pan asked. "I know that Rica likes me to be here for the new arrivals...I can come back this evening, welcome everyone properly, but I have something I need to do today."

"Getting your jobs done before winter sets in?" Newt smiled and winked. "I can handle this, Pan, go, do what you need to do. We will have a feast tonight and celebrate our new friends." Pan gave him a grateful smile before taking a breath and aiming for the sky again.

Since Raesh had died more and more people arrived to Neverland by the day. It was as if they knew that the magic that was once there had returned, it was finally a safe place for all those that were lost to find refuge again. The arrivals did tend to dwindle in the colder months though, this would be one of the last big intakes of the year. The cool air that was settling over Neverland was the first sign that Peter picked up on—how he knew that winter was on the way. It was crisp and soothing, dancing across his skin as he flew through the sky. He liked to fly as high as he could and look down on the island he called home. Neverland. Beautiful Neverland. It was starting to grow again now, new life finding its way through the fighting and fear from before. The fairies returned to Spire, protected the trees and wildlife like they used to.

The people foraged for food on the outskirts of the forest, caught fish in the bay towards the East. The fish were plentiful along with scallops and shellfish, the whole island was flourishing. Some days Peter would see a lot of the younger children paddling down in rocky pools with a wire as they caught crabs to take back to their settlements, their laughter echoing around the island for all to hear.

The lagoon was warm and sunny like usual. A few different coloured flowers had started to grow since the last summer, bright yellow and pink ones that Pan had stared at for a while until they made his eyes water and made him sneeze. As he walked past them he battered them out of the way with his foot, not to crush them, but just to let them know that no stupid flower was allowed to make him cry.

The lagoon was a strange place for him to visit, although it was bright and beautiful it now felt forever tainted, and even though more merfolk lived on the shores now than before it felt like an empty place for him. It was his duty to visit, though. Part of one of the rules from the new leaders of Neverland. Priya would be there waiting.

"Hello, Priya," Pan said as he carefully sat down beside her as she bathed on one of the rocks. She opened her eyes then tilted her head to look at him.

"Peter." Her voice reminded Peter of silk, delicate and soft. "Can you believe it has been three years already?"

"I try not to think about it."

"It is impossible for me not to." Pan sucked in his bottom lip as he looked at her. "I have thought about leaving these shores. Everything here reminds me of that day. The screams from the cave still haunt me."

"Is it any consolation to you are now a hero of Neverland?" he asked.

"No," she said bitterly. "No one cares about me, only about you."

"Come on, that's not true Priya."

"Why does no one else come down here like you do to pay their respects to me then?"

"People don't like coming here. It is a place of fear for them. Raesh met his end here but the crocodile didn't." Pan glanced over to the waterfall and entrance to the cave. "They are scared that if they come here they will die too."

"Then they are cowards."

"Maybe." He shrugged. "But give it time, people will get their confidence back."

Priya held out a closed hand to Pan who frowned at her, expecting a different kind of response. "I think it is time I returned this," she said and opened her webbed hand to reveal a small thimble. Pan's eyebrows raised in surprise and he picked up the small item tentatively. "I know it was payment from Rica, but I know it really belongs to you."

"Thank you," he said softly. "Do you not want to keep it? I know how you like your trinkets"

"It wasn't Rica's to give was it?" Priya smiled sadly. "She found it in the old King's belongings, did you give it to Raesh?"

"No. No, no,no," Pan laughed. "I gave it to Nat, Raesh found it when he searched his room."

"Oh." A concerned look of guilt spread over Priya's features. "I'm sorry, if I had of known that it belonged to Nathaniel I would have returned it to you much sooner."

"It's okay." Pan put the thimble into his tunic pocket and swallowed back the urge to cry. "I will get it back to him."

"You going to see him today?"

"Tomorrow. I have too many newcomers to welcome this afternoon, he will understand though." Priya reached out and place her hand on top of his.

"Try and spend more time with him, you are lucky, you get to see Nat, you get comfort knowing that he is alive."

"I don't know if it would be easier if he wasn't," he admitted.

"You don't mean that." Priya sighed and removed her hand. "Trust me, you don't. He might not be where you want him to be, but he is never far."

"Thank you, for the thimble." Pan cleared his throat and forced himself to give the mermaid a smile. "It's nice, seeing you, Priya."

"It is nice seeing you too, Peter."

Rica took a deep breath as she looked out at the many new faces that made their way into Spire. She smiled at each person, welcoming them personally no matter how long it took her. This was the reason she stayed in Spire; it was the closest to the docks and the new arrivals. She had been voted to rule the city after Raesh was killed. She took the throne with grace. Democracy was a new concept to Neverland, something that at first had made her nervous, but once she realised that it was best for everyone she joined with the other leaders to vote for who they felt was best for the island.

She hoped that with time they could put the vote to the people, to give them more of a voice, but there was time, that was something that they were all blessed enough to have. Neverland had the potential to be great.

"I request ten of the newcomers," Hook said angrily. "You promised me ten last time and I only got four!"

"Hook, some people just don't want to become pirates," Rica sighed at him. "I can't force people to join your crew."

"How am I meant to get a crew together strong enough to beat Pan, hmm?" he asked incredulously. "That little rat thinks he has escaped me, but I am fed up with him flying around my boat shouting obscenities at my crew."

"Shouting obscenities?" Rica smirked. "Oh come on Hook, you need a better reason than that to attack him."

Hook curled his upper lip in annoyance. "It won't be long until that boy does something to really make my blood boil. I will get him, just you wait."

"I don't doubt it, Hook."

"Excuse me?" a young girl said and tugged on the hem of Rica's trousers. "I don't know where to go."

Rica smiled at her. "Well now we can't have that can we?" she said as she knelt down beside her. "Did you come here on your own?"

"Yes," she said with a nod.

"Okay, so tell me, what do you like to do for fun?"

"Um..." The girl chewed the inside of her cheek as she thought of an answer. "I like to play outside, my brothers used to help me climb trees."

"How do you like sailing, and treasure?" Hook asked with a wide smile that made the girl shuffle behind Rica in fear.

"Hook, stop!" she tutted at him. "You like climbing trees?" Rica beamed and offered to take her hand, which the girl gladly accepted. "Come with me, these people over here will be travelling to a place called Nova tomorrow, the trees there are beautiful, I used to climb them all the time. You will be so happy there. See you later, James." The pirate looked at her thoughtfully before nodding his head and allowing her to pass. She led the girl over to a group who sat around a small fire eating bowls of fruit. "Sit down with us?" She sat herself down and after a moment the girl tentatively sat beside her.

"We are telling the story of the Lost Boy who discovered he could control fire," one of the other people sitting there said warmly. "You want to hear?"

"Yes please," the girl said and picked up an apple to eat. "I love stories."

"So do we, and we are never short of them," Rica said then looked down at her own hands as frost sparkled on her fingertips.

Nathaniel pressed his forehead to the cold window pane and puffed out his breath against the glass to create a mist on the surface. He brought his finger to it and drew a circle which disappeared as his air evaporated from the glass. There had been a steady snowfall for the past two hours which was now staring to lay over the ground as the evening afternoon sun turned to night. Outside there were twinkling lights that kept jogging a memory in the back of his mind but as soon as they came close enough for him to grasp the memory faded right back into darkness.

It was Christmas, a time when everyone raced around the streets with bags full of gifts, trees were cut down to be placed in homes and people drank a hot wine and called it 'festive'. The small room he had set himself up in for the day had been decorated with paper lanterns and ribbons, with sparkling tinsel dancing around the window panes. The whole idea of Christmas was something that he took no interest in learning about; the season seemed forced to him, though, he sometimes caught a glimpse of child like wonder on a young person's face and that would light a fire in his chest and make him smile.

He had told Pan to visit at this time of year just so he could see what Nathaniel really meant when he described the holiday to him. When he had first mentioned trees in houses decorated with various ornaments Pan had burst out laughing and had questioned whether Nat had gone crazy.

That was one of the frustrations of being in London and not in Neverland. Neverland was a magical place, where almost anything could happen, but if Nathaniel mentioned something that happened in London, Pan would dismiss it as fantasy. In some ways being in London had ruined the wonder of Neverland for him. Life was different in England. People worked, went to school, went to bed, woke up and repeated the same day over again. On the outside it felt horribly mundane, but the more time he spent there the more he realised just how content people seemed in their routines. There was love, birth, heartbreak, anything you could imagine could happen and in a way that was far more magical than seeing a fairy fly in Neverland. Not that he didn't love the magic from back home. He missed it all. He wanted to see it thriving, see how Rica was making positive changes in Spire. But, he had yet to return.

Part of him felt that he was no longer good enough to be there. He was damaged, he failed everyone. He didn't remember much from that night, but he remembered waking to searing pain in his arm and looking down to see that only the top half of his left arm remained. It was a phantom feeling, he was sure he could feel tingling in his fingertips, his pulse racing through his wrist. But he couldn't. He had screamed and Pan had to pin him down onto the bed with the help of some other people from Spire. It was such a foreign feeling and he didn't know how he survived the whole ordeal either. He was sure he was going to die back in that cave, that he was never going to see Pan again, that he had met his end in such a sad and gruesome way.

Returning to where he had been born was Pan's idea. Weeks passed after the night Raesh died and Nathaniel didn't leave his room in the palace. It was difficult adjusting to his newly altered body; his balance was off and he repeatedly woke up thinking that it had all been a dream. There was a deep conflict inside of him that he couldn't seem to overcome. He knew that nothing had changed, not really, that him losing an arm would never change the way that Pan felt about him, and Pan assured him of that everyday. The tentative relationship they had started to build again seemed genuine, like they both knew that they needed each other. That made him happy sometimes.

Another part of him felt deep sorrow, not because he had been injured, but because he wasn't strong enough to complete the plan. He wasn't quick enough to move away from the crocodile before it bit him. He wasn't good enough.

"I think you need a change of scenery," Peter said one rainy afternoon as he sat on the edge of Nathaniel's bed. "It isn't doing you any good being cooped up in here."

"I'm not going to the Nova or Ipsling if that is what you're suggesting," he mumbled.

"I was actually thinking somewhere a bit further away." Nat turned on his side to look at Pan with curiosity.

"Where?"

"London."

"London?"

"Don't you think it would be nice to see where you were born? To learn something about a place other than here?"

"Are you sure that is even when I came from...why are you trying to send me away?" he asked as his lip started to tremble. "Are you banishing me?"

"No!" Pan said quickly and cupped Nathaniel's face in his hands. "No, never, no." He kissed his lips lightly, for the first time in forty years. "I just want to see you smile again, being here is not making you happy."

"But...Rica has chosen you as her adviser, you can't leave her after everything that happened," Nat sniffed and blinked back some tears.

"You're right, I would have to stay here."

"So, you want me to go on my own?" his face creased with sadness that tugged at Pan's heart.

"I can take you. You can stay for as long as you want. A day, a week, whatever you want. I would never take you there and leave you there, Nat, never."

"But what would I do in London? I have no purpose there."

"You could find out about your family, you could see if anyone is still alive, I don't know Nat, it was just an idea." Pan sounded defeated, his voice tired and strained. Nathaniel wanted to just tell him to run away with him, they could both go to London and stay there forever, they never had to think about Neverland again. Deep down he knew that would never work. Peter belonged in Neverland, he was part of the island and he was sure that if Pan wasn't there then Neverland wouldn't even exist. To remove him from his home would kill him, he would see the life sucked out of him every day he had to be away from the island and although he wanted Pan to himself, he couldn't see him fade away like that.

However, he was fading with Nathaniel being there. He could see it in his eyes, that beautiful light them was no longer there and it was because of him. He knew that his own sadness could be all consuming. His sadness was now eating away at Pan and dragging him down to a place he didn't deserve to be. This was a time for celebration, Peter had defeated Raesh, he had saved Neverland and saved Nathaniel too. He was a hero, the people had welcomed him back into their ranks with great fan fare. People felt liberated by him and were finally able to breathe. Peter was Peter Pan again. He was a thing of legend, people would tell his story for centuries to come, it was his fate, his destiny to be the hero that he was.

Nathaniel couldn't see himself in the narrative. He couldn't see how anyone would talk of Peter and have his name come out of their mouth beside him. It was never his story. It was Peter's. It was his fall from glory and phoenix-like rise from the ashes that everybody needed to hear about. Nat was a supporting character, a piece in the puzzle that would get Peter back to where he belonged. He didn't resent playing that part, he never wanted to be the protagonist in an adventure, he was much happier being in a backseat role. What role did he have now?

Going to London was a solution, a short term solution. He could work on himself, get his strength back and then re-evaluate the place he had in Peter's life. It would hurt. It would hurt more than having his arm ripped off by a crocodile, but he loved him. He had to go.

Twelve

When Pan took Nathaniel to his childhood home there was nothing that he could remember of it. He still wasn't even sure if it was his home, he knew Pan as remembering more and more by the day but he still had a flicker of doubt in his mind. It was nestled between other houses, all of them tall with multiple floors and large windows that had iron railings on the outside to protect the occupants from falling out. They were frightening, Nathaniel had never seen anything quite like them, they felt incredibly intimidating and ominous. The middle house was where his mother died, according to Pan. It was where Peter had taken him and Henry from the top floor window and whisked them away to Neverland to save them from their father.

Nathaniel stepped up to the front door, a big red wooden thing with large gold knocker in the center of it. He looked over his shoulder at Pan who gave him a reassuring nod and he lifted the knocker in his hand then brought it back down to the door loudly.

The woman who opened the door was old. Nathaniel couldn't put an age on how old but her skin was creased with decades of wrinkles, hands like that of a skeletons with dark brown and red blemishes all over them. She looked at him through thick rimmed silver spectacles, her eyes such a light brown that they looked yellow.

"Can I help you dear?" she asked and wrapped her long red cardigan around her petite frame to protect her from the wind outside.

"I don't know if you can." Nathaniel fumbled with the sleeve of his jacket anxiously. "I used to live here."

"You did?" She frowned at him then gave a croaky laugh. "I think you might have the wrong house, I have lived here all my life."

"Oh, I'm sorry..." he turned to leave but Pan shook his head at him from where he was standing and gestured for him to keep talking. "Actually, it was this house." The old woman looked over to where Pan was and let out a soft gasp.

"It can't be true," she said and placed a hand over her chest. She stepped out of the door, her bare feet connecting with the cold pavement and she took tentative steps over to him as he gave her a smile.

"Hello, Alice," he said and Nathaniel heard her let out a cry and she wrapped her arms around him tightly.

"You came back," she cried as he held her in his arms.

"I promised that I would, didn't I?"

"You look so different." She pulled back from him and placed a shaking hand to his cheek. "Why, Peter, you look magnificent."

"Come on, let's get inside, you will catch a chill out here." He took her hand and helped support her weight as she walked back to the door. Nathaniel looked between them with a furrowed brow, unable to understand what was going on, but there was a comfort knowing that Pan knew who she was.

Alice placed two cups down in front of them. She picked up a pair of silver tongs then dropped three lumps of sugar into each of the cups and added a drop of milk. She pushed a small china plate of biscuits towards them that Pan took hungrily and started to stuff them into his mouth without offering them to Nathaniel. Nathaniel picked up the mug but quickly placed it back down when it burnt his fingers. Alice let out a laugh and shook her head at him.

"It's hot."

"Yeah, I kinda got that," Nathaniel said and glared at the steaming cup suspiciously. "Why would you make something to drink that is that hot?" He thought back to the fire that used to flicker in his palm.

"It is tea," Alice told him. "Tea is served hot. And with proper sugar, none of that stuff from a plastic tub. Sugar should be served in cubes." She looked at Pan and tutted. "Good grief Peter, stop eating like an animal." His eyes widened as he looked at her then cautiously set the plate back down on the coffee table.

"Sorry," he said, sending a mouthful of biscuit crumbs flying into the air.

"Well," Alice rolled her eyes and pushed her glasses further up her nose. "I must say, this is a very unexpected visit. You were meant to come back for me seventy-two years ago. You come to be now, Peter, now that I am old."

"I'm sorry," he said, genuinely looking remorseful.

"Seventy-two years?" Nathaniel asked and touched his mug again, this time he was satisfied with the temperature and brought it to his lips. "What did you say this was, tea?"

"Yes," Alice nodded but her eyes were on Pan. "Where did you go, Peter?"

"I had some adventures to go on, Alice."

"I told all my friends about you," she said with a smile on her thin lips. "That you said you would visit again and take me to a place called Neverland. When it never happened I lost all hope of magic. I put it down to a very imaginative dream."

"Pan used to visit you?" Nathaniel asked.

"A few times, very forgetful back then though," she laughed. "He used to come here asking for Wendy, each time I had to say that no one called Wendy lived here. Of course, I knew who he was talking about."

"You did?"

"Everyone knows about Peter and Wendy," she said and brought her own tea to her lips. "It is a cherished story in our family, my mother thought it was adorable when I said I had met Peter Pan."

"Alice," Pan said seriously. "I know it has been a long time, I should have come back for you, and I have no right to ask you this. But, Nathaniel, well..." He reached over and took Nathaniel's hand into his. "He needs your help."

"How can I help you young man?" Alice asked, her eyes focusing on their intertwined hands for a brief moment. "I don't know how much help an old lady will be to you."

"I can't be in Neverland right now...I need time to heal...Pan said this used to be my old home. That I could be here..." The room filled with silence, only broken when Alice placed her tea back on the table and cleared her throat.

"What was your name?"

"Nathaniel."

She blinked. "Nathaniel?"

"Yes." Nathaniel nodded and held onto Pan's hand tighter. "If what Pan has said is correct, then, this is the house he took me and my brother from."

"Henry?"

"Yes Henry!" Nathaniel smiled. "You know us?"

"Well, not personally," she said and stood up from her seat. She took shaky steps over to a wooden sideboard and opened a drawer. She rummaged around for a few minutes before pulling out a small leather bound book and made her way back to her seat. "This, this is my family tree." She held out the book for Nathaniel to take. He was holding onto Pan's hand so tightly he just stared at it until Pan took it with his spare hand and opened it for him to see.

"I...I'm sorry I can't read the writing." Nathaniel's cheeks flushed as he looked down at the swirling handwriting.

"Oh, well, pass it back-" She held out her hand so Pan passed it back to her. She flicked through a few pages before finding the one she needed and placed the book down on the table for them all to see. "This-" she said and pointed to a name. "This is me. And this, well, these are my parents and their parents." She waved her hand in the air dismissively. "If we go back even further..." She flicked through a few more pages. "To here...well...this is Graham Darling," she looked at Nathaniel but he showed no signs of understanding. "Graham was my Great Grandfather's brother. It says here that he was married to a Jemima Scully and that they had two children." Nathaniel was holding onto Pan's hand so tightly that his knuckles had turned white. "Henry and

Nathaniel Darling." Nathaniel looked from the page and back to Alice.

"So, Jemima and Graham...they were my parents?"

"It would appear so," she said and turned another page. "You will see here that your father, Graham, was the son of Michael Darling, who was the brother of Wendy...Peter's Wendy."

Nathaniel looked at Pan and took a deep breath. "You were right."

"When am I ever wrong?" he grinned.

"No one knew what happened to you and Henry. Jemima was killed by Graham, it was terrible, all over the newspapers. No one knew why and he never told anyone why he did what he did. He also never said where the two boys were...though...now I realise what had happened."

"Peter saved us," Nathaniel told her as the realisation settled for him. "He took us to Neverland to save us from our father."

"Is Henry still there?" Alice asked.

"No, he died a long time ago." Pan pressed a kiss to Nathaniel's cheek when he saw the man's expression fall. "We have both been through a lot," he explained as he looked back at the old lady. "Nathaniel...he needs some time to recover."

"Recover?" Alice frowned.

"I have so much to tell you Alice..." Pan saw her face turn serious. "Let's just say that if it wasn't for Nathaniel then there would be nowhere safe in Neverland."

"That's not true I-"

"It is," Pan said to him sternly. "But he got hurt in the process. He needs to be away for a while to recover in peace. Please, Alice, can you help?"

"Are you asking if he can stay here?" Alice looked between them with a slightly amused expression. "Because if that is what you are asking then I will not turn down a handsome young man."

"Really?" Nathaniel asked in surprise. "You would let me stay here with you?"

"Technically, Nathaniel, this house is yours. Though, I don't think you could really have any claim to it now as you really should be dead." She let out a laugh but Nathaniel and Pan failed to see what was funny. "Sorry," she said and waved her hand in front of her eyes to compose herself. "I didn't mean that in a spiteful way. Just, really, you would be dead if you had of stayed here. Or the oldest man alive."

"Oh." Nathaniel gave a small understanding nod.

"But, yes, you can stay here. This is your home, Nathaniel, you can tell me about all of your adventures with the amazing Peter Pan."

It was a thirty minute walk to Kensington Gardens and it was a walk that Nathaniel made at least once a week since living in London. It was a beautiful part of the city that had so many beautiful areas to explore, he was sure that he would never get to discover all of it's secrets.

It was New Years Day that he discovered a statue there that he had never seen before. It wasn't exactly in a hidden place, it was quite out in the open for all to see. From a distance he couldn't make out what it was, but with every step closer he took the details became more and more refined until he stood right in front of it with tears in his eyes. He looked down at the plaque and sounded out the letters in his head as he read it.

"Peter Pan, the boy who would not grow up," he said quietly and drew his eyes back to the statue. At the base there were small animals and fairies with a playful look about them that caused Nathaniel to smile. The boy at the top of the statue could have only been about eight years old and appeared to be playing some kind of flute. There was something so whimsical about it, but it didn't resemble Peter. When he first knew him, at that age, he had such a mischievious way about him, this statue was too innocent to really be Peter.

"Lovely statue isn't it?" Nathaniel turned his head to see the park keeper with a broom, sweeping up leaves behind him. He smiled at Nathaniel and took a step closer as he blew on his hands to warm them up. "Though, not many people know this, but Peter Pan did grow up."

"He did?" Nathaniel smiled back politely and wrapped his right arm around himself protectively. "But that plaque says that he would not grow up."

"He didn't want to, he was stubborn," the man laughed. "But he did, and then he had even more adventures."

"Why is this here?"

"The statue?"

"Yeah, I mean, why does he have a statue?" The man looked at him curiously, there was a sense of sadness in his eyes.

"Well, to many children he is a hero. Defying adults, being a child forever. I don't know all the stories people tell about him, but, I think that they bring people a lot of happiness."

"Just a child's story though, right?"

"That depends, do you believe in magic?"

Nathaniel laughed and shrugged his shoulders. "It's nice to believe isn't it?"

"You know, you remind me of one of the characters in the Peter Pan story," the man commented. "You might not know about him if you don't know the stories anyway, and not many people talk about what happened after Peter grew up, but he had a very good friend called Nathaniel."

"Nathaniel?"

"A Lost Boy with messy hair, just like yours, no offence though lad." Nathaniel stared at the man as he spoke. "Freckles dotted across his cheeks, bravery that no one else could ever possess. He used to be able to control fire, until he no longer needed that power."

"Did he have a happy ending?"

"Yes, I believe he did."

"Nat!" Nathaniel turned in the other direction when he heard his name called and waved to the black haired man who was coming towards him. When he looked back to say goodbye to the park keeper he had gone.

"Do you have to shout?" Nathaniel scrunched up his nose as Pan got closer to him.

"I needed to get your attention." Pan smiled and pulled the shorter man into his arms to kiss him. "And it worked."

"I guess," Nathaniel scoffed as he pulled away from him. "Hey, I never knew you had a statue."

"Wonderful isn't it?" he said proudly as he looked at the piece of art in front of them. "I think it really captures my spirit."

"Nothing could really capture your whole spirit." Nathaniel watched Pan as he looked at the statue. His skin had been kissed by the sun, even his hair looked lighter from the time he had clearly been spending out in the warm rays. It must have been a good summer in Neverland.

They walked together throughout the gardens, both of them enjoying the quiet of the new years morning without having to say much to each other. Each time Pan visited it got easier, the first few times Nathaniel had felt beyond himself with grief each time he went back to Neverland he didn't think he would be able to get through it. Time helped. The visits became further apart and for shorter amounts of time. Pan didn't stay the night like he used to. They didn't share the same space like they used to either, their bond was still as strong as ever, but physically they were holding on by a thread.

"I have something for you," Pan said after a while and they came to stop by a bench to sit down. "I know you told me not to bring you gifts, but I think you will like this one."

"I just didn't want you flying here carrying stuff," Nathaniel explained as he sat beside him. "But, go on, show me."

"Close your eyes and hold out your hand," he instructed. Nathaniel let out a small huff as he closed his eyes and held out his hand impatiently. He felt Pan place something small in his palm and when he opened his eyes he looked down at the small object intently.

"The thimble."

"The kiss," Pan corrected him. "Priya gave it back to me." Nathaniel turned the thimble around in his hand and thought back to when Raesh had said he had found it under his pillow. The fear he felt at being confronted by him felt like a million years ago, he wasn't sure he could even remember Raesh's face despite it only being a few short years since he died.

"You didn't feel like leaving it under my pillow this time then?"

"No, I was trying to be discreet before," Pan said in amusement. "Don't really have to be discreet now, do I? Everyone knows I would give every kiss in the world to you." Nathaniel tipped his head to look at the man beside him. He didn't look any different from when he left Neverland, he hadn't aged anymore, nothing had changed.

Nathaniel was changing. He could feel his body dying, not a rapid decline, but he could finally taste his mortality and for the first time he didn't wonder about *if* he was going to die, he knew he would. The longer he spent away from Neverland the more distant it became, the more out of reach his life with Pan became.

"What are you thinking?" Pan asked as Nathaniel placed the thimble in his jacket pocket. "I can see something in your eyes that you are not telling me."

"Do you not think that you should maybe give those kisses to someone else?" Pan opened his mouth and closed it again in response, no words coming to his mind to say what he felt about what Nathaniel had just said. Nathaniel felt a pang of guilt as he looked at him. Not being with Pan wasn't what he wanted. If he was even with him. He knew he loved him. He loved every single inch of him and would until the day he died. That was the problem.

"I love you," Pan finally said which made Nathaniel want to take back every thought he had of letting him go. "I never stopped loving you. Not for one moment."

"I love you too."

"Then why would you say something like that?"

"Because what can I give you by being here?"

"That is a stupid question." Pan looked panicked, he took Nathaniel's hand into his and held tightly. "You give me everything. Do you want me to stay? I will stay here Nathaniel. I would move one hundred moons if you asked me to. If Neverland isn't where you want to be then let me be with you."

"Alice told me that you would eventually forget, that you would forget everything and you would no longer come back here. She didn't say it with any malice, but she wanted to warn me."

"I never forgot Alice."

"But, you forgot Wendy."

"You are not Wendy."

"And you forgot Tinker-bell." Pan looked away from him and dropped his hand. He breathed in the air deeply then looked up at the sky.

"Back then I didn't remember anything that wasn't in my face everyday. I won't forget you. I won't forget *us*. I know how you think. That you think you are putting me in danger by being around me. Raesh is gone, Nathaniel, there is no danger." Nathaniel observed him. Was he right? Was there no danger anymore?

"I'm terrified of losing you."

"Don't you think I feel that same fear?" Pan asked. "We have spent years without each other. But...all that anger and resentment has gone, it was temporary," he explained. "This-" he said and gestured to the gardens around him. "This was all meant to be temporary too. I understand if you are not ready to return home, but remember that Neverland is your home. Not here. And remember, *you* are my home, Nathaniel, where ever you are is where I belong."

Pan stayed that night. He held Nathaniel in his arms until the brunette fell asleep and pressed gentle kisses to his forehead lovingly. Nathaniel felt warm against his skin, his body always ran hot, he was radiating against him giving that warmth to Pan. He glanced over the room and out of the bay window. The stars shone brightly in the sky and he picked out which one led to Neverland. It was a long flight, a flight he would have to make in the morning. He had decided that was going to be the last time he flew back to Neverland. He would return and make sure the foundations were there for Rica, then he would say goodbye to the island for the last time.

He looked back down at Nathaniel who was breathing softly, his head on Pan's chest as he slept. He would never know just how beautiful he was. He was brave, determined and clever, Pan was so incredibly proud of him that he could never put it into words.

He also knew why Nathaniel was staying away. He understood that Nat was scared of what faced him back in Neverland. The people still didn't trust him, despite knowing the truth of what happened with Raesh and Hook, and how Raesh had treated him when he was working by his side. What he didn't understand was why Nathaniel couldn't see that none of that was his fault. He tried, that was more than a lot of people would do. He put himself into the path of danger for the people of Spire and for the island–knowing full well that he might not make it out alive.

He wanted to scream at him, grab him by the shoulders and shake him until he understood that he was the hero, he was the only reason that Pan and all the others were alive and free. There was no arrogance from Nathaniel, he wasn't like Pan or Raesh or even Rica.

He understood the pain he had gone through, both physically and mentally. He couldn't image what it must have felt like to lose a part of your body, what that must do for your own self-esteem. It didn't change a thing for Pan though, he didn't look at Nathaniel in a different way, didn't find him any less beautiful. He needed Nathaniel to know that he loved him, that he would be with him every day and tell him just how amazing he was. He couldn't let his light fade.

Neverland was an incredible place. It held magic and wonder for so many people who ended up there. They were allowed to live now, they could be happy and fly with the fairies while creating their own adventures that they could have only dreamed of before. Pan couldn't deny that the days where he ran around Neverland with no fears or cares were bliss, not having responsibilities was a gift that only children could really possess. He would never go back to it though, he would rather suffer heartbreak than never having loved. Nathaniel was the best adventure he ever had, and he was not going to see it come to an end. He knew that he had often been called selfish, that he only thought of himself. What he was planning now could be considered self-absorbed, leaving behind everyone else, but he didn't see it that way. He had given enough of himself to the island, Nathaniel had given even more. It was their turn to finally have a happy ending, even if it meant not living forever. To live and die with Nathaniel by his side would be an awfully big adventure.

"You're coming back?" Nathaniel asked as Pan opened the large windows and stepped up onto the railing outside. Pan looked at him and gave a nod, a smile spread over his lips.

"I won't be long. A week at most."

"Are you sure, Pan?" Nathaniel reached for his hand which he took willingly. He pulled the man closer to him and tiptoed up while Pan leaned down to kiss him.

"As sure as I will ever be. Besides, I know all of Neverland like the back of my hand. London is a new place to explore. Just think of the adventures that we will have."

"You can't fly around London," Nathaniel warned.

"Then we will get...what are those red things called?"

"A bus?"

"A bus!" Pan exclaimed happily and pressed his lips to Nathaniel's again. "Now, a bus sounds like a very fun way to get around." Nathaniel laughed and let go of his hand so Pan could stand properly again.

"Sure, you can press the bell to make it stop and everything."

"The bell?" Pan pulled a confused face. "That needs a lot more explaining, make a list of things to teach me about for when I get back."

"Fly safe, Peter Pan."

"Keep your window open for me, love."

Acknowledgments

I must admit, I never thought I would be writing an acknowledgment page for this book, because I never thought I would finish it.

I don't know how many forms this story has taken, it started off as something I was writing to distract me from another story I was struggling with. Once I started I couldn't get Nathaniel and Pan out of my head and now here they are, for everyone to see.

The original story of Peter Pan is one that I cherish; it reminds me of my childhood, of Christmas time and going to see a pantomime. Everything about it screams familiarity and warmth, yet deep down I always knew there was a certain sadness to it, that Peter was destined to actually live a lonely life while those around him grew older. I think that was what drove me to write this story. There was so much to explore in the island of Neverland and I wanted to expand on the mythology and create my own characters to inhabit it.

Firstly I need to thank the incredible A.M.Hubbard, an outstanding author who I have the honour of calling my friend. Without you I would not have finished this book. Your unconditional support means more to me than you could ever know. I hope that I can give you the same inspiration and encouragement with your own projects.

I would also like to thank Laurie. Your patience with me is second to none! My texts of "Should Hook die?" to "Is Pan too much of a dick?" always went answered and helped shape this story. Thank you for reading my drafts and giving your feedback, Hook survived (this time).

I also want to mention the artist Venessa Kelley. While editing I received incredible artwork from Venessa that was inspired by Pan and Nat. To see my characters come to life in such a beautiful image made me cry, thank you for giving them such care and attention. They look perfect.

A huge thank you to GG and Arli Barli. The two best people anyone could ever ask for. I love you both so much.

And finally I would like to thank you, for reading. It is a scary process when you send your book out into the world, you don't know how people will react to it, but you hope that it falls into someone's hands who will enjoy it. I sincerely hope that you enjoyed this adventure as much as I enjoyed writing it.

Ilya